Joyce Windsor began her career working for the Inland Revenue while writing in her spare time. But after taking a creative writing course, she now writes full time.

KEEPER OF SWANS

In 1997, five acquaintances gather at The
Glebe retirement home in a quiet corner
of Dorset. Each is troubled by the shadow
of events that took place twenty-seven
years before. Against her better judgement, Bird Dawlish, proprietor of the
home, takes in a widower, Hereward
Parstock, who was once her lover. Connie
Lovibond, Hereward's sister-in-law, who
has never been satisfied that her sister's
death was natural, is convinced that Bird
and possibly Rita Parry, an old travelling
woman, can help to discover the truth.
The tragic death of Princess Diana
heightens emotions and helps to bring
about crises of love and violence that
affect residents and villagers alike.

Books by Joyce Windsor
Published by The House of Ulverscroft:

AFTER THE UNICORN

JOYCE WINDSOR

KEEPER OF SWANS

Complete and Unabridged

ULVERSCROFT
Leicester

First published in Great Britain in 2003 by
Robert Hale Limited
London

First Large Print Edition
published 2004
by arrangement with
Robert Hale Limited
London

The moral right of the author has been asserted

British Library CIP Data

Windsor, Joyce
    Keeper of swans.—Large print ed.—
    Ulverscroft large print series: general fiction
    1. Old age homes—England—Dorset—Fiction
    2. Large type books
    I. Title
    823.9'14 [F]

    ISBN 1–84395–349–8

Published by
F. A. Thorpe (Publishing)
Anstey, Leicestershire

Set by Words & Graphics Ltd.
Anstey, Leicestershire
Printed and bound in Great Britain by
T. J. International Ltd., Padstow, Cornwall

This book is printed on acid-free paper

For Maureen Witt
with my love

1

At The Glebe retirement home, of which she was both owner and proprietor, Bird Dawlish watched a hired car pause at the gates then make its way up the drive. She was expecting no one. A visitor for one of her residents, perhaps? But the tiresome clairvoyance of an ex-mistress cut in on her thoughts with the certainty that the single passenger was Hereward Parstock. Since she could not remember giving him a conscious thought for years, she dismissed the suspicion that she might have half-hoped, half-expected him. He had messed up her life once. Now that she had rebuilt it, he had no right to invade her peace. The sad, spiritless July day of flat grey sky and sneaking wind was scarcely designed to revive ancient passions. Her care and her emotions belonged now to The Glebe. Hereward was a complication she did not want.

Defensively she froze, summoned up professional cordiality and waited unflustered until he had been announced and was seated opposite her. She allowed him to speak first. A moment of uncomfortable silence passed.

'Do you realize, Bird, that it's been twenty-seven years?' he asked at length, glancing over her head at the various framed nursing certificates displayed on the wall behind her desk as though he could not manage to look directly at her.

'The arithmetic is easy enough,' she said with uncustomary dryness. 'Why have you come here to me? Why The Glebe? There are hundreds of good retirement homes.'

'I saw your advertisement in *The Times*, a vacant apartment.'

'You weren't in my mind at all. If you imagine I want to relive the past, you're entirely mistaken.'

'But I ran into poor Miles Alban. You've taken *him* in. He tells me that this is more a place of peaceful retreat than an institution. If he's happy here, it really must be. Having his homosexuality made public in that seedy fashion destroyed his life, don't you think?'

'Obviously, Hereward, I can't discuss anyone's private concerns, certainly not their sex lives. This isn't a prison camp. The sick are well nursed, the disabled are helped to enjoy their last years in every way we can find. The rest are perfectly free to come and go as they choose.'

'Aren't they mostly too old for sex?'

'Are you?' asked Bird, sorry that she had

2

mentioned sex at all. 'Is there a switch-off point? Miles is barely sixty I believe.' And he had, for a while in the memorable summer of 1970, been passionately in love with Hereward, who fortunately, had not noticed. The very idea would have shaken the Parstock pride. He, as with most of Miles's old friends, lay very low when he might have saved him from despair. Rescue of their wrecked and perishing friend was left to one woman, Connie Lovibond, Hereward's sister-in-law.

He said, 'But surely you don't allow, hum, that sort of thing here?'

Did he really now think in terms so prudish? Yet he had indulged in plenty of 'that sort of thing' in his time, and gloried in it. Somehow she had never once, in all the dead years between them, imagined him old, all passion spent, a compulsory convert to chastity. An impulse to make a vengeful remark came, then went, because she couldn't think of one. She was useless at putting people down. Carefully neutral, she said, 'Miss Lovibond looked after Miles when he had that breakdown. She still does. He's staying with her now.'

Unaware of reproach, he frowned. 'Connie? I had no idea they were friends. I haven't seen her since Winifred's funeral. A dreadful time, Bird. As you know, we had decided to

3

divorce, but after you — your mother — well, there seemed no hurry, on my part at least. We remained fond of each other, Winifred and I, and affection and friendship are always worth preserving. Yet I felt that Connie somehow blamed me for her death.'

'You're mistaken surely,' Bird said in her briskest nursing voice, 'but if you stay here you're liable to meet Miss Lovibond again quite soon, at the end of next month in fact. Her father died. She's coming here for a rest. If that makes you uncomfortable you could look for a more congenial place, with a bridge club perhaps, or close to a golf course.'

He brushed this aside. 'Why should it bother me? I like Connie. You have every right to hate me and send me packing, Bird, but it seemed such amazing luck that you were running this place. I'm weary and hag-ridden. Swan House is lost; pulled down and replaced by a gimcrack housing estate. I need a haven very much.' The sublime confidence in his ability to arrange everything according to the heart's desire had gone. He was too highly coloured. Heart, she guessed. His rough fair hair had lost vigour and faded to streaky white. Bird certainly did not hate him but, by the grace of Heaven, she no longer loved him as she had once done, extravagantly, ruining a good fifteen years of

4

her life before she managed to forgive her own stupidity.

A sense of the inevitability of the past troubled her. A few dream-like months, the half-forgotten heart of her youth, had begun a reprise, disturbing to her peace and aggravating to common sense. 'Which particular hag is riding you?' she asked, guessing what the answer would be.

'Stella, Stella Worth she is now. So persistent. You remember her?'

Bird did. In glorious weather she, the outsider, had remained detached from the house-party, watching the glamorous people glide like swans through the summer heat. Swan House; well and aptly named, and Stella, a notable actress, twice married, twice divorced. Also darkly beautiful, and Hereward's other mistress. The discovery of their shared status had driven Bird away. That was twenty-seven years ago, as he had reminded her, in the year which seemed to have encapsulated as much as she knew of romance. Peaceable himself, he trailed with him a suggestion of violence. The Glebe was not for him.

Her face was more revealing than she knew and he was watching her. 'I did you a very grave injury, Bird,' he said; 'believe me, I didn't know at the time how grave until your mother told me what she must also have told you. You'll have realized that our situation was hopeless.'

'Hopeless? Are we talking about age difference, class difference?' Her tone was bewildered and angry. 'Or a tendency of my family to gibber at full moon? My mother hated me all my life and only spoke to me when she was forced to it. I have no idea what she may have told you, or why she bothered to talk to you at all.'

'Oh dear God,' he said. 'Was she lying? What have you been thinking of me all these years?'

'It hardly matters now. I was nineteen, immoral, pregnant and dumped. That was enough to worry about.'

Old men cry easily. His eyes misted over and he looked desolate and lonely. 'Bird, you're a loving person. Don't punish me too much. Paris was unforgettable, however wrong. You were an enchantment, as ethereal and lovely as your name.'

'I detest my name,' she said coldly. 'I don't care if it was your grandmother's; it's infantile and stupid and you are manipulating the situation.'

'Of course I am. You mean to turn me down and I don't want you to. I'm an old man. My need of you is desperate.'

'You aren't being fair. It's unfair to mention Paris at all. Pointless now, and still as embarrassing to me as it was at the time.'

'But amazing? You do remember, even after so long?'

'Yes,' she agreed absently, drawing a form towards her and writing his name neatly in the space provided. Fatuous question; she most certainly remembered. It *had* been amazing. Bird shivered, as though she were still bracing herself against the chill of the wind funnelling up from the Seine. She could not possibly turn him away.

★   ★   ★

Walking between rows of shuttered, secretive houses, bleached like washed-out cotton, she had never known where she was. Empty streets in nowhere land; corner cafés where they were not wanted, where locals huddled at the bar, throwing out remarks in French too rapid for her to follow. Long walks by the river to quays where working boats tied up to take on cargo. Not the Paris of tourists and glamour. 'Don't you have any other clothes?' Hereward had asked, examining her grey school skirt and nylon blouse and rejecting them. Getting to Paris at all in the face of her mother's opposition had been miracle

7

enough; asking for new clothes as well was to risk a thunderbolt from Heaven! So he bought her a blue and white dress with a mini-skirt and matching shoes and took her to the Eiffel Tower and Napoleon's tomb. In the dusky evenings he kissed her a lot and stroked her breasts, which made her both shrink with timidity and wish for more.

Eventually, on a wet May morning of 1970, Hereward seduced her in the grotto of the Jardin des Plantes. Bird was tremendously surprised. Her ideas on the subject of sex were vague. Flowers, wine and the privacy of a softly lit bedroom drifted into her mind and out again. Anguished by love, she did not for all that enjoy her initiation a great deal. Was she supposed to *do* anything? Touch him, take all her clothes off — or his? He seemed to be managing without her help, easing her pants down and over her feet. One of her shoes came off. Bird tried to retrieve it, but Hereward began kissing her so vigorously that she gave up. As he bore her passionately to the ground, she tried to peer through the assortment of fronds and spikes and other aggressive greenery to make sure that they were alone. The path through the grotto was uncomfortably damp and chilly. She was nervous to the point of coma.

An old man, solitary in the rain, glanced

through the distant gates and passed on. It was not the weather for gardens. Yet Bird expected at any moment to be discovered. Around them water spilled from the sky, spattering and dripping on to leaves and stones. The vegetation smelled rankly of earth and graveyards. She seemed to be experiencing hallucinations, hearing alarming, inhuman cries. Only later did she discover that they came from the animals in a nearby menagerie. And then, fatally to pleasure, she remembered her mother's religious mania and mad rejection of life. 'Stop, oh please stop,' she murmured. But it was too late.

Hereward concentrated on the moment while she remained distressingly aware of the vulnerability of her exposed body, fearing both detection and a chill from the damp concrete beneath her. 'My little Bird, how I love you,' he said as he helped her to her feet. He turned his back to make adjustments. His courteous technique throughout possessed an old-fashioned flavour belonging more to 1930 than 1970. After all, he was forty-three. He smiled tenderly, looking like a conqueror, immensely pleased with himself. At that moment her chief concern was whether she had telltale mud stains on the back of her new dress, but the paralysing shyness that ought to have kept her safe from marauding strangers made it impossible for her to ask him. She managed to find her shoe. The whereabouts of her knickers was unknown until Hereward produced them from his pocket and waited — oh God, the awkwardness and intimacy of it! — while she put them on.

Bird, in Paris with three college companions to improve her atrocious French, was not quite nineteen. She had known Hereward for less than two weeks. A sharper girl might have noticed some discomfort behind his smile. As it was, she simply felt that she might enjoy her new experience better in retrospect and wanted to be alone to think about it. On the next day they were both leaving Paris, never, she thought, to meet again. 'I must go back now,' she whispered sadly, but with some relief. 'The other girls will be expecting me.'

'Do you love me, even though I'm so much — even though I'm rather older than you?' He did not look his age and invited contradiction, which he did not get. She nodded, having never been age-conscious or aware of unwritten rules concerning the seduction of virgins. She simply wished that she might stay in Paris forever. Where else would she run into a god on a river-bank and be swept up by passion and adventure? At that time, Bird's simple ignorance was colossal.

Hereward, who was flying home, appeared at the Gare du Nord to see her on to her train. She hoped he would not ask where her new dress was. Not daring to take it to England, she had, on her way to the station, stuffed it and the shoes into a convenient dustbin. Other things were on his mind. He drew her behind a barrow with a striped awning and kissed her in the shelter of piled-up fruit and filled baguettes. The food was wrapped. It exuded a strong smell of cheese and smoked ham. She was aware of hunger and the avid stares of her three companions. An inquisition would follow. She murmured a confused goodbye. 'But we shall meet again soon,' he said. 'I don't think you have the remotest idea of who I am, do you?'

'Didn't you say you were Harry Wood? I thought that was what you said.'

'You're too timid to listen properly; you're nervous of asking questions and only speak when you're spoken to. Really, Bird, that's dangerous. I'm not Harry Wood, for God's sake. My name's Hereward, Hereward Parstock, and your mother is one of my tenants. She married the farm bailiff.'

Bird, suddenly wide awake, glowered and

pulled away from him. French history that composed her evening reading, came alive and mocked at her. 'You knew, didn't you? And you weren't going to tell me if — if you decided I was going to be a nuisance.' Then to his discomfort, she laughed aloud. '*Droit de seigneur*. Oh help, what a fool to be taken in. No wonder my mother hates the Parstocks.'

★   ★   ★

Hereward did not care to be thought shoddy and cynical. He might have been ashamed, except that he knew, inconveniently and against all probability, that he had fallen in love with this odd child. To touch her smooth, thin body shook him with adolescent fever. She wore for travelling a cotton dress under a hand-knitted white cardigan. Over her arm hung a crumpled plastic mac. Among the Parisians she looked dowdy and very English. In spite of the appalling clothes, there was an airy, newly created radiance about her that drew the eyes of passing men. At the thought of her departure he felt breathless. Panic gripped him. She had become an essential element, like oxygen, and he could no longer imagine going through the ordinary stuff of living without her.

Hereward liked women, not girls. He had not expected to want Bird so fiercely, nor to encounter virginity, not in these times, nor to love so helplessly. 'If I'd told you, you would have run away, and as it is, I can hardly bear to let you take that train. We could fly home together.'

'Impossible,' Bird said, 'think of the questions. Girls talk and you're married, I know you are. My mother would kill me. You can't imagine how powerfully she dislikes me.'

'Do mothers ever dislike their daughters? Surely not.' He grasped her very tightly. 'Are you in love with me at all? I do hope so, because very much against my inclination I love you. I'm behaving badly and babbling like an idiot, I expect.' The food-seller made an impatient French noise and began to rearrange his wares, wanting them to buy something. Hereward picked up a roll that sweated camembert and salad within its plastic, thrust it into Bird's hand and passed over francs. The train whistled urgently. 'It will be all right, I promise you that. Don't worry about Winifred. She's a dear and I shall always love her as a friend. But marriage bores her. We're arranging an amicable divorce.' Even to himself none of this rang true, though true it was. 'Please say something, say you love me.'

13

Did she, though, love him properly? Did she even believe him? A moustachioed man sitting on a folding stool began to squeeze out a tune on an accordion. Between the other noises came occasional bursts of something that might have been 'Under the Bridges of Paris'. Or not. Bird tried her best to think of it as the voice of romance. 'Yes, I do, I expect,' she said, 'but — '

'No buts, darling. We shall meet in Dorset, swim, play tennis, learn about each other. You mustn't be embarrassed. It's not suitable.' He kissed her so thoroughly that she dropped her baguette and trod on it. 'My wife will like you very much.'

That last statement sounded ridiculous. Loved and unsuitable, Bird blushed, hung her head, blinked and he was gone, vanished like a pantomime genie, or Zeus jetting back to Olympus. 'There's no future in this,' she muttered after him. 'How can there be?'

'You lucky bitch,' said one of the girls, a clergyman's daughter who, in her own words, knew her way around a double bed. 'He's gorgeous. Good at it too, I bet.'

'I don't know,' muttered Bird, feeling that her experience in the botanical gardens was scarcely a fair test.

'Didn't you even try? Oh my hat, listen to this girls. Talk about square, she's positively cubic. Paris in the spring, a man to die for, and little Miss Muffet here lets him get away.'

They studied her as though she were a particularly strange exhibit in a museum. Traitorously, she said, 'He's just someone who knows my family. Besides, he's quite old and he's married.'

'Old? Not the way he kissed you, he wasn't. Come on, we'll buy you a glass of milk and tell you the facts of life.' Bird enjoyed the milk and listened with interest to accounts of their experiences. It seemed that in Paris there were hotels that let rooms by the hour. No questions asked. Imagine! That might have been a degree better than cold concrete in a manky old grotto.

★   ★   ★

Back in the present, a helicopter clattered low over the roof of The Glebe and out to sea. Watching Bird's downcast face as her pen hovered over the inevitable form, Hereward accepted that he had disgracefully tricked her into loving him. He could not decide whether he also had been tricked. No act was too spiteful for that bitterly preposterous woman, Bird's mother, who had reduced him to

15

something lower than a worm. Forcing on him the knowledge of what he had done effectively destroyed him. Hereward had not encountered hatred before and he had believed every word she spat at him. But if she had lied? What better punishment than to leave for Bird the humiliation of a young girl fooled and then forgotten?

And yet she appeared to be unembittered, artless still and still with that elusive incandescence. Her charm was carefully muted. She wore a version of a nurse's uniform that removed her into a professional remoteness. It surprised him that she had never married. Lovers, surely? Or had there been no man who measured up to him, her first love? Secretly he preened himself. 'Did you abandon your career as a scientist, Bird?'

'It abandoned me. I could hardly turn up at university three months pregnant.'

His momentary self-satisfaction vanished. Of course, the child. For years he had paid substantial sums in maintenance, yet when the payments stopped he forgot that he was a father. Only an old fool would need to impress, want Bird to love him forever like a character in a cheap novel. A surge of desire, the one emotion that he had not anticipated, dismayed him with its sudden intensity. 'I suppose not. I'm sorry. Our child — it was so wrong of me. Had I known.'

'Known what?' She glanced up at him in vague alarm. 'One thing you must accept is that Hannah is *mine*, not ours. My mother invented a dead father for her and brought her up, while I trained for nursing. She bitterly resents her illegitimacy and blames me for not being there while she was growing. You are never, never to intrude on her life. I hope that's clear.' Hannah lived now, with her young son, in the old lodge-keeper's cottage at the front gates. She resented that too, resented the need to accept help from Bird.

'I make no claim on her. My silence was pledged to Mrs Dawlish in 1970,' he said, a slight huffiness in his voice. 'She should have explained.'

'If there's something I ought to know, can we get it over with now, please?'

'I'm tired,' he said. 'We'll have plenty of time to talk once I move in.'

'You may not be happy here. My fees are high to those who can afford to pay. They subsidise those who can't. There's no compulsion to stay if you feel that's unfair. I can recommend other places.' He simply shook his head. As she recorded Hereward's answers on her form, she recognized that she had probably made a foolish decision. Stella Worth needed sex as fish need water. She

17

would scarcely still be chasing him (another husband or two later) if she believed that he was a waste of her time. Already his air of defeat was fading. His back straightened and with a rapid return to his calm, authoritative self he said, 'Should Stella manage to track me down, you must keep her out. I don't want to see her, d'you understand?'

'Perfectly,' Bird said, with the beginnings of anger. 'I certainly don't want her here and she will as certainly find you. Visiting is not limited. Guests who are able come and go as they please and order their own lives. You must deal with her yourself, Hereward, and make sure that she causes no upsets or the police will become involved.'

'The police?' He stared, astonished and displeased that she was no longer biddable. She was unimpressed. The Glebe could not afford more scandal. When she chanced upon the estate it had been a place of evil reputation. The house and its outbuildings stood in neglect and gloom and the previous proprietors were serving long prison sentences. In the graveyard of Wynfred Abbas lay the bones of those elderly people whom they had robbed before hastening on their passage to the grave. Social workers were then wrestling to move the remaining residents to a council home. Failing to tempt Bird with the grounds and the numerous follies, arches and arbours, the estate agent named a bargain price, shrugged and abandoned her in favour of examining the view to the sea.

Wandering about on her own, she found the nursing unit at a moment of maximum chaos. Collapsed in a hard chair opposite to the door an old, old woman slept, dribbling a shining trail over her chin and on to the front of her dress. At her feet was a bundle of clothes, tied up with string. A gang of men, fussed at by a pest control officer, heaved furniture to and fro, throwing stained and distressingly thin mattresses into a pile The smell, to which in a much lesser degree Bird was accustomed, scalded the back of the throat.

'I wonder if we could burn that lot on site,' said a girl with a clipboard. 'If you want to look around, go ahead. I'm waiting for the ambulance to come for *her*.' She nodded towards the sleeping woman. 'She's been sitting there day after day I'm told, waiting for someone to take her home. I dare say she'd be dead if she weren't drug-resistant.' In spite of — perhaps because of — her youth, the girl sounded irritated rather than shocked.

'Does she have a home?'

'Her family sold it over her head and

dumped her here. We've found her a place; not ideal. This is a private home yet it's costing a bomb in social security. We shouldn't have to be doing this, but I suppose someone's got to.' The desolation of lonely, uncherished old age caused Bird to shiver. The place was haunted by misery. 'We've only two more. They were the ones who spoke up and put a stop to the racket. Now they refuse to move out. No chance of you buying it, I imagine?'

'None.' What miracle could exorcise the ghosts of the abused and the dead?

'Pity. They're pinning their hopes on a buyer. I expect they're in the kitchen getting their lunch. Lizzie Greengrass and Charlie Bean; the long and the short of it, I call them. Would you mind telling them yourself and say that there's a lovely place in Bournemouth I can get them into, if they'll just co-operate?' The girl's impatience was plain. 'I can't leave here until I've got *her* off. Oh, and I could murder a cup of tea if they're making.'

The dreadful smell followed Bird as she passed the empty rooms. To walk through double doors into the kitchen was like a homecoming.

'Meet the two elderly delinquents,' said Lizzie Greengrass, presiding at the stove. 'I suppose she's still on about the lovely place in Bournemouth. She needn't bother.' At a nod from her, Charlie Bean unfolded his stork's legs, and stood to offer Bird a seat at the table. Lizzie grinned. 'Eat with us. It's quite safe; I cooked everything myself.'

The atmosphere of irretrievable misery receded. Bird stepped out into a world of sunlight and bird-song. The conversion of the buildings took months, but her decision to launch into the retirement home business was made at that moment. She had fallen a little in love.

★ ★ ★

Hereward moved into his suite at The Glebe towards the end of July. Three days later, tea was being served to the residents in the lounge and to Bird in her sitting-room when Stella Worth arrived, lightly glazed by alcohol and exuding a mixture of Chanel and gin. 'Ah, there you are, whatsername. Hereward's here, Hereward Parstock. Tell him to come on out. I'll be wanting a room.' She fumbled for a cigarette and dropped it. 'Shit, where's it gone? No matter.' Her theatrical career was over, but her voice, rich and resonant, rattled the teacups. At her peak, that voice and a bold exaggerated loveliness had charmed as Juliet, thrilled as Desdemona and brought a definitive wantonness to Kate. Bird had never seen her in the theatre. 'Foul-mouthed and common as muck, nowadays,' Miles Alban once said; 'dripping primeval slime. But a wonder on stage and quite sweet as a girl, they say. Not that anyone knows where she came from; Mars, Venus, take your pick.'

Stella attacked the cucumber sandwiches with ferocious appetite. 'I don't have a room for you, Mrs Worth,' Bird said; 'this is a retirement home, not an hotel. Another cup of tea before you leave?'

'Couples, you take couples. I'll share with Hereward.'

'Married couples, yes, and he wants peace; he's very tired.'

'Tired,' she repeated, 'aren't we all?' The broad face wore a defenceless expression and her attention seemed to wander a little. 'What's this about? I don't remember you all that well, but I know we've met before somewhere.'

'At Swan House,' Bird said briefly, feeling a retrospective hatred. 'I can't force Mr Parstock to see you, but a maid will tell him that you are here.'

★ ★ ★

Hereward gave Stella a reluctant nod, but neither spoke nor smiled. Half the buttons on her shirt had come undone, whether accidentally or deliberately he neither knew nor cared. 'We're never alone nowadays,' she muttered. 'Can't we go to your room?' She patted her diaphragm and belched with genteel thoroughness. 'Just a quickie?'

Unutterably dismayed, he knew that sick or well, he was never to escape that continual crying-out for love, for sex, which had not happened between them for a long time. Her physical presence so frightened him that it seemed inconceivable that he had once desired her. 'We're old, for God's sake,' he said. 'It's damned unsuitable at your time of life to be forever harping on about sex. And go easy on the cucumber sandwiches if they give you wind. Take up knitting or jigsaw puzzles, but leave me alone.'

'You're screwing bloody Nest, is that it? Or a nurse, or one of the maids. Or is it Miles Alban now? He used to fancy you. Oh God, you've destroyed me, do you know that? All my life has gone.'

'Bird, not Nest.' Hereward had learned to endure jealousy, rage and her terrible devotion, but he had never discovered how to get rid of Stella. Whenever he had refused to see her, she wrote him letters, full of entreaties and vile accusations, laying curses on him, as though he were not already cursed enough. 'Do up some buttons, can't you?' he said, peering distastefully at her tanned and withered breasts. 'You've more wrinkles than a bloodhound. Get married again if you're so obsessed.'

'Christ, just listen to you,' she said. 'What did you ever live for but to lay any woman in sight? Now, where's this Bird person? Oh, there you are. Show me my room, will you?'

Hereward shook a little as his heart began its heavy uneven pounding. He was not a particularly subtle or sensitive man, except in the provision of his own comfort, though he understood and resented the emotions of a rejected woman. Yet surely there was something *weird* about Stella. Bird said at once, 'I've already told you, Mrs Worth, that I can't take you; we're full.' He breathed out slowly, relieved. Stella's determined acts of possession had begun to terrify him. He knew death to be close. All in all he did not mind too much. Simply, he longed for a time of composure before dying. She would never rest, skidding along like a fast car out of control, towards a precipice from which she threatened to hurl herself.

The first fault was his. Just the same, he did not feel that he deserved a lifetime of torment from an unshakeable succubus. 'God help me,' he muttered so quietly that only Bird heard him. She put an arm across his shoulders and rang for the maid to take him back to his room. Stella said, as quietly, 'Why do I do this? It's the very devil.' He did not notice the quivering misery in her face. He could have wept.

2

Before Hereward met and fell in love with Bird he was already out of date. He felt no push towards employment or achievement. Deficient in self-analysis, he simply carried on life as he believed his father had lived it, enjoying the comforts of a large house staffed adequately to meet his needs, taking a desultory interest in his estate, shooting a little, ordering plantings and prunings and leaving gardeners and bailiffs to carry out the work and collect the rents. The difference between father and son was that Parstock senior had a gift for making money, while Hereward's talent lay in spending it. He went through his inheritance at a tremendous rate. When letters from solicitors, banks, accountants or stockbrokers appeared with his breakfast, he handed them to his dismayed young wife. 'Win, darling, you're clever with business. Can you make head or tail of this? I'm sure I don't know what they're on about.'

Although he knew that Winifred was a rich woman, he married her without guile, for love, finding her witty and wise as well as good to look at. By a subtle rearrangement of the features possessed also by her plainer sister, Constance Lovibond, she achieved a beauty that made Hereward proud. 'How I adore you; so much, so deeply,' he said each day, until, reassured by her loving responses, he began to forget to mention his adoration. Quite soon she despaired of trying to teach him to live within his income. Insistence on discussing practical matters clouded his handsome face and spoiled his charm. When she began using her own money to maintain his idle, happy days he did not even notice.

Since his eighteenth birthday, when his father had taken him to spend a holiday with old friends in America, Hereward had enjoyed a satisfying and varied sex life. He lost his virginity on the edge of the surf at Long Beach to his host's importunate thirty-eight-year-old daughter, and much of his father's hidden dollar investments in the casinos of Las Vegas. The anger of Parstock senior at both these activities struck him as amusing. He insisted on telling the story to Winifred. 'Poor Father never sowed a wild oat in his life. Even his affairs were businesslike. He thought it bad form to carry on with the married daughter of a friend, but she was by no means a virgin and she did absolutely throw herself at me.'

'You sound proud of yourself,' said

Winifred in a dry tone. 'I hope you don't propose to while away the evening hours on a regular basis with stories of your sex life. I should much prefer you keep past encounters to yourself.'

'Nonsense, my darling. I hadn't met you then and there was nothing unpleasant about it. The family are good style, and at that time, *faute de mieux*, it might have been a truly sordid encounter with a prostitute.' He lifted her hand to his lips. 'We are one; I feel that I can tell you anything and everything.'

Winifred sighed deeply. 'But I prefer not to know everything. Sex is utterly boring unless one is doing it oneself.' Perversely, such indelicate frankness from his wife upset Hereward, who half believed that to talk of sex was a male prerogative. When he began taking mistresses, he did not, of course, tell her everything, or indeed anything. She knew nonetheless. To his further discomfort she mentioned that she was inclined to leave him. 'I beg you not to, my darling. My love for you is too deep to be shaken by indiscretions. They are stupid impulses that mean nothing. Forgive me. It will never happen again, I swear.' But inevitably it did. And she, too, was guilty of not telling him those things that he had a right to know. To secure the property from his creditors, and taking advantage of his willingness to sign any document she put in front of him, Winifred had bought Swan House over his head. She was not anxious to confess this deception, as she would have felt compelled to do had she left him. In any case, she was immensely fond of Hereward; his liaisons never lasted and posed no threat to their marriage. By the time that the obsessed and determined Stella Worth came along, Winifred was too bored with a life that excluded the excitement of art and the discovery of new painters and writers to give a damn. 'I feel that we should divorce, since we no longer amuse each other,' she said, not entirely without malice. 'Stella seems to love being married, while I don't. She will provide you with plenty of entertainment.'

After some argument, Hereward's resistance weakened, though he managed to make Winifred's discontent seem unreasonable. 'There's no hurry, surely? I still love and admire you, but since that is clearly not enough to make you happy, do as you wish, but let it be without acrimony,' he said: 'We need not be enemies.'

'Naturally not, and it may not be simple. The grounds are shaky since I've waited so long and condoned so much. But I'm sure that I can rely on you not to give up adultery at this stage.'

He had not thought of grounds, disliking Winifred's sardonic tone and the idea of his private matters becoming public gossip. 'There's all the time in the world,' he said. 'You know and forgive all my faults and *I* know that I can never replace you. I don't want to lose you or to remarry and I wish you would stay with me.' But then, in Paris, he met Bird Dawlish.

★　★　★

The first rumour of Bird's pregnancy was fed to Hereward by Stella, who, when bored, nosed around the house and estate and kept a sharp eye on her rival. 'Something's up with your little friend,' she said. 'There's a great deal of praying and argument going on at that hovel she lives in. It wouldn't surprise me if you've got her pregnant, you dirty old sod.'

'Nonsense; I don't believe it.'

'Then why hasn't she been near this house for days?'

'You know perfectly well that you made a scene to upset her. I can't reach her to talk about it. That cottage is like a stockade. There's not even a telephone.' But Hereward's confidence was sadly dented. Would even Stella's insults have kept Bird away for so long? In his limited mental vision he saw his girl, composed of light and air, become heavy and earthbound, the slight body invaded by an anonymous, importunate being, himself excluded. Although his passionate love for Bird was genuine, it was now touched with resentment against her. And his disappointment was fed by the slightest feeling that, in loving her, he had condescended to a social inferior. He certainly had not bargained for a child. Even had he been free to marry, the idea of a hasty, hole-in-corner wedding offended his dignity. What *would* his friends say?

Stella could afford not to argue with him. 'We'll see. If I'm right, don't get any noble ideas. Just remember that you are committed to marrying me if Winifred decides to divorce you, and I won't go quietly. Better buy the girl off.'

The arrival of a coldly vengeful Mrs Dawlish, seeking an interview, confirmed the acuteness of Stella's observation and consigned Hereward to a role slightly less worthy than that of a frog in a puddle. Under her onslaught of controlled rage and contempt, his self-respect and masculine pride shrivelled away to nothing. Was he, with the rest of the Parstocks, a perverted destroyer of young girls, a near-rapist who should be burned alive on earth as he would surely burn in

Hell? His ultimate intentions had been honourable. Accustomed to being loved and admired and serenely certain that Bird was his, the awful complication of her mother destroyed the last of the summer idyll. 'It isn't the cynical act that you describe, Mrs Dawlish,' he said. 'I love her and I must explain, help her somehow.'

'You are never to approach her again. You will arrange to pay to my solicitors such amounts for her maintenance and the child's as I decide. Your name will not be mentioned in connection with either. Do you understand me?'

Hereward understood. A coward he might be, but he could find no way of fighting the bitter diktats presented to him, and to defy them would make things worse for Bird. The loss of her broke his heart. He denied to himself the faint sense of relief that tempered the pain. His solicitors were instructed to pay whatever was asked of them and he consoled himself with the assurance that she and the child would want for nothing. He had no means of understanding the full extent of Mrs Dawlish's malice. Had it not been for Stella lurking and ready, he felt sure, to sue for breach of promise when circumstances seemed favourable, he would have kept the whole disastrous tale from Winifred.

Always in the past, his liaisons had been discreet, the women involved were happy with impermanent pleasures. Stella, a twice-divorced actress, ought to have been the same. Thinking of her dark, captivating vivacity revived for an instant the violence of his passion for her that had swept caution aside. Until she insisted on following him to Swan House, he had not noticed her strangeness. Even his love for Bird left her unshaken and the more violently determined to marry him. He was aware that first with Stella and secondly (and worse) with Bird he had crossed an invisible boundary of taste and acceptability. The last thing Hereward wanted now was a divorce. He did not look forward to facing Winifred with a plea for delay.

Telling her was even worse than he had imagined it could be. She listened silently, but with an expression of distaste reflecting that of Mrs Dawlish. 'I can't apologize for falling in love with Bird,' he said at length, hoping to move her to pity. 'It was as unexpected and painful as a lightning strike. That in no way diminishes my abiding affection for you. I felt unhappy about you, but as we had already agreed on divorce, I saw no harm in loving again.'

'And at precisely what point did you fall

out of love with Stella, she asked, her anger obvious, 'and decide to destroy the life of an impressionable young girl? Your emotions seem to become shallower with middle age; the male menopause, perhaps?'

In spite of a dull answering anger at her questions, and a suspicion that he was not the god Bird had believed him to be, he spoke quietly. 'I can't analyse what's wrong with me, Win. I know only that I am being punished for it; Stella waiting to pounce and that dreadful Mrs Dawlish with the knives out! All I can do is throw myself on your mercy and beg that you won't divorce me yet.'

'You deserve Stella. Neither of you has the slightest regard for other people's feelings, mine least of all. I'm thoroughly out of love with marriage and with you. I was so much looking forward to being with my family again and now you ask me to give that up to act as a kind of bodyguard against a discarded mistress and the mother of a pregnant child. How lucky you are that neither has had you shot.'

'Winifred!'

'What a pointless man you are. Instead of considering the girl whose youth you've wasted, you think only of saving your own skin. Do you wonder I'm in a rage?'

'Please,' he said, 'don't hate me. Stay with me. I need you.'

'I really cannot be bothered to hate you, any more than I can be bothered to love you. It's a waste of good emotion. Now please go away and let me think.' The conclusion of Winifred's thoughts was that for the time being she would substitute a judicial separation for divorce. 'I won't stay with you, Hereward. Lead your own life, such as it is, and I'll lead mine. By Christmas I intend to be in London.'

Stella's single shriek of rage when he told her the news startled the crows out of the trees. 'God knows why I love such a slippery cheating bastard,' she hissed, pushing her face within an inch of his and showing every one of her strong teeth. 'Men have died for less.'

Hereward retreated into dignity. 'I do wish you would stop calling me evil names, Stella. Surely we can be friends?'

'Friends? I don't want any more bloody friends. Get out of my sight, I'm going for a swim to wash some of the slime off me.'

'Sorry, Stella, the cover's on the pool,' he said, feeling feeble, as though he were recovering from a serious illness.

'I don't want your nice bland pool; it's only fit for this damned morgue. I need the sea, something to fight, power that has to be defeated before it defeats you.'

Hereward thought of the sea, full of dangerous living things and dead men, and decided that he did not much care for it, nor did he trust Stella when she was angry. She swam as easily as she walked and he preferred to avoid drowning. 'I hope you don't expect me to go with you.'

'I'll break your arm if you try,' she said, in a tone that he recognized as truth unvarnished, and walked off. He saw her car speed down the drive and turn into the road without pausing. She was away for two days. Returning, she ignored him, wandering around alone. Her restless prowling exasperated him to wretchedness and he wished that Winifred would ask her to go. Eventually she was called to London for rehearsals, occasionally turning up without warning, expressly, he thought, to make him miserable. He longed for Bird's adoration that had made him feel half his age and phenomenal. Yet, now that he was losing her, he had never loved and admired his wife more, clinging to the thought that a separation could easily be set aside.

But with the approach of Christmas, Winifred died her cruel death and he was devastated by it. He forgot his fear of Stella who, confronted with his rage of despair, said with simple heartlessness, 'She was going to leave you anyway, so what's your problem? You'll soon get over it and when we're married it'll all be forgotten.'

He turned away from her, noticing through the window an old creature moving around at the edge of the arboretum. Who was she? Perhaps he was haunted by evil spirits. 'Marry you?' he shouted, outraged and unnerved, 'I'd sooner marry a rattlesnake. I don't know where you came from, but you can fuck off back there. You're weird, Stella, do you know that? Bloody weird; without humanity or a soul.' Tears began to trickle down the grooves in his cheeks.

'Perhaps the devil was around when I was begotten. Who knows?' Her voice reverberated as though she were on-stage. 'Cry as much as you like, but don't think you've seen the last of me; you haven't.' She made a splendid exit, lifting an arm gracefully and pointing at him. The old woman had disappeared. The emptiness of house and garden was both restful and dreary. A few months later, Stella married a third husband, a millionaire property-developer with a reputation in the City for unparalleled miserliness, and haunted Hereward no more.

It was something of a surprise to him to find that he had inherited Swan House from

Winifred, since as far as he knew it had always been his. She left him no capital, only an annuity for life. His solicitor talked seriously and made Hereward listen. His income, reduced by the charges upon it, and the annuity were not, together, enough to keep up the house. 'But I don't understand how it came to be Winifred's,' he said.

'If you paid the slightest attention to business matters, you would know that she bought it from you to safeguard it from your creditors. The proceeds are what you have been living on. Unless you fancy the Labour Exchange and a pittance from the State, the house will have to be sold again. There's plenty of land; I daresay a developer would pay a decent price. I will advise on investments to ensure you a good living.'

Hereward held out for a couple of years. In the end, it was the silence and a sense that he was gradually fading from existence, as much as the shortage of money, that persuaded him to sell. He leased an apartment in London and for a time enjoyed the renewal of a social life among friends. Rumours began to circulate that Stella's millionaire had gutter tastes in women and was offended at his wife's ill-concealed disgust when he returned to her with gonorrhoea or a colony of body lice. Divorced again, Stella found Hereward and took up a cautious pursuit. When she wanted to be she was a sparkling companion, persuading him to attend her first nights, luring him into her bed, making him laugh. But she was soaking up gin like a mop in a bucket and beginning to take on a quality that sometimes frightened him. One morning far too early, he awoke to find her looming above him. The suffocating mass of her black hair hung over his face and touched the pillow and he could have counted the faint lines around her eyes. She said, 'Winifred's been dead for more than ten years. You may be a prize shit, but you're the only man I truly want to marry.'

Alarmed, he rolled out of bed so suddenly that he left her sprawled face down and cursing. 'You've had three stabs at it already and it never works. It's getting to be a habit. We do well enough as we are for the time being.'

'Until when?' asked Stella.

'I must go; I'm lunching with friends. We'll talk about it again tomorrow.' Hereward dressed and left the house. He visited his bank and the nearest branch of Thomas Cook. Returning to his apartment, he packed bags in time to catch a late flight to Milan. In the south of Italy he settled, relaxing in the balm of sun and wine and indulging in a little light fornication among those wives who spent their summers in expensive villas, while their husbands stayed at home making the money to pay for them. Obscenely libellous letters from Stella were sent on to him. He burned them. The months passed pleasantly enough uncounted, extending into years when he travelled a little, tried his hand at oil-painting and wood-carving (unsuccessfully), and went to festivals and exhibitions. Occasionally he ran into old acquaintances and entertained them in his house overlooking the Bay of Naples.

Reading in an English newspaper that Stella had decided to retire from the stage to marry yet again, Hereward noticed that he was missing England. Feeling older and rather tired, it occurred to him also that he was almost seventy and had felt no need of sex or sun in several months. 'Do I want to die in Italy?' he asked himself aloud, looking around at the overbright sky and sea and flowers and women. He did not. When his time came, he wanted to lie with Winifred in the darkness and peace of the family vault. Peace; a comforting ideal in a dull muddle of a world. With that blessed promise of rest, it should be safe enough now to return home.

The new husband was, it seemed a young and aspiring actor, less than half Stella's age, who, if the burblings in Press reports were to be believed, worshipped at her expensively shod feet and would adore her forever, richer or poorer. (Picture on Page 4.) But, thought Hereward, examining the photographs, particularly richer I should guess. 'Fourth time lucky,' said the bride, leering out of the smudgy picture. 'I'm very, very happy. We hope to act together when the right play comes along.'

In Hereward's absence, London had grown in noise and traffic and people and violence. He felt ill at ease there. His doctor, diagnosing a heart weakness, advised him to move to the country. 'A hotel that accepts residents, perhaps, or one of the new retirement developments.' But where? He thought he might advertise the remainder of the lease of his apartment for sale, but in the end did nothing other than worry about himself.

But the fourth time of marriage had not proved to be at all lucky for Stella. Her husband's career had taken off, while hers was in decline 'for lack of suitable parts', and he explained publicly that she was over jealous and drank too much. Her reply, tidied up, was, 'He's a — little beetle who stole my money, my jewels, anything he could get his hands on. Now let him sue me, if he dares.'

Experience, thought Hereward, failed to sour her belief that some parasite looking for easy money would make her happy ever after. This last remnant of hopeful trust both irritated and touched him. He did not expect her to want to find him after so long, but find him she did. He scarcely recognized the haggard, over-strung creature she had become, knowing that instead of a lover in his prime, she now looked with dismay at a sick old man. 'You need livening up,' she said. 'Let's do a show and take it from there.'

'I'm ill, heart trouble. I've nothing to offer you, Stella; I don't even go out these days.'

She fidgeted around the room, disturbing it with her own neurotic energy. 'The same old brush-off, isn't it? Christ, men are swine. I thought that after all these years we might manage to get some kind of relationship going, a quiet marriage even.'

'What is it with you and marrying, Stella? You live life as though you're in an unending drama. Four duds ought to be enough for any woman. Surely you didn't expect that weasel-eyed youth to last?'

'What's wrong with hoping for permanence?'

'It's out of character for you to be so gullible. Whatever demon drives you, it's to a kind of madness. You're gin-soaked and self-destructive.'

'And why not?' she asked 'Loving you has been ruinous. You're shrink-wrapped in plastic, Hereward, visible but useless; creating nothing, feeling nothing that requires effort, simply passing the time and drifting through life like a damned jellyfish. Yet I was desperate to get you and I want you still. Come and live with me.'

In a sudden fury, Hereward bellowed, 'Insult me as much as you like, Stella, then clear off and don't come back. In some way that I can't fathom, you've managed to destroy my life as well as your own.' He had to fight for breath, clutching at his chest. 'Go on, before you kill me.'

'Right, but I'll be back tomorrow.' From that moment he was under siege. He gave orders that Stella was not to be admitted and stopped taking her abusive telephone calls. Her letters remained unread and unanswered. Hereward despaired of ever being free of her.

Since he had sold Swan House, he thought of Bird only in unguarded moments of loneliness or boredom. He experienced a shock when he came upon an advertisement in *The Times* for a luxury apartment vacant at The Glebe retirement home, proprietor Bird Dawlish. From the page came an acute reminder of her physical presence; the sight, the scent, the feel of her slight body against his, the thrill of taking her. The newsprint seemed like a beckoning, a sign from Heaven. A secluded place by the sea was the perfect solution to his problems. Time had surely expunged the guilts and sins of the past, yet he thought it prudent not to mention in advance his decision to visit The Glebe.

It was a lovely place, standing tranquil in its gardens. Here he could rest and be forgiven. Until Bird reminded him, he had quite forgotten that he was the father of a child of hitherto unknown sex, a daughter whom he had never seen.

3

At her home in Rye, Constance Lovibond, Hereward Parstock's sister-in-law, listened to Miles Alban babbling excitedly while his breakfast egg went cold. He had just telephoned The Glebe to announce his return that day. 'Isn't it amazing, Connie, that Hereward should be there. Such an old friend. Just when I was missing your dear father so much I shall have someone to talk to about my book. He won't mind about me being you-know-what, will he? Everyone's out nowadays.'

'If you don't make a point of it, I'm sure he won't,' said Connie. 'I haven't seen him since Winifred's funeral. It will be interesting to meet him again.' Miles had been writing his novel, a love-triangle between three men, for over a year and it sounded quite dreadful. He loved to read his work aloud, with expression. She doubted whether her father listened to a word, though he suffered the burden politely, wearing the smile with which he dismissed poor art. 'Yes, good, good. Thank you for letting me hear it.'

'You puzzle me, Connie. I'm delighted to

claim you as my guest, but why leave a perfectly lovely house for a retirement home? You always seem to me to be definitely a four-star hotel type. Not that I can complain: Bird has a capacious wing, if you will forgive a feeble joke. I live in luxury. Yet you are neither infirm nor particularly old, and now that your father is gone, you have absolute freedom.' Connie did not point out that, with her help, he had retreated to The Glebe soon after his fiftieth birthday. She understood him. The wounds of the past went deep and had barely healed. He spoke of being 'out', yet he was quite unable to cope with openness or his sexuality and he struggled to be celibate. One snub would send him right back in again.

'It isn't to be permanent, you know. Bird is only taking me as a favour. I need a rest and some kind of mental stimulus.'

In 1970, the young Miles had been an actor of promise, a glorious creature, sleekly aglow. Connie had loved him then, desperately — and hopelessly as she had known perfectly well. Miles might enjoy, even depend upon, the company and devotion of women, but he remained firmly homosexual. For a few weeks a kind of wild, uncomfortable romance had infused her reasoned life, showering sudden bursts of light and colour like exploding fireworks. At thirty-eight she should certainly have shown more sense. She passed him the toast, grateful that her freakish passion had died in time to save her from the absolute tedium of unrequited love.

'That summer,' he said softly. 'I wondered at the time how much went on between Bird and Hereward. I was stupidly jealous, having a bit of a thing about Hereward myself, though I think he would have killed me had I made the smallest sign.'

Connie, watching Miles, had noticed when she partnered him at tennis how his eyes followed Hereward and how he wilted if Hereward snapped at him. She said, 'Somehow I feel that between us we damaged Bird. That extraordinary brilliance, yet it came to nothing.'

'We were too wrapped up in ourselves to do her much harm, though I think that, even then, she saw us as we are, flawed and pathetic.' Miles spoke more loudly than he intended and glanced apprehensively at Connie for fear of offending her. 'She's awfully compassionate.'

Connie laughed. 'Flawed, pathetic? Really, Miles, that's a bit much.'

'Aren't we, though? You're rich, you never married. All your time until now has been spent in looking after your father and, of course, me. Hereward never had a mite of business sense. Everything gone except what Winifred salvaged for him while she was alive. And I managed to make a complete balls-up of my life and work. As for old Stella, her obsessions and appetites are beyond normal understanding.' The actor's voice retained its charm. He added, 'We can't have impressed Bird too much or she would have stayed around longer. There's a daughter living in the lodge cottage, you know. Not *simpatica*. They don't get on.'

His career had foundered on a small and entirely unimportant indiscretion in a public lavatory after his first theatrical triumph. A police officer, routinely spying, arrested him on a charge of importuning. The newspapers took little interest. It was 1979. They were feasting on the Thorpe trial. But Miles, achingly sensitive as he was, suffered a nervous breakdown that spelled the death of his self-esteem. Connie stepped in and rescued him. She had taken care of him ever since, managing the shreds of his career, and finding him nowadays infectiously prim and Edwardian. She censored her conversation with him as she might have done for a bishop. 'Truly, Miles, my dear, I haven't the temperament for marriage. Men do tend to demand the mind and soul as well as the heart and that I couldn't endure.'

He enjoyed gossip too much to be interested in her opinions. 'I wonder what Stella will do now. Husbands have never stopped her from pursuing Hereward. It must be years since they were lovers and, like a bulldog, she will *not* let go. We can expect high drama.' His smile held faint malice. 'Promise me, Connie, that you'll still let me come here, even though your father's gone. It's my refuge. I adore staying with you, and the unusual little shops, and lunching at the Mermaid or the Hope Anchor. There isn't a commonplace object in your house. You never sneer at me or make me awkward and you let me talk about art.'

Connie viewed him with dispassionate kindness, thinking that her ache for him had been a particularly silly joke on the part of fate. How desperately she had longed, in the heat of that distant summer, to take him in her arms, kiss his alluring mouth and stroke the bright curls of coppery gold that grew thickly down to the nape of his neck. Such hair as remained fluffed in downy sparseness over a pallid scalp. He had lost teeth. As an old friend, she now had leave to kiss him and avoided doing so. Age had its compensations! 'Of course you'll always be welcome. Having you here has helped me through a dismal time. As soon as Bird's care and protection pall, I shall come home.' Patiently she supervised his departure, closing the door on him with relief. She considered, though only momentarily, cancelling her visit to The Glebe. It was always good to be alone. Yet this gathering together of the 1970 house-party, insignificant at the time, had the distinct feel of a summoning. Not by Winifred, who was dead. Who then? A rational woman, accustomed to regarding life as a series of random events, Connie disliked any hint of the supernatural. She needed a change of scene. If anything, acquaintances would be less challenging than strangers in her present frame of mind. But she could not entirely dispel a sense of compulsion.

★   ★   ★

A herring-gull stood one-legged on top of Connie's car. She would miss the gulls. Strident and vulgar, they owned Rye, screaming at night as well as by day. The Glebe was closer to the sea, but Dorset gulls were probably genteel birds who went discreetly about their affairs and never squabbled. Her house, built in the reign of the second George, looked its loveliest. She felt a terrible reluctance to leave, even though she had determined on going. 'I have an urge to get to the bottom of things,' she told the gull. 'I've waited a long time. Wish me luck as a discerning resident in a retirement apartment of the first quality. No, don't crap on the car, curse you, it's just been cleaned.' The clock on the church opposite the house struck ten, followed by the rare longcase clock in the hall. Her father had made his fortune from art, which was both his business and his passion. He had possessed neither a wireless set nor a television. Even the kitchen paraphernalia came from a past age, other than the electric stove and lamps that Connie had insisted upon. 'Sixty-five years old,' she informed the clock, 'I've never yet owned a plastic washing-up bowl or an amusing coffee-mug, I look like hell on earth and I'm getting into the habit of talking to myself.'

After Winifred's death, their father took up perpetual mourning and bought yet more paintings, some of them morbid in theme. The walls became full. He stacked the overflow in the attics, changing them around so frequently that Connie no longer bothered to look at them. He rarely left home except to attend sales. Unmarried, devoted, wearied, Connie had been trapped. Nevertheless, she locked the door behind her with regret. Rye on its hill was a siren town, luring travellers and holding them fast. She would be back. As she approached the car, the gull hopped unconcernedly down on to the road under the front wheels and began to investigate the cracks between the cobblestones. Cautiously, with the bird waddling ahead like an undertaker's mute, she bumped away.

★   ★   ★

For a Sunday morning, the High Street and The Mint were unusually busy. A steady stream of people, many of them weeping, climbed the hill, carrying flowers. Why? It was 31 August, not, therefore, a wartime anniversary. Presumably someone had died. Connie tried to look for a newspaper billboard, but found that she needed all her attention to negotiate her way out of town. Travelling westward on minor roads, she lost most of the traffic and forgot the mourners. Her ambling speed gave her time to decide that she was doing a crazy thing. Never mind. If it helped to exorcize the summer of '70 and its aftermath, she would be content and free.

Five people were at Swan House, six including Bird Dawlish, who had become significant because they had made her so with their tangled and quite pointless emotions.

They had patronized, flattered and disparaged her in gentle voices. Youth and wild loveliness, allied to a burning intelligence, needed somehow to be cut down to size, so they praised and damned her in the same breath. 'Why this love-in for a country nobody?' Miles had asked, petulant because he had expected to be the star of the party. 'I know she lives on the estate, but must we talk about her all the time? Stella's in a raging temper and tennis is a farce. Neither of you girls has your mind on the game.'

'It's just too bad about Stella, nagging at Hereward all the time to take her down to the sea so that she can get him on his own. It's thirty miles, for heaven's sake, and who wants to drive in this heat?' Connie replied, glad that he had not noticed the reason for her distraction. 'Attention is tedious unless directed at one's self.'

'Isn't it, though?' He smiled. 'I suppose it's because of Stella that Winifred proposes to leave Hereward. She's pretty blatant.'

'There's no single reason. Winifred has never thought highly of marriage. Quite simply, she's had enough and wants to live her own kind of life. It offends the masculine sense of possession, I know, but it isn't always men who tire of domesticity.'

In a mild way Winifred had wanted

children. She had said to Connie, 'Five years ago I was distressed not to produce an heir, now I'm relieved to have avoided that complication. Of course I knew that Hereward was bound to be unfaithful; all Parstock men are. If only he wouldn't bring his mistresses home! Look at Stella, jealous as hell and terrified of losing him to the point where civilized conversation is impossible. Illicit sex turns women into vulgar bores. He's a bore too, poor dear, marriage is a bore, and I refuse to go on pretending to be blind, deaf and stupid, or that I care what he does.'

Connie laughed, though she was concerned. 'Do I preach at this point that love suffereth long and is kind?'

'Please don't. For the first five years I adored Hereward. I still like him as much as ever. Generally he has rather a nice nature and an almost hypnotic charm. Also he has the sudden Parstock rages; a savage streak that I hate.'

'There's not another man, I take it?'

'I'm simply out of love. Sex day and night for a while, fine; I enjoyed it. But it's scarcely a life's work. As friends, he and I can meet or avoid each other when we choose. To be married implies the acting out of roles set generations ago and laughably out of date. I firmly believe that lust causes temporary softening of the brain!'

'True,' Constance had sighed, thinking of Miles Alban and feeling an immediate acute desire. She managed to concentrate her wandering attention on his hands. They were ugly. Ginger hair grew thickly on their backs, his touch was flabby and moist, he had stubby fingers and bit his nails. That had calmed her down.

'How lucky we were to grow up among musicians and artists and writers,' Winifred said. 'Father knew how to furnish our minds and, God knows, there are plenty to let with vacant possession. If only someone, anyone, good and kind, would take Hereward off my hands. After a fashion he still loves me. I'm his anchor and his alibi.'

'You think he won't leave you?'

'I know he won't, not yet. The very last thing he wants is to be free to marry Stella. I shall have to be the one to go.'

After indifferent weather, June had flamed and burned. Solid objects appeared insubstantial and fragile in the dense air. The sun mesmerized. Connie, made imaginative by frustrated love, was decidedly surprised to feel quite suddenly that in the languorous heat that slowed their movements lurked a subtle and sinister threat. She immediately took two aspirin and a dose of Epsom salts, a remedy for many things, but not for superstitious fears. Her unease remained. Eventually she decided that the true cause of her discomfort was a depraved yearning to be dragged behind a bush by Miles and thoroughly debauched. She felt anxious, also, over the unpleasantness faced by her sister. Love, sex and marriage were a complete bloody nuisance. Her father needed help in preparing an autumn exhibition at his gallery, where passion seldom intruded unless set in paint or stone, and in July she fled to London. 'Come back with me now,' she had begged her sister. 'Don't waste any more of your life. We'll be thrilled to have you home.'

'Not now — soon. For Christmas at the latest. There's a lot to sort out first.' Connie planned festivities that were destined never to take place. For the remaining years of his life, her father ignored the feast.

At Ditchling Beacon she parked the car by the roadside to order her thoughts, considering food and voting against it in favour of a cigarette and a discreet sip or two from her small flask of brandy. A sudden tension caused her heart to jump violently under her sensible dark suit. Memory was a roller-coaster ride pitched between Heaven and Hell, and in late December of 1970 she had sat helplessly, holding her sister against her shoulder as she died, worn out by the appalling violence of gastro-enteritis. Hereward wept. They tidied Winifred away on a shelf in the Parstock family vault. Snow fell heavily. The roads into Dorset were blocked and there were few mourners.

Hereward had not married again. Stella persisted, but failed, and now Bird had him in her care. Surely he had loved Bird? He was free, yet nothing came of it. They had met and separated within months. Why? Unguarded expressions, actions half-witnessed, words spoken more than a quarter of a century before, began to spin in her mind. She considered the Parstock capacity for anger that she had not so far encountered. What frustrations might set a spark to savagery? Had there been a pattern, a hidden evil at Swan House to cause her own flight? Probably not. Most things that happen to most people are chance, and true wickedness is rare.

Well, at least my motives are clear enough, Connie reminded herself; to discover my old age of course, and then to know whatever there is to be known, what exactly happened between Hereward and Bird and Stella, how Winifred came to die in mid-winter of a summer infection, everything.

She drove on, stopping in Romsey for a late lunch. The town seemed to be in the grip of a hushed and hopeless desolation. Only then did she discover that the Princess of Wales had been killed in an accident, so sudden and devastating that the counties were in shock. From the back of the restaurant came the voice of a commentator. The BBC, of course. Odd how the whole world trusted them for truth in momentous times.

The eyes of her waiter swam with tears as he said, 'It's the waste of a loving heart that gets me down. When I was in the navy, we grumbled sometimes about the spit and polish for royal visits, but never for her. She was human. It's hard to believe that she's gone.' He picked up a menu, then put it down again. 'No good showing you that. Chef's Italian and he's in a worse state than the rest of us. You're going to have an awful meal. I'd advise you to go somewhere else, except that you're too late for the pubs and most other places are closed.'

The food was as bad as he predicted. Her spaghetti bolognaise confirmed that the chef's heart was not in his work. Left over from yesterday, I bet, thought Connie, struggling to get it down. Extraordinary that there should be so much public grief for a stranger. And yet, out there, anonymous and unregarded, were many thousands of women, cheated, robbed and betrayed, who resented for the princess the cynicism of her marriage and her public rejection. However rapaciously pursued, total happiness and eternal life were impossible goals. Connie foresaw another slump in the already devalued Prince Charming market. To her intense astonishment, for she could never be described as a sentimental woman, a deep sadness gripped her, not for a single individual, but for the cheapness of modern dreams and the idiot's mess that was the world.

The royal house, protected by adulation, had always stepped delicately, treading on no toes too heavily. Not, at least, until those ill-advised attempts to snatch back popularity and justify bad behaviour by airing publicly what were essentially personal matters. Overconfidence in their own *rightness*, of course. They were unused to the rude shocks that life deals out generously to lesser mortals. Small wonder that they were not remarkable for imagination or an excess of emotion. So what now? A very nasty dilemma that was not about to go quietly away. There would be consequences, reverberations, constant rakings-up, and the republican hounds baying for change, a tedious prospect for an old and non-political woman, thought Connie. A waste of the dwindling, precious days. She smiled at her own selfish views and overtipped the waiter, hoping to dry his tears.

4

The Parstocks were a large family and, in the main, a close one. They declared that they could trace their ancestry back to before the arrival of William the Conqueror, though no document was ever produced to support the claim. Evidence was scarcely necessary. Belief in their superiority featured strongly in the Parstock natures. Had anyone cared to look for the basis of this belief it would have been hard to uncover. They followed ordinary occupations. In Suffolk, the county of their origin, they lived close to each other and became lawyers or accountants or ran small successful businesses. 'Joined at the hip,' said an interloper from Ireland, audacious enough to court a Parstock daughter. He retired gracefully, squeezed out with relentless politeness, a lucky escape from a lifetime of tyranny.

English men and women all, they married only others of their own kind. It disturbed and alarmed them when Hereward's grandfather became engaged to a foreigner, a Dutchwoman, and resisted all their gentle arguments against the unwisdom of so rash a departure from the family tradition. She was a beautiful girl, tall, fair, rounded of figure. The other wives sneered secretly at her names, which were Bird Sasha, feeling put-down by their inability to be superior. They treated her with effusive patronage that was worse than hostility.

The black sheep, having his full share of family arrogance, did not care overmuch for his relatives, for offices, shops and warehouses, or for Suffolk. He looked further afield. Eventually he came upon a large rundown house in Dorset, where he could indulge his two passions, building and books. He set about restoring the property and establishing his library. The land was enough to bring a living. His wife created for them a small model farm that provided milk and eggs, fruit and greenstuffs. For a while other Parstocks wrote, sent invitations for Christmas, weddings, christenings and the occasional funeral, and met with polite refusals. Eventually the renegades were forgotten.

Without these grandparents, Hereward probably would not have met, let alone have married, Winifred Lovibond, whose ancestry was a good European mix and who was a woman of character and intellect. The Parstocks distrusted intelligent women. Hereward's father reverted sufficiently to ancestral type to marry the daughter of a Suffolk clergyman. She was a sunny-natured, acquiescent girl, though not robust. Soon after her son was born she developed pernicious anaemia and, when he was fourteen, she died. Bird Sasha survived her daughter-in-law by two years. After her death, the three generations of men pursued their separate lives together at Swan House, creating a new superiority of Parstocks.

The Lovibonds were few, but tightly knit. As for the Dawlishes, they were fewer almost to the point of non-existence, and clutching grimly at grievances. Arnold Dawlish communicated only with farmers. At home he was silent. Bird never knew him, as he died within weeks of her birth. Soon afterwards, Mrs Dawlish came under the influence of an itinerant evangelist and colporteur, adopted a religion of unparallelled malevolence, and withdrew into a general hatred of her fellows, especially if they were Parstocks. Her days were spent in prayer, obsessive house-cleaning and reading. The travelling library called once a fortnight. Mrs Dawlish read methodically from A to Z, beginning again after Zola, whether the books were new to her or not. How Bird (odd that she had been given a Parstock name) managed to grow up loving and giving was, Connie Lovibond concluded, one of the mysterious tricks of heredity.

Following the unfenced road across the clifftops, she negotiated a sharp bend and arrived abruptly at the gates of The Glebe. There she stopped the car and composed her thoughts. On her left stood the church, flag flying at half-mast, and beside it a row of cottages. Before her, a single street, empty of life, fell steeply away towards rocks splotched with green and, beyond, the streaked blue of the sea. No seagulls, no sound. Behind low windows sat the population, imprisoned by the blue, jittery light of television screens. That was the world, encapsulated. Nevertheless she found herself watched by a small boy, standing motionless in the garden of the lodge. He gazed at the car with a half-smile of pure pleasure. Connie moved on slowly, smiling back. 'Hallo,' he said and might have said more, except that a young woman emerged from the house, favoured her with a long, unfriendly glare, then grabbed his arm and led him inside.

This, then, must be the daughter with whom Bird failed, unsurprisingly, to get on. A brief glimpse produced an impression of plainness; an arched, arrogant nose under

64

frowning eyebrows, pale hair that hung long and straight past the shoulders. Vaguely Connie wondered who had fathered her. According to Miles, Bird was given married status by courtesy, but her name remained Dawlish. The girl might, of course, be adopted. There need be no reason why Bird should not have picked up a baby during her nursing career. Adopted children often grew to resent their adopters. Or she could have married and divorced. Or have had a hundred lovers, but sensibly remained single. With these faintly acid thoughts, Connie accelerated and swept at a dignified speed up the long gravel drive between rose-beds to the elegant front door.

★　★　★

While Connie Lovibond idled along the Dorset roads, struggling to digest a malevolent knot of dried-up spaghetti, Bird waited in the garden, breathing in the restorative silence. For this brief interval she was unnecessary. Most of the residents were welded to the television sets, waiting for some explanation of an inexplicable tragedy. Unaccountably, Hereward had locked himself in his room and refused to leave it. This withdrawal could not, thought Bird wryly, have much to do with the royal family: the Parstocks had always been royalty enough for themselves. He seemed to be in a curious state of mind, half accepting the nearness of death, half resentful of those excitements he must one day miss: the journeys abroad to France and Italy, the pleasant rivalry of intelligent discussion, the books forever unread and, above all, the beautiful women unseduced. If he grieved, it was for himself.

Her mind began to drift. The dead princess, Hannah, herself, tangled themselves together, emerging as one child, to all intents motherless and damaged. She was aware of a growing agitation. Events and conversation rose up hauntingly like small, distant tumps in a flattened landscape. This death, so disturbing to her old people, pointed up the dangerous vortex of desire and the negative currents of emotion that flowed around it. Faithlessness, cruelty, indifference diminished the spirit by slow attrition. Bred into Bird by the tyranny of her upbringing was a strong sense of good and evil and, under pressure from the past and the shocking present, she tried to assess the degree of her own guilt. Unearned hatred is hard to fight. Yet she should have fought more fiercely for Hannah.

Her mother never relented towards her own daughter, yet against all probability she had cared for her granddaughter. But Hannah grew up and fell in love. Mrs Dawlish could not compete or control, however much she wore out her knees with angry prayer. God did not strike the intruder dead, nor cure the wickedness of lust. Hannah ignored her tantrums. One morning she announced that she was leaving and by the evening she was married.

In her last illness Mrs Dawlish did not send for Bird. She had no friends, but Rita Parry came closest, being a travelling woman who disappeared for months or years, turning up with uncanny promptness when she was needed. Her passport to the closed Dawlish house was a knowledge of herbs and cures. Some of them may have been effective. By word of mouth, several mouths in fact, Rita (she had never been known to read or write) got a message through to Bird, who returned at once to Dorset. Reduced and powerless through illness, Mrs Dawlish said to her daughter, 'I didn't ask you to come. Go away.'

Bird nodded, tidied the bed, inspected the unlabelled bottles (Rita's dubious remedies) on the bedside table. 'I'll call the doctor.'

'You won't. I can die without his help or yours. You ruined my life by being born. I couldn't love you.' Her hurried breaths were loud under the slope of the ceiling, making her voice sound softer. 'Don't stare at me. It wasn't your fault.'

A weakening of the citadel; not much, not enough to pay for the dead years, but something. 'No, it wasn't. I should have loved you if you'd let me. Do you want a drink?'

A shake of the head. 'Keep Hannah out of here. A beer-swilling labourer; disgusting. She'll get nothing from me. I refuse to see her.'

'Don't worry, she won't come near you — or me.' An ache for her lost, rejected child fanned Bird's resentments. 'You did a thorough job of making her hate us. I just wish you hadn't lied to her about her father. I can never remember what his name was supposed to be and now I can't tell her the truth.'

The fierce eyes closed briefly and her mother's face sank into tormented weariness. In a hoarse whisper, so low that Bird could scarcely hear, she muttered, 'Truth and lies, it's all the same in the end.'

A bald statement to which there could be no answer, and Bird did not trouble to question. 'Do you want to see your parson again? He's put another load of pamphlets through the door.' On the doorstep he had also tried to get inside, kissing Bird and pushing a hand under her skirt. Sighing, since she was reluctant to hurt anyone, she had put into practise the self-defence tactics taught her when she became a nurse in London, and kneed him smartly in the groin. He used a non-ecclesiastical expression and clasped himself tenderly as he hobbled away.

'Throw them on the fire and him after them if you like. Now keep quiet,' said Mrs Dawlish.

Rita spoke from the shadows. Conversation with her had a surreal quality. She talked of the ancient past, the present, fact and legend as though she had lived them all and had lived forever. 'Riches aren't potatoes and no meat.'

'What?'

'You understand well enough.' Bird didn't follow this at all and talk of riches in that beggarly house seemed crazier than most of Rita's pronouncements. Yet after a life lived in near penury Mrs Dawlish left behind her, when she eventually managed to die, a substantial and mystifying fortune, not to the banished Hannah but to Bird. She explained nothing. Rita knew most things, but she was a keeper of secrets and it did not occur to Bird to question her. After the cremation in Salisbury she had disappeared about her own affairs.

Returning alone, Bird felt the cottage to be

as empty as though it had never been occupied. Incuriously she had stowed into her mother's old carpet-bag the meagre bundles of papers from the bureau to take to the solicitor, rejecting any idea of clearing the house of clothes and chattels. The room was without ornaments. She sat down, avoiding the Windsor chair with its faded red cushions where Mrs Dawlish customarily read or stared blankly at the wall, trying to summon up some tender memory, a kiss, a hug, a hand to cling to, a candle against the dark. Nothing to recall, nothing to feel. The kitchen range was cold. Her mother had left no ghost, friendly or malignant, behind. After a few moments, Bird had climbed the bare wooden staircase to the bedrooms. The sickroom was already cleared. In Hannah's room, once her own, some effort at softness had been made; white net curtains, tied back with ribbon, a flowered bedspread, a doll, too big and splendidly dressed for a child to hold, sitting stiffly in a rocking chair, a bookcase holding a few books. Love had invaded here for a while and been defeated. At last sadness dampened her eyes. The stupid doll simpered at her with unchanging sweetness. She had had an impulse to smash the china smile to fragments.

And now came Connie Lovibond and the

spirit of her dead sister, the last link in the chain that bound her to the past. At that point the present abruptly claimed her attention. Ahead of her, a shell-grotto, decorated by an unskilled hand and of surpassing ugliness, had been tunnelled into rising ground towards the seaward boundary: a claustrophobic place, little visited. In a round chamber, a crude plaster statue leered blearily through streaks of green mould. Its subject might have been anyone or anything, monster, nymph, god or devil. Lizzie Greengrass said, with a degree of spite, that it reminded her of Harold Wilson, an ex-Prime Minister whose tax measures she had deeply resented. A few steps beyond, a protective iron grille cut off the passageway from a small cave, giving a keyhole view of rocks and the shifting tide. A dank, insanitary, unsafe place for the old. Raising clouds of dust in front of the wooden door, which stood ajar, Wally Spratt swept.

At Bird's approach, he pushed the door to and leaned on his broom, watching her with a meaty benevolence touched by unease. Wally inspired in her an unreasonable discomfort. A relic of the old regime, there was something about him, a well-nourished conceit, that brought to mind her mother's creepy evangelist with the roving hands. And like

71

that man of God, Spratt was clever but jumpy. While the various authorities had argued about the dismissal of staff and the disposal of the sick; and struggled with awkward customers like Lizzie and Charlie, he effaced himself and was forgotten. On the day that The Glebe reopened, he rolled into Bird's office and handed her a small sheet of paper. 'Wally, head gardener, missis, and this is due wages. My card won't have been stamped for a while.'

'But I haven't hired a gardener,' said Bird, who had not noticed anybody working in the grounds. 'I need to know more about you: and oughtn't you to have a form P45 for the tax people?'

His broad red face shone on her. 'I bin working here eight years. I weren't never laid off, so I'm owed me money.' There followed a sequence of protests, questions, propositions, from which Bird gathered that Wally had considerable nuisance value and enough dependants to make him tax-free for life. She suspected that there might be a lot more to know. This was the time when she feared that she had taken on more than she could handle, that the old reputation of The Glebe would overcome her and that the residents would never like or trust her. This was also the time when she should have been firm. But gardeners she certainly needed. Wally made it seem reasonable to pay the arrears and keep him on.

Unable to take affection for granted, Bird avoided the trite view of her community as a family, yet there were resemblances in the spats and arguments, the jokes and loyalties, the closing of ranks against critics. Spratt prowled the edges of their enclave with the air of a famished dog. Often she considered sacking him. The prospect of arguments and tribunals, claims for unfair dismissal and redundancy payments put her off.

A hint of appeasement lurked in the smile he turned on her now, before examining the handle of the broom with extreme care. She said, 'The grotto is supposed to be kept locked at all times and the key taken only with my permission. What are you doing in there?'

'Leaf-fall do make work, missis, blowing every which way. I keep a few bits inside, a spare besom and a tool or two. 'Tis safe from thieving and saves me a powerful lot of walking and time-wasting.'

'I can't think of anyone here likely to steal such things, can you? We'll get them out now and lock up again.'

He heaved the door back reluctantly. Inside, lined up against one sweating wall, stood buckets of flowers, her flowers. 'They old folks will be wanting to go to the church with a few blooms, what with the upset and all. Best pick'em now, I thought, and carry them up to the house when I finish.'

'You weren't thinking of taking them down to the village, naturally?'

He took exception. 'That's not a thing to ask of a man what works his fingers to the bone,' he said. 'Howsoever could you begin to think a thing like that? It was to help, that's what, to help.'

Bird snorted and made a mental note to keep a close eye on the October apple-picking and the bottled fruit stored in a pantry near the back door. 'It would have to be someone pretty low to rob the elderly, I think.'

'That would, sure enough. Lucky to be some folks and well looked after. Got sitting-rooms each nowadays, bungalows even, more than my old mum's got in her place.' A demand hung in the air, though without a threat to give it force. Bird did not answer. With a dozen vacancies she would not have cared to accommodate Wally's old mum or any other member of the Spratt family. He looked past her and his mood deteriorated. 'You got company,' he said, 'the witchwoman's here. I hoped she was dead.'

A spry old figure swathed in an assortment

74

of ragged cardigans skittered up to them. 'Well, well, if it isn't Wally Spratt and not in gaol,' said Rita Parry. 'High time I paid a visit. I'm looking for an outside place for Ched. He's my cousin's grandson and a good worker.'

'When was I ever in gaol?' asked Wally, with a virtuous resentment that came from the heart. 'Us don't need her kind working here, spying and that. I can manage on me own like always.'

He had a way of making the undergardeners Bird engaged disappear without notice. Whatever his little rackets, he wanted no observers and a young man backed by Rita would take some dislodging. 'Nonsense,' said Bird. 'You were just complaining of the extra work. If you're not happy here, you can leave. Nice to see you again, Rita. I've been wondering about you and where you had got to. Send me Ched by all means. I hope he'll stay.'

'Exit Wally Spratt, scattering blossom,' said Rita, mildly humorous, as he departed for the house with the buckets, slopping water and plastering his boots with stray petals. 'I've known him a long time and he's frightened I'll tell on him.'

'You love having secrets, don't you? I wish you would give me a cast-iron reason to get rid of him, but you won't, I suppose?'

'Try asking some time, though I don't promise. Knowing things is the only power old women have. Speak out too soon, and our lords and masters up top think we're mental until they find out different. Keep Wally nervous enough and he'll give himself away. Now, I've been travelling since your mother died. For a while I'm bedded down in a condemned cottage behind the High Street. No rent, no rates. Any news?'

'Hereward Parstock's living here and Stella Worth is renting a cottage in the village. You know how obsessed with him she is. Divorced again, too. And Connie Lovibond's due to arrive for a visit at any moment. It's an odd feeling. Like opening a forgotten door and walking back into the past.'

'Past, present and future, they're all the same,' said Rita in a down-to-earth tone. 'Didn't a Roman legion pass me by last night on Winfrith Heath, clattering and shouting?'

No, Bird thought; it did not. The infuriating thing about Rita was the sheer impossibility of catching her out. Asked to describe these visions, or mystic encounters, whatever they were, she would do so fluently and with historical accuracy. 'How long will you stay?'

'I'm very old,' she said. 'It's best not to die

76

in a field and get gnawed over by animals. Time I settled.' When Bird did not respond she grinned. 'I wouldn't mind living here myself, but I can see you're not thinking of asking me. Ta-ta now.'

Civilization and Rita were not acquainted and Bird had no great faith in her ability to settle down. The distress of recalling the past had begun to evaporate. From the separate nursing wing emerged an old-fashioned double invalid carriage, pushed by a nurse. 'It's his hour in the lounge,' she said, indicating her charge. 'Heaven knows what he'll make of all the to-do. His clock stopped when Fred Astaire hung up his dancing shoes, poor love.' Against the tartan blanket, his hands lay white and flat-fingered, veined with blue, belonging less to flesh than to a painted medieval saint. Bird touched them gently and smiled at him. The sudden radiance of his face was saint-like too. He had reached ninety-nine and looked forward, when he remembered, to a telegram from the Queen.

'Is it the Coronation?' he asked. 'I've seen that.' The nurse smiled and nodded, not trying to explain.

Beyond a thicket of trees and shrubs lay the broad cliff and the sea, often turbulent, but today a gentle, milky blue. On the still water, a pair of swans inclined their heads, resting. My old ones are as slow and graceful as swans, Bird thought with love; gliding through the last days of their lives towards safe haven. She locked the grotto door and dropped the key into her apron pocket. Joshua, her grandson and her pride, emerged from the lodge cottage. He looked in her direction, smiled and waved vigorously. A fragile happiness flowed over her. A red Sunbeam Rapier turned into the drive and Bird pulled herself together. Miss Lovibond had arrived.

★ ★ ★

As Connie approached journey's end, she wondered whether she would recognize Bird. It had been a long time. Her mind's eye retained still the vision of an intensely radiant creature, always half-poised for flight. She found an unremarkable woman in her forties, still good enough to look at, but firmly encased in healthy flesh under a blue and white nurse's uniform, and a little on the defensive. Connie felt faintly cheated. The change in Bird pointed up the changes in herself and made her feel that after so long she might have made more sense of her freedom by joining a bridge club in Rye (though she hated cards), taken up embroidery for which she had no talent, delivered meals on wheels, occupied her time in any way rather than look for answers to unasked questions.

The sudden death of a royal young woman who was none of her business ought not to have so unsettled her. In Romsey, the collective and suspicious mind had already been at work. 'She was a nuisance to them,' the waiter had said. 'She was supposed to keep quiet and just fade out. Now she has. Convenient! It'll all be hushed up.' Connie had listened non-committally. 'I'd like to know what MI5 were up to. We need to be told if there was any funny business.'

Un-English and unreal, yet she understood how he and others might burn for truth. She had always been unsure about Winifred. There was no parallel. Or was there? She felt that she could not go to her grave wondering whether or not her sister's death also had been the purest of mischances. Had she stood in someone's way? If so, whose? Not Hereward's. Somehow Bird, the girl, the unconsidered outsider, must be the key to all the events of that summer and what came after.

She said, 'It's been many years, Mrs Dawlish. You were quite a child when we first met. Not that I'm completely out of touch. Miles gives me news of The Glebe and you and, of course, Hereward. I hear that you have children, a family. How nice.'

'Child,' Bird said, perhaps a little stunned. 'Hannah, my daughter. She's grown up now, married with a son. The rooms are ready, so I'll show you up. Would you mind waiting here while I get your keys?'

Connie heard through an open door a television announcer speculating about the imminent release of the Princess's body from the Paris hospital. She stepped into the room. Still as a corpse, an old man slept in an invalid chair. From behind the window curtains protruded a bare, sinewy leg of indeterminate sex, probably female to judge by the smallness of the booted foot. A short woman whose head, due to the ampleness of her bosom, appeared to rest on her shoulders without the intervention of a neck, sat beside a huddle that on closer inspection turned out to be a thin, bald man with a newspaper. 'Good evening,' Connie said.

The woman didn't look up. 'Just a tick. He and her sisters have gone to Paris to bring her home. They'll be out any minute. Bit late for him to show concern, though I suppose he feels he has to for the sake of those poor boys. They were so close to their mother.'

'And very sad, too. I beg your pardon for interrupting.' The Prime Minister appeared, recorded, with other images of the day, and spoke. Sincere and moving, of course. The pity for politicians was that they used up so much sincerity as a career commodity. Connie, automatically looking for shiftiness and self-interest, the practised smile, was shamed by the shabbiness of her thought. On this cataclysmic day, everyone spoke from the heart. Meanwhile the populace milled around in London with flowers and heart-shaped balloons, a man clung to the railings of Buckingham Palace and wept, a pressman was surrounded and told that it was all his fault. There were snippets of tributes from here and there. In time, the doors of the hospital opened and the coffin, draped with the royal standard, was borne down the steps to the waiting hearse and eventually the procession drove away.

The small woman fished a handkerchief out of a thicket of ribbons (purple and black, very suitable) and assorted jewellery and dabbed at her eyes. 'Not much for an hour or more until the plane gets here.' She screwed her head towards Connie. 'You're new,' she said accusingly. 'Visitor or resident?'

'A temporary resident. I'm hoping to rest for two or three months.'

'You'll be comfortable here There's only five of us in the main house, though we see quite a bit of the convalescents from the nursing wing. A couple of men lease the cottages behind the house, but they're nothing to do with us. Bird likes us to mix, but no need if you don't want to. You're not ill, are you?'

'Not at all. Just wanting a change of scene.'

'What's your name? Mine's Lizzie Greengrass; make what you like of it.'

'Right,' said Connie; 'I'm Constance Lovibond, Connie to friends.'

'Sister to Mr Parstock's late wife? We heard you were coming. Not much of a beginning to a holiday is this, with everyone shaken to their boot-soles. Back home in Portsmouth they love the royals and especially her. They made her a freeman of the city and we saw a lot of her one way and another. Everyone turned out to wave.' A weatherman and a map of the British Isles appeared on the screen. Lizzie Greengrass gave them both an incurious glance. 'I wish the Queen, or one of those Palace spokesmen we're always hearing about, would say something, I really do. They didn't treat her too sensitive when you come to think of it and it's a terrible thing for her sons to remember how their own mother was slighted. *He'll* have to keep his trap shut, of course. Whatever he says, he can't win now. It's a rotten world.'

Connie wondered whether it would be possible for her to avoid conversations on this theme. Probably not. The affairs of royalty, usually of transcendant dullness, had never much interested her, and she felt that they might, with a little sense and better advice, have avoided dramas of this magnitude. She ventured to suggest to Lizzie that the princess had embarked on an unwise friendship. 'Wasn't it asking for trouble?'

'What kind of trouble did you have in mind?' She injected her question with huge sarcasm. 'Stoning? Public hanging for treason? A bomb from MI5? So she wasn't perfect, the mean way they turned on her makes me sick. He was the one that married her out of the schoolroom and still kept his bit on the side. How was she to know that his vows didn't mean a damned thing? Sure as eggs is eggs she didn't ask to be dead, did she?'

'I suppose not.'

At that point the reader put down his paper and ran a hand over his pale, hairless scalp. 'Come off it, Lizzie. She found someone else pretty quick, several somebodies, and if she'd stayed alive and gone off and married a Muslim you'd have been croaking on the other side of your face.'

Lizzie's eyebrows rose almost into her hair. 'Don't bother acting tough with me. I heard you sniffing behind that paper. You may not have been all that keen on her, but you're as upset as the rest of us. She'd never have married a foreigner. It was a bit of life after years of stuffed shirts, that's all.'

'Marvellous how you always know best about everything. I've got a cold coming on; why shouldn't I sniff if I feel like it?'

She smiled at Connie. 'Take no notice of him; he's Charlie Bean. You know — Bean's Eazie-Change bog-roll holders. I used to sell them in my shop. He fancies himself as being political and balanced, the old devil.'

'At least I've travelled the world, and I didn't think much of it,' said Charlie. 'And there's no need to be vulgar. It's Bean's Bathroom Accessories, if you don't mind. Just one of my interests. Bean's have long roots.'

Connie supposed this to be a stock joke, though she was uncertain whether to smile or not. Fortunately Bird reappeared and led her upstairs. 'Ah, you've met Lizzie and Charlie. They are more or less the reason for the survival of The Glebe. A stroppy, argumentative pair, and brave too. I love them. If you don't already know the previous history of this house, they'll tell you.'

The guest suite was beautifully appointed. On a table beside the telephone stood a blue bowl of late roses, huge and heavily scented. Connie could also smell lavender polish and the fresh starch of Bird's apron. The first awkwardness had passed. 'How pleasant this is. A view of the church too. Isn't it dedicated to Saint Winifred?'

A trapped bumble-bee buzzed crossly in the window. Bird walked over and flapped it outside. 'All Saints, but she's got a side chapel with some old wall-paintings. Funny, since she was Welsh. It was the nuns, I suppose. They came from that part of the country. Then Queen somebody or other gave the land away to a French abbey and monks came over from France and walled off the women into one wing. At the Dissolution they were all turned out. The village clung on to its church and its saint.'

'My father died recently. Now there's nobody much, just a few distant relations I've never met. Winifred was my sister's name. I miss her terribly.'

'I remember. Students are always hard up. She paid me just to make up tennis fours and bring the chairs in at night, that sort of thing. I thought how sad it was that she died. It seemed so — unnecessary.' Her sympathetic look had a transparency that hid nothing. 'Mr

85

Parstock's apartment is on the other side of the passage, overlooking the sea, and Mr Alban is next door and very upset. I hope you'll be comfortable. There's a bell. Please ask for anything you need.'

'Thank you. It's an odd coincidence surely that Hereward should be here?'

'It wasn't planned, not by me. He saw my advert in *The Times*.' The ghost of a smile crossed Bird's face. 'That brought Mrs Worth. She wanted to move in with him, but I wouldn't take her, so she found a house in the village. Poor Hereward, he's a disaster with determined women.'

Connie, liking her, smiled back and decided to jump in at the deep end. 'This will sound impertinent, but I have a reason for asking. Were you lovers once? There's your daughter to consider, of course, and not to be upset by misunderstandings.' A barely concealed second question hung on the air: whose child is she?

The anxious, almost frightened look on Bird's face answered for her. 'I won't have her bothered. As far as she's concerned her father's dead. She suffers enough from being illegitimate.'

'And Hereward takes no interest in her or in her upbringing? Yet there's no barrier to acknowledging her now.'

This time the silence lasted longer. Bird had flushed. 'It has nothing to do with you, Miss Lovibond. Why are you here anyway? What's the point of going over it, now that we're getting old?'

'I'm not at all sure that there is a point. You're the only one who can tell me what I might have seen for myself if I hadn't been blinded by my own infatuated state.' She smiled as Bird's eyebrows rose in enquiry. 'Miles Alban; I knew I was wasting emotion.'

'Perhaps it's all a waste. What can I tell you? The sun and the heat made it unreal, dreamlike. I wasn't thinking about right and wrong and other people's feelings; I wasn't thinking at all. And I wasn't the only one in Hereward's life.' Bird's lips compressed as though silence had become habitual.

Cautiously Connie said, 'You've never been able to talk about him, have you, and what happened to separate you? And all these years I could never speak of Winifred because it distressed my father so. There are times when her memory troubles me.'

'It doesn't matter about me, and I can't help you, Miss Lovibond, truly I can't.'

'You can trust me, tell me — I don't know what — everything. We can help each other. As you say, the sun and the heat, then my own emotions. I ran away.'

'As I ought to have done. Mrs Worth made sure that I knew how out of place I was in your world. Yet, in the end, it was harmless, except to me.'

'Not at all,' said Constance. 'My sister died. Somewhere there was wickedness.'

She had intended to shock. Bird's sudden pallor and incredulous eyes made her sorry. Plainly, the protective impulses that had driven Bird to buy The Glebe drove her also to take to herself not only her own guilt but that of others. It was a poor beginning, a clumsy effort to take advantage. Connie considered apologizing, then decided that she could only make matters worse. She changed the subject.

5

Monday morning, and Hannah Marsh, Bird Dawlish's daughter, came in from worming the goats and cleaning their hindquarters, then she spent ten minutes washing her hands and arms. The solicitor's letter that had come with the morning's post still lay on the kitchen table. Could she simply ignore it and let events happen remotely, without getting caught up in them? Her tidy, conscientious mind rejected that as a solution. Some time she would have to explain to her son. For once she felt glad that Joshua was out for the day at Beavers' camp, safe and playing harmless games. A great deal of her energy drained away in worry for Josh's safety. Often she lay awake at night, thinking of the awful fates that might happen to him, reminding herself to keep a watch on strangers in the village, worrying about his health. Hence the two goats in the paddock behind the lodge.

In Birmingham, living in a high-rise council flat, she had read that city children were often addicted to junk foods or allergic to the residues of antibiotics in cows' milk. Once within Bird's compass she set out to show her neglectful mother how mothering ought to be done. The problem was that she knew nothing of keeping any animal, vaguely believing that goats would be roughly comparable to large dogs. She grew quite fond of them. Unfortunately they seemed not to return her affection, liking her no more than people did, yielding milk reluctantly, trying hard to escape, and presenting her with enormous vet's bills. Soon they would need to be mated again. Annoyingly, Josh took a calm interest in this embarrassing procedure while much preferring to drink unwholesome pop. She blamed her failure, as with all things, on her illegitimacy and not being a country person. In the goats' company she recalled that her husband had once called her the most incurably miserable bitch on God's earth. There must be some reason why nothing worked for her. Other women didn't give a damn for their homes or husbands and left their children to bring themselves up, yet everybody loved them.

Idly she spread out the newspapers, covering up the long, whiter-than-white envelope. Depressing? Oh God, were they not. Aristocrats and royalty did not normally excite her compassion, yet here was another idealistic girl, for all practical purposes motherless, doing her best to please a ham-fisted, flat-footed family of in-laws and never accepted or supported. Once the princess had produced a couple of heirs that was goodbye. Oh, I know how she felt, thought Hannah, mourning for herself. Knocking at doors that slammed shut in her face, rejected publicly, and then dismissed into a second-rate existence of isolation and extinguished hopes.

Princess Diana (Hannah did not approve of familiar abbreviations) got herself a new life in the end. Now that was taken away from her. What was the use of fighting? Welling with self-pity, she was braced to note that the Tory tabloids, caught out by a censorious public, were crawling on their bellies to save their circulation. She felt a moment's triumph. It vanished when she noticed that the Socialist Press was up to the same ignoble trick. When you had a mother who could not see that every retirement and nursing home should be properly controlled and run by the State, and when you relied on her for a roof, it was less than easy to hold on to a vision of an egalitarian world based on sound Marxist principles. All her beliefs broke down in Wynfred Abbas.

The damned letter seemed to be burning a hole through the newsprint to get her attention. She scowled in its direction. Time was passing. A few more years and she would be thirty, the kind of woman she despised, aimless, purposeless, frightened of being alone without a man, over-doting on her son. Josh ought not to remain an only child. Hannah took a huge breath, wanting to break her self-imposed bonds and be rid of the conviction that she had lost her ability to fall recklessly in love. Her face, that was not constructed for merriment, expressed blank misery.

Hannah did not at all resemble her mother; she did not even seem like a product of the twentieth century. Her considerable beauty was distinctive and archaic. A high, rounded medieval forehead gave to her face an elongated, inbred look, emphasized by her bundle of straightish pale hair. She cut it herself, inexpertly, and tied it back with a belt from an old cotton skirt. Modern clothes sat oddly on her with a suggestion of fancy dress. She smiled rarely. When she did, her whole body seemed to smile, lit up like a sudden pure beam of lamplight. Her coolness concealed an exuberant sexuality of which she was more often than not ashamed. She hated her looks.

A vague idea of shopping crossed her mind. Or the doctor. He was new. Was she supposed to register herself and Josh all over again? She shoved the letter into the knife drawer and went out. It had rained during the night. Under a white sunless sky the puddles gleamed like polished steel, dizzying her eyes. Her feet did not quite belong to her. In the mini-market a single subject obsessed the shoppers. Their voices roared and faded: prince, mistress, disgusting, poor Di, queen of our hearts, *they* didn't care, oh well, say what you like, it wasn't nice, going with an Arab; she'd have finished up worse off than ever, if you ask me! The lights over the frozen food began to jiggle unpleasantly. Hannah picked up a tin of baked beans, dropped it and, ignoring a talkative and helpful shop assistant, she fled.

As her head cleared she found that she was sitting on a damp bench outside the Duke's Head, fallen sideways against a purple cardigan. She sat up abruptly. 'Been a few years since I saw you,' said Rita Parry. 'You all right, my dear? A bit bloodless, no doubt. Marshwort, sweet cicely and watercress, they're the thing.'

In spite of a degree in sociology (disappointing to her mother and grandmother, who had expected better) and five years spent as a social worker, Hannah could not be comfortable with the old. Rita had always quite definitely frightened her. Her ghastly potions, forced down a reluctant, gagging throat, had a horrid familiarity from childhood. At times she seemed seriously deranged. In her professional social services capacity, Hannah would certainly have recommended forcibly taking Rita into care. She shivered. 'I can't stop. I have to see the doctor.'

'He can't cure man-trouble any more than I can. Give me your hand, I'll read your palm.'

A guess, of course, but infuriatingly accurate. Hannah's marriage, that began like a forest fire, had slowly frozen to death in the middle of the North Sea and she knew that it was her own fault. Muscular young men acted on her as a potent aphrodisiac. When she first saw her husband, stripped to the waist, brown and beautiful, smelling of sweat and engine oil, she had felt almost sick with love. He could encompass her waist with his hands, yet she could subjugate him with a kiss. What she could not do was to steer his attention away from beer and football and nights out with his mates, or change him into a Socialist hero. They married within weeks in the face of her grandmother's fury. A year later, by the time that Joshua was born, Hannah had fallen out of love and her husband had taken a job on an oil-rig to get away from her. His leaves were disastrous.

She responded coldly to his advances and the intervals between his visits home grew ever longer. Josh scarcely knew his father. And the letter in the morning post came from a solicitor in Aberdeen, informing her that her husband wanted a divorce, now, at once, so that he could marry again. He invited her co-operation.

'Fortune-telling is rubbish,' Hannah said, with a flaring look of contempt. 'I'm not giving you money to spend on drink.'

'Your grandmother never turned me away, though she was careful enough. We helped each other. She wanted great things for you. It broke her heart when you went off and married a mechanic.'

'Leave me alone. It's none of your business.'

'Of course it's my business. You were a miserable kid, forever squalling like a kitten. I was the only one that could get you quiet.' Mrs Parry shot her a malicious look, then her eyes clouded over. 'Miracles happened to me that year. I met a great one on the road; Joseph, who carried the cup to Glastonbury and planted his thorn staff there.'

'Oh damn, haven't you got over that nonsense yet?' said Hannah feebly, wanting to throw up, but controlling her rebellious stomach. 'I wouldn't tell people you're seeing saints and druids and two thousand-year-old Romans if I were you, I really wouldn't. They'll take you off to a nice geriatric ward and lock you up.'

'No compassion, have you? Angels walk this world. Take care you don't offend one and find the gates of Heaven slammed shut on you.'

Hannah surveyed her ancient face, dyed bronze by the sun, crisscrossed with seams and channels like a dry river delta. A line of hairs on the upper lip was mottled black and white and grey. It was difficult to guess precisely how old Rita was, since she had existed in the same state of preservation as long as Hannah could remember. 'Just at the moment,' she said carefully, 'what I need is a tonic. I can do without lectures and visions. Now I'm going to the doctor's. He's new. I hope he'll see me.'

'You must take after your father. There's nothing of your mother in you.' Rita made this a condemnation. 'If you change your mind I'll be here when you come back.' From a pocket deep within her muddle of clothing she drew a battered, handrolled cigarette and set fire to it with a gold Dunhill lighter. A small flurry of sparks and blackened paper blew away and the cigarette went out again. 'What you looking at? Oh, this lighter. I suppose you think I stole it? Well, I didn't. A present, that's what. Your mother's not the only one with high-up friends.'

As she walked away, Hannah stifled an impulse towards penitence. A solitary, slightly touched, muddleheaded old woman ought to inspire sympathy, not resentment and anger. It must be true that she lacked compassion. She would have liked to ask Rita about the father who had died before she was born, omitted to marry her mother, and was never spoken of. So much lay outside Hannah's experience. Brothers and sisters might have been nice; connections and awful family Christmases, rivalries, quarrels and reunions that other people complained about. But why worry when she was too lousy at relationships to keep her husband? Nothing of that brilliant passion remained. Divorce was hateful and wrong. Everyone got divorced, including half the royal family. She had disapproved. Now she, too, was about to become a statistic. Her life was over.

Also, she had missed morning surgery. A man stood on top of a ladder, painting the old stucco a pleasing shade of apricot and whistling quietly to himself. He wore a torn T-shirt over blue jeans. Hannah, who had gone off workmen, regarded him stonily. 'Do you know what time the surgery will be open?' she called. The ladder began to lean to the right. She grabbed the bottom of it, then jumped back as a loaded brush flew sideways and fell at her feet, splashing paint on her shoes. Inevitably the young man followed, leaping the last few feet and catching the ladder before it hit ground. Hannah scarcely noticed. She was looking down at her ruined shoes and weeping.

'Damn; I'm so sorry. Please, don't be upset.' A hand reached out to pat her arm and withdrew as its owner noticed that it was smothered in smears of apricot. 'Come inside while I clean us up.'

'No,' she wailed. 'It's the doctor I want to talk to.'

'Right. There's a splash on your nose. Better get that off.' He hurried her through to a wildly untidy kitchen, lowered her into a chair and knelt to take off her shoes. Her tears fell in heavy drops on to his cropped dark hair. A small, reserved corner of her mind noted that it curled and that she found the nape of his neck attractive. 'Stormy weather,' he murmured to himself, fishing a tin from under the sink and washing his hands vigorously. A reminiscent industrial smell pervaded the room. Hannah felt a humiliating stab of acute desire for the memory of her Adonis of machine parts who had vanished the moment she married him. The house painter approached with a cloth, dabbed at the smear on her nose and wiped it with a towel. Her tears turned to sobs. She clutched at the towel and buried her face. 'Good lord,' he said, 'whatever's wrong? A blob of paint and my ungraceful descent didn't bring this on, surely?'

'No, it's nothing. I'd better go. I'll come back when the doctor's here.'

'Hang it, I *am* the doctor: Gus Early. I'm too hard up to have the house decorated unless I do it myself. There's no afternoon surgery today, but if you'll wait while I change I'll see you now. You don't look very bright.'

Feeling intensely foolish, Hannah emerged from the towel and said, 'I only wanted to know whether I need to register again because of the change of GP.'

'No. All the patients will get a letter. You'll remain registered with me, unless of course you prefer to go elsewhere.'

'There isn't an elsewhere in Wynfred Abbas!'

'Exactly. It gives me an advantage, don't you think? What else brought you?'

'Sorry, I expected someone older. Just give me my shoes, please.' Stray tears still slid down her cheeks and she guessed that her eyes had turned to red slits. 'Can I — ' The sickness in her stomach returned with imperative force. She stumbled past him and threw up her breakfast bran cereal with a liberal dressing of curdled goat's milk, into the paint-stained sink. Her humiliation was complete.

'Be a good girl and make a cup of coffee, will you?' Dr Early said. 'In the right-hand cupboard with the mugs. I'll polish your shoes and then we'll talk. If I let you go in this state you'll put the customers off.' She hesitated, then did as he asked.

'It's not a bit of use looking for your records,' he said in the surgery, hooking out a chair for her with his foot. 'The old boy who was here before left everything in the devil of a mess. I must see about finding a secretary. And a housekeeper. Begin at the beginning; when you're ready of course.' He took great gulps of coffee, watching her with a relaxed concentration that was either flattering or aggravating, she could not make up her mind which. Once or twice she opened her mouth like a stranded fish. The silence began to get on her nerves. Soon the whole village would know of her inadequacies as a wife and dislike her even more. This doctor might as well be the first. And if he precribed valium or sleeping tablets she would probably kill him.

She said, 'I don't believe in divorce, but I heard this morning that my husband wants one. Somehow I have to tell Joshua and I can't.'

'Your son?' She nodded. 'Close to his father, is he? Fond of him?'

'I wouldn't say so. Josh barely knows him. He works away on an oil-rig and hardly ever comes home. It's the failure that's so destructive.'

'Ah,' said Gus Early very gently, 'the parents' failure, not the boy's, and I imagine that's what you find hard to admit. Divorce is no great disgrace. It happens in the best-regulated families nowadays.'

'Mine isn't — well-regulated I mean. It's a mess. We're all peculiar,' Hannah said, irritable now. 'My grandmother lived like a pauper and left a fortune; my mother's spending all the money subsidizing a bunch of misfits at The wretched Glebe and I'm an about-to-be-divorced bastard. I never knew my father, I don't even properly know who he was and I don't think I care. My mother can barely remember his name. What are you grinning at?'

'Better rage than tears,' said Dr Early. 'What you find so upsetting seems fairly normal for these times. Look how fashionable illegitimacy is. We're bringing up a whole generation of bastards and fathers come as optional extras. Not a trend I like much, but there's no point in quarrelling with reality. Of The Glebe, I can't yet speak. I believe I'm the attendant physician and the word is that Mrs Dawlish — your mother, yes? — cares for her old people as though they were family.'

'She's not really a Mrs; she isn't married, and we're her family, Josh and me. That place should be run for the benefit of the elderly poor. I used to be a social worker and I saw awful squalor; pensioners who died alone and weren't found for weeks, old ladies who couldn't fend for themselves and starved, men with Parkinson's or Alzheimer's who daren't go out because of brain-dead youths who tormented them. Why should five or six fat cats enjoy so much space and luxury when the council could fit in a dozen or more?'

After a long scrutiny that allowed her to examine her remarks and wonder if something was wrong with them, Gus Early said, 'What do you want for your own old age, Hannah? I know that I'm going to feel reluctant to face a life that has diminished to a share of one small room. Better to aim high than low — for everyone.'

'That's not practical, and it isn't better to be dead.'

'I'm not sure. To be alive is more than simply breathing. Now, if you feel up to it I'll run you home. Talk to your son today and bring him in to see me tomorrow.'

Hannah looked about her. She was a great giver of unwanted advice and always ready with practical help. The ladies of Wynfred Abbas cared not at all for her criticism of their flower arrangements or the relative lightness of their Victoria sponges, yet whenever judges were required Hannah was among them. This had a great deal to do with the men, who found her cool beauty provocative. And her readiness to tackle useful and dirty jobs like cleansing the local footpaths of dog-droppings, heaving soiled mattresses and bundles of rags from ditches, picking up litter from the beach, impressed them and further annoyed the women. Often Bird prayed that Hannah would not discover and be hurt by her unpopularity. A wasted prayer, since she already knew.

She said, 'No thanks. You can't function properly in this muddle and you'll never get a secretary to take it on. I'll start getting the records in order while you finish your painting.'

'It's only an hour or so to lunchtime and I don't much feel like starting again.'

'Lunch can wait. Get the job done while you can. I'll let myself out when I've finished and come back tomorrow in surgery hours.'

The hard work pleased her. She felt her pride redeemed and it took her mind off husbands, lovers and sex. While she still had wings, she floated home, considered her terms and wrote to Aberdeen agreeing to an immediate divorce.

★ ★ ★

Rita Parry sat patiently until the Duke's Head opened its doors. She bought a small rum and pep at the bar and stared so hard at the pies that the landlord threw in a stale one for nothing. She took her meal back to the outside seat. Bursts of sound from the radio set came and went with the customers. Interest still focused on the news bulletins, but she barely listened. Death had not much disturbed her for a long time. It was close, but she felt convinced that it had visited her before and that there were other lives to be led and other deaths to die.

Rita meditated on Bird Dawlish and her mother. That was a strange, sad history; the sins of a prideful woman had been cruelly visited on her child. Knowing the whole of it, Rita was content to keep the knowledge to herself, expecting that it would come in useful quite soon. The word, blackmail, did not enter her head. Her stratagems were practical. She liked Bird and wished her no harm.

The Social Services knew nothing of Rita. Never in her life had she cumbered herself with insurance, rent, rates, or any permanence, and she certainly had no way of paying a fee for one of Bird's apartments. Yet even the independent and the free need a place to die. In the recesses of her mind Rita believed, with Hereward Parstock, that where Bird lived was home. She had tried to protect the child against the mother's unreasoning hate, she had never betrayed them, and the dead woman owed her a debt for her silence.

The small world of the village went about its affairs. Hannah Marsh hurried towards the Duke's Head, swinging her shopping-bag and looking quite cheerful. Cheerful enough to part with the price of a drink? No. The girl was too highminded to encourage what she thought of as bad habits. On the opposite side of the High Street, the door of Wally Spratt's cottage opened. Stella Worth emerged. She picked her way rapidly through the assortment of old tyres, rusting bicycle parts and rags that composed the front garden and sped, grinning, up the hill towards The Glebe. The back of Rita's neck prickled with a warning of evil. That was a creature of the dark she would not much care to cross without strong magic. She stored away the unlikely conjunction to think about later. Wally shambled to his gate and shut it. His smug expression changed to one of deepest suspicion when he noticed her. 'What you looking at me for, you old hag?' he called. Rita bit into her pie and did not answer, watching him with a fixed, black gaze that penetrated his slow exterior clear down to the concealed store of cunning and avarice. She fished a piece of gristle out of her teeth and smiled. He flinched. His door slammed shut.

The wall of the Duke's Head felt easy to her back. Her eyes began to close and on the edge of sleep she half remembered all the events she had witnessed from the beginning. She thought of her births, lives and several deaths. Dreams — all her family had been great dreamers — or perhaps she was a witch as they said. The New Forest where she had last been born had a name for witches. More likely I'm mad, like Hannah thinks. The giver of the gold cigarette lighter believed she had the art of casting and removing spells. Rita knew that she possessed no such power. No such power had ever existed. Good or ill, everything comes as it pleases and none of it matters, she thought, warmed by rum and the last of summer. I have a vision in my head of glory. If I can get into The Glebe, if Bird will care for me, I can go to my next death at ease.

The landlord of the Duke's Head came out, collected her glass and closed his doors. She did not notice him. The afternoon wore on while she slept and opening time came round again. The evening sunshine slanted low across the sea below the village, bathing her in golden light. She might have been dead. Nobody spared her more than a glance or stopped to find out.

6

By the time that Winifred Parstock died, Bird
had put behind her the loves and longings of
summer, and her conviction that at any
moment Hereward would rescue her from the
plight for which he was responsible. Once
again Swan House became a foreign land,
populated by mythical beings of whom she
knew nothing. And they knew even less of
her. Long hours of nursing and home to a
bed-sitting room in Clerkenwell ensured that
their paths never crossed. The swingers and
the flower-people had been evicted from their
squats and London had become a depressing
place of strikes and potential violence. Yet
Bird flourished there. She accepted people
and was accepted by them, which she found a
pleasant change from the constant carpings of
her mother. The intrusion of past misery into
her happiness was something of an irritant.
Fires that had burned in her years ago were
out and she did not want to stir the embers,
nor try to revive dead emotions. Yet Connie's
mention of wickedness disturbed her. Why
should a death that seemed so transparently
natural now raise questions and suspicions? It

was nonsense, yet events at The Glebe under the old regime proved how easily murder might be hidden.

In the house, the weekend's events had caused disturbance enough. People wandered in and out, from the convalescent wing, from the bungalows, even from the cottages, exchanging opinions. Bird crushed a brief anxiety that the health of her charges might suffer, wondering whether a completely tranquil life was desirable, even for the old. The Glebers had lived through war and seen homes and lives wiped out by bombs. They had gathered up shattered bodies, witnessed unspeakable things, battled against fear and hunger, and never afterwards recaptured the excitement. This royal drama was meat and drink to them. Beneath the sadness lay a deep, animating stimulus that detracted not at all from their genuine regret.

After overseeing their medication and their mid-morning drinks, she slipped away to the broad green sweep of cliff beyond the garden and to her favourite seat, a stone dolmen warmed by the sun. Rock falls had tilted it to a comfortable angle. A deep and narrow chine cut off the small promontory from Wynfred Abbas, driving the coastal path inland. A solitary swimmer powered towards the hidden beach; Stella Worth who loved the sea and, when sober, talked of one day reaching the brightness of the horizon. Bird was utterly private and undisturbed. There she brooded, trying to recapture, beyond the damage of passion, the exaltation of youth and love and innocence. How would she have fared, married to a man older than herself, who might or might not have been a good and faithful husband? Although she had tried, she had never managed to fall in love again. One single burst of overwhelming emotion had left her as fragile and useless as an empty eggshell, ready to collapse inward at a touch.

Waiting, she allowed her mind to drift. An irrational woe for the regiments of dead whose bones layered the Dorset fields, for Hereward, for herself, brought her close to tears. Far below, the sea moved like silk over drowned settlements. Stillness flowed down from the high slopes beyond the village and the earth seemed to draw her in, reaffirming her as part of this ancient land. Her thoughts stopped. There was no haunting or betrayal here, only a peaceful enchantment.

'A spell-binding place,' said Connie, from a bench half-hidden by a tangle of wild clematis; 'violent once, if old tales are true, though I don't believe it. Tell me about Hereward.'

Bird slid from her stone. 'You startled me. I

don't know why I should tell you. I don't at all want to talk about him.' She sighed. 'It lasted so short a time.'

'Perhaps this is the right moment and place. It isn't mere curiosity, but a part of a whole. I need to understand.'

Bird considered her closely. There would be no sentimental reproaches from Connie. 'Very well then. Will it content you if I begin at the beginning, in Paris, when I was supposed to be learning the language? I didn't, of course. I was far too inhibited to speak to anyone in any language whatsoever. What Hereward saw in me is still a mystery.'

'You may not have known, but you were amazingly like your name; shy, quick and vivid as a kingfisher,' said Connie. 'It wasn't Hereward's style to prey on youth and ignorance. He behaved like a shit and he deserved to suffer for it.'

Bird, weary of hearing that she once resembled her name, was inclined to agree, except that she did not intend to be regarded simply as a victim, even if she was. 'Youth? I hated it. You can't imagine how much I longed to be old. This didn't happen in the Dark Ages, Connie; it was 1970, when everyone but me seemed to know about flower-power and sexual freedom and drugs. I'd been stuck in an all-girls college, a byword for strictness. Holidays were worse. My mother resented every moment that I was in her sight. There's no defence against a hatred that seems to have no point or reason and I quite thought she was mad.' The tied cottage in a wood had the picturesque qualities of a fairy-tale and every inconvenience devised by men for the wearing-out of women. Bird had dreamed of escape and longed to be advised about love. If she remembered anything of the emotion, Mrs Dawlish did not choose to impart her knowledge to her daughter. Furiously she swept and scoured and polished and rarely spoke. Bird now voiced her perpetual puzzlement. 'How was I to guess that she had once been brilliant? Hereward told me that she first went to Swan House to catalogue his grandfather's library, but I've no idea why she stayed if she was so miserable. She fought me over France. I was of age and for once I rebelled. If I disgraced her I was to throw myself in the river.'

'A monstrous suggestion,' Connie said. 'Rivers are cold, wet and unreliable. Where did Hereward manage to find you?'

'Oddly enough, by the Seine. I was watching the barges and the *bateaux-mouches*. Under the bridges of Paris sounded so alluring. They turned out to be a bit disgusting. Tramps must have sheltered there at night and used them as lavatories too.' And as she wandered under the shadowed arches, Hereward approached out of the sun like a conquering god. She mentioned this with a smile, recalling his extreme good looks and sophistication and the explosion of emotion that had overwhelmed her. 'I was dazzled. Not that it was nearly as romantic as it sounds. We were both dodging a particularly horrible mess and collided. If he hadn't grabbed me I should have fallen into the water. Until it was too late I had no idea he was one of the Parstocks.'

At that point she had intended to stop her confidences. The clergyman's daughter who had discovered the convenience of hotel rooms let by the hour had no inhibitions about describing her sex life. ('Curates are a country-girl's best friend, if you can overlook those dreadful ecclesiastical trousers!) A single episode in the botanical gardens scarcely made history. Bird smiled at the remnants of her old embarrassment, shedding guilt and shame. 'If you want the rest,' she said, 'you must give me a good reason. You aren't in need of care or a home. Why have you come here? Was there truly a question about your sister's death?'

Connie frowned. 'I have absolutely no idea,' she said. 'The questions are all in my own mind. Have you ever before heard of a death from acute gastro-enteritis in a bitterly cold December in England?'

'No, though I imagine it's not impossible.'

'Arsenic poisoning gives much the same symptoms. Many a wife, and occasionally a husband, has been quietly disposed of by that means.'

The tranquil green of their surroundings took on for a moment a frozen unreality. Bird relaxed and shook her head at Connie, regarding her with an air of rueful disappointment. 'Hasn't it occurred to you yet that I may be reasonably intelligent, certainly intelligent enough to know that you don't believe that of Hereward. There's no need to shock me into revelations. It would serve you right if I clammed up on you.'

*　*　*

Blast, thought Connie, so it would: I should have got out more since 1970. She had once known, better than most, that people who are complete fools over love can be perfectly sensible in other things. 'Sorry, Bird,' she said; 'that was disgraceful. Trying to make myself seem interesting and what a forlorn hope that is! It takes true evil or hidden madness to kill by poisoning. And a blind egotism. There's not an ounce of malevolence in Hereward that I've noticed, and several other people were in the house when Winifred was taken ill. I don't know who. They made themselves scarce when I arrived.' A wasp, sleepy with the ending of summer, settled on her knee. She flicked it away. 'At the time I was too concerned with my father's distress and my own even to be curious. If I'm altogether wrong, asking direct questions now is pretty offensive. If I'm right, what purpose am I serving?'

'Did you never discuss it with Miles? He mentioned once that Mrs Parstock let him take friends there while they were rehearsing and hard-up, until the day she died.'

Connie silently cursed herself. There she went again, arrogantly assuming that Miles existed only through her. Out of her orbit she had never allowed him a life. In flight from that idiot fixation she forgot him for years, until he needed a friend. She had rarely turned up for his stage performances, and yet he had shown tact and delicacy, avoiding any mention of Winifred in her father's house. 'Bird, as a detective, I'm a wash-out. And I dare say the whole business is simply the maunderings of a neurotic old maid. Yet I feel that you are the reason for — what? Some oddities of behaviour? I don't know. What exactly did happen in Paris? Were you and Hereward lovers then?'

Bird sat down and kicked off her shoes; rubber-soled, flat-heeled, sensible for a nurse's tired feet. For a second or two she wriggled her toes. (Nice legs, thought Connie, regretting her varicose veins and thickish ankles.) 'One affair, one measly little affair, and my whole life was taken up by it,' Bird said with faint irritation. 'I didn't talk to anyone. I didn't make a fuss about being pregnant and ignored. I should have done. Perhaps it's time I got it off my mind.'

Connie took a packet of cigarettes from her pocket and offered it to Bird, who shook her head. She lit one herself. 'Hereward had no right to expect you to keep quiet for his sake. I can see that Hannah needed protection, but not why she had to be told lies about her father.'

'There's something, some reason. I don't know what. Another stupid muddle, I expect. Everything was a muddle from the beginning, as you'll see.' Startlingly, as she began her story, the luminous, brilliant child shone out of her maturing face, drawing Connie into a romantic Paris that she knew to be an illusion. In cold and rain it was as dreary as any city. Where in the dripping emptiness of the botanical gardens had been Hereward's sense of occasion?

'He might have made an effort and taken you to his hotel,' she said at length, while Bird paused and seemed ready to lapse into silence.

'He was staying with friends. It quite startled me that sex could be done out-of-doors, especially with a god. I hadn't known that it happened like that. Mythology is misleading, don't you think? Zeus showered Danae with gold. I got a touch of lumbago from the damp.' She laughed. 'Ignorance is shaming when you're young. The other girls thought I was half-witted to let Hereward go. A trio of street-wise swingers was never going to believe that the only man I had ever met socially was a creepy evangelist who dropped to his knees at the slightest provocation and prayed on the doorstep.'

'I deeply distrust gratuitous prayer,' said Connie. 'Why do it unless your mind is on sinning? It's quite plain that Hereward genuinely loved you, or he wouldn't have told you who he was and taken you into his house.'

'All the same, I felt awkward there, a goose among swans. If he had left me alone, I should probably have got over him in no time. In a few months I would have been at university.'

'His place took a lot of keeping up without live-in staff. Having students to run errands helped, though I imagine it never crossed Winifred's mind that he had made love to you. He rather disliked young women except as tennis partners, and, of course, there was Stella, always on guard and intent on marriage. Yet you managed to avoid her?'

Bird smiled slightly and shook her head.

★ ★ ★

Many significant events are soon forgotten, yet Bird remembered vividly, long after her passion for him had died, the white, rolled-up sleeves of Hereward's shirt and the hairs on his arms, glistening bright and damp in the sunlight. But he had intentions other than tennis and Bird, moved by love beyond fear, beyond prudence and intelligence, had few defences. He did not intend her to resist his fierce approaches. She submitted, at first reluctantly then rapturously. They had been wildly indiscreet. Hereward made love to her on library tables, the floor of the picture gallery, on much of the drawing-room furniture, awkwardly across the steps of the servants' staircase, in the kitchen garden among the cabbages, or in the arboretum, where he waylaid her as she was returning home. He was proud of his virility. She swung from peaks of bliss to deep troughs of shame. It did not occur to her that she might be watched.

In a summerhouse behind the croquet lawn, Hereward lay heavily across her. It had been a day of stunning heat. Bees buzzed in the climbing rose that half obscured the narrow doorway, and an uneven floorboard and the hem of her rolled-up skirt dug painfully into her back. Time was at a stop. Sated, she drifted between dreams and substance.

'I thought so.' The shadow of Stella had loomed, casting them into satanic darkness. All senses suspended, Bird watched the grey-white flashes of her bared teeth switching on and off, unable to think or move. 'Get off her, Hereward, you pathetic shit, you look ridiculous.' Stella's voice resonated hollow and distant as a sibyl in a cave. She kicked him violently in the ribs, reducing them to a tangle of arms and legs and clothes. Bird made a rapid journey back from dreamland. She tried to get up. A stiletto heel ground agonizingly into her stomach. 'Stay there, Nest, or whatever your damned silly name is. I've not finished.'

Hereward lost his temper with her. 'Bloody awful bitch,' he shouted, frightening the life out of a wren that was nesting in the summerhouse, 'I've a good mind to break your neck. What right have you to spy on me? Pack your bags and get out of my house.'

'When I'm ready.' And conversationally to Bird, 'This object has been my lover for two years. I imagine he forgot to mention it. Now bugger off, dear, before I get angry.'

Hereward did not fly to Bird's defence. He nodded. 'Better run along while I sort this out. It's not important, sweetheart, I promise you. Don't be upset. I'll see you tomorrow.'

Upset? That was scarcely the word for her desperate humiliation. 'No you won't,' she said; 'not tomorrow, not ever. Disgusting people.' As she sauntered away with unconvincing lack of concern she thought, They're old, sophisticated, rich and they've made a fool of me: I hate them. But where the path disappeared among shrubs she glanced over her shoulder, hoping just a little to be called back. Hereward, sorting out his dignity, wasn't even looking her way.

Two days later she was violently sick when she got out of bed. Not just a fool then, but a pregnant one. Her mother went crazy, dropped to her knees to harangue God, and threatened to kill Bird if she didn't have an abortion. She refused. Hannah was born in a home for unmarried mothers that closely resembled a prison: by no means a tender, life-enhancing experience. In the teeth of savage pressure, she also declined to sign away her daughter for adoption. The nursing staff tried to make her life hell. In this they proved ineffectual, lacking as they did the relentless spite of Mrs Dawlish and her direct line to a vengeful heaven. Did they sell the unwanted babies? Bird wondered; was she depriving them of profit? By this time she had become suspicious of motives.

Not that Stella Worth had been hard to fathom. She wanted Hereward, then as now, and cared very little whether or not he wanted her. 'It was such a slap in the face, Connie. Deserved, of course. I didn't go to the house again. Almost immediately I discovered that I was pregnant and that was that. Until he turned up here, I hadn't seen Hereward for twenty-seven years.'

Bird watched a rowing-boat as it put out from the shore with a regular creak and splash of oars. The solitary occupant dropped a line, sat back, lit a pipe, waited for fish. In The Glebe a gong sounded. 'Heavens, lunch-time, I must go.' Bird led the way to the gate. 'I hope your curiosity is satisfied.'

'Why, oh why did Hereward never marry you? I'm beginning to see how divorce at that time would have left him inconveniently free for Stella.' She stumbled a little on the rough ground, clutching Bird's arm to recover her balance. 'One more question: what made you buy a private retirement home? It can't be enormously profitable.'

'It doesn't have to be. My mother left a great deal of money, and I've spent most of my life nursing the old. I never got to university. The Glebe was a sad and sinister place when I came across it and Lizzie and Charlie deserved a good home. It's a matter of loving those who need it, if you like, a habit I can't shake off.'

'Love is a keeper of swans,' said Connie, smiling, 'or so we're told. Not that I've ever understood quite why. The poem has a where-are-they-now bias; the title says it all, I think.' Bird's attention lapsed. There were books in her bedroom, but any poetry she had ever known, she had pretty well forgotten.

In the grounds, a vision awaited them under a broad-brimmed hat, weighed down with a festoon of roses. Stella Worth sat on a bench, leaning against a dripping bathing-suit, her straw bag at her feet. Beside it stood a bottle, and a single glass. Her dress, a designer's retrospective fantasy of country weekends in the 1920s, burst from the waist in billows of blues, greens and pinks and reached her feet. She had forgotten her underwear. Under the wet, semi-transparent bodice, her breasts lay flattened like uncooked buns. From a dreamy distance she wrenched her eyes into focus. 'Hey you, maid person,' she shrilled, 'bring me out a tonic and some ice, will you? We'll have a little drinky together.'

'We maid persons aren't allowed to drink on duty, thank you, Stella,' said Connie. 'Go home and sleep it off.'

Words took a while to penetrate. Stella brooded peacefully. Her mouth opened and closed as though she were engaged in animated conversation. At last she said, 'Good stuff this, after a swim. Gets to the vitals. Hereward could use some, the mouldy old sod.' Her painted eyelids drooped. A fly settled on her head and began a meticulous cleaning of its legs. She snored loudly and it flew away.

They left her there. Wally Spratt rolled back from his lunch, stopped by the bench and spoke. Stella sat on. It occurred to Bird that she might have to do something, though heaven knew what, about her. The council welfare services had suffered some nasty criticism over the activities of the previous regime at The Glebe, and now they made inspections zealously and often. Stella, obsessed and dwelling in her own never-never land, was going to take some explaining. With her dangerous inclination to love the lost, Bird knew that she would have been wise to turn Hereward away. But the signs were in his face. He saw, rightly or wrongly, the end of his life and because there was no one else, he had come to her to ease his dying. Her role had changed from lover to mother and nurse. She could not let him end his days among strangers.

★   ★   ★

It was late in the evening. Stella had disappeared. Bird, touched by loneliness and not entirely happy, stood at her window, looking out into the half-dark. Since the arrival of Connie Lovibond, she had begun to feel haunted. Alone in a darkening room, she would glance over her shoulder and reach for the light switch. Now, as she drew the curtains, she imagined that she could see a black, faceless figure standing in the shadows by the dense screen of trees at the far end of the garden. Through a high bank of rhododendrons a shifting light came and went. Bird blinked and looked again. There was no one, only clouds moving across the moon and a faint, pale glow rising off the sea. I'm becoming fanciful, she thought: a beautiful icon has died, reviving emotions I would rather not feel. But she went downstairs and through her routine evening check again. The gates were shut, the gardens empty. Once more she locked and bolted the outside doors. Inside the house no one was stirring except for the night sister on duty. 'Any problems? she asked.

'Everyone on medication's had it; Mrs Worth came in and was treating us to Shakespeare, rather loudly, but we packed her off while she was still on her feet. Mr Parstock's snoring. Miss Lovibond is playing cards with Mr Bean, and the others are quiet. You're not worried about anyone, are you?'

Bird shook her head. 'Not especially. They related so to the princess and they're disappointed in the other royals. Once the funeral is over perhaps they'll settle down.' Back in her room, she undressed with a grateful sigh, listening for sounds outside. It was impossible to separate them from the chatter of Lizzie's powerful wireless set in the room next door.

Lying back, Bird began to go over the things she must remember to do the next day. The telephone beside her rang. 'Sorry it's a bit late, Mother. Hope I didn't wake you.' Hannah's voice. 'Josh was playing up. The princess's death can't mean a thing to him, but he knows how to take advantage.' Here came a long pause while Hannah cleared her throat and rattled a cup.

'Yes,' Bird said cautiously, 'children usually do.'

'What I wanted to say — I just wanted to tell you that I've been offered a part-time job as Dr Early's secretary and receptionist. I've accepted. Can you have Josh occasionally on Saturday mornings?'

'I'd like that very much,' Bird replied, not wanting to show too much enthusiasm in case the treat was snatched away from her.

'Oh, by the way, Grandmother wins; I'm getting a divorce and I'm getting rid of the damned goats too. Good night, sleep well.' Amazed, Bird replaced the receiver. Had she imagined a slight warmth and kindness in her daughter's voice, and had Hannah of all people almost made a joke? An awareness of death had a way of infusing new life into the living. Sceptre and crown must tumble down and remind us of the precipice at our feet. Bird smiled. Pomposity doesn't suit me at all, she thought. It was awesome enough that some stimulus had jolted Hannah into activity, reminding her that time was passing and that she still had a life to live. Not by any account a bad thing.

7

On the morning of Wednesday, Lizzie Greengrass woke before her tray of tea arrived. She lay still, then moved carefully, testing her joints for pain and grunting softly at their stiffness. The hip that needed replacing was troubling her. At intervals, Charlie Bean nagged at her to get it done, but The Glebe had just begun to be interesting, whereas hospitals, Lizzie firmly believed, killed off their patients by boring them to death. The radio, which had been on all night, muttered beside her. She switched it off, feeling that she had mourned enough for Princess Diana; rather more, she realized, than she would have grieved for her own daughter, who did not much love her, but dearly loved her money. Lizzie had won over £500,000 on a football pool. She had intended to share her windfall, but before she could do so her upwardly mobile son-in-law came forward with his plan for her future which, stripped of concerned waffle, was that she should give her daughter power of attorney. He would look after the capital and dole out expenses. He did not know Lizzie very well. Her body might be arthritic, but there was nothing wrong with her brain and her comments on this plan were forthright and bruising. She sold her shop in Portsmouth and decamped to a retirement home. The pair did not visit her and she was glad.

As much as she hated plotters, she liked a fighter. If dominant women were to the taste of royal princes, the Princess should have exerted herself to become tougher and seen off the intruder, as Lizzie had done when her late husband took to bringing home barmaids. She admired the Queen and the Queen Mother. Now was the time for their advisers to show some gumption and ensure that they did the tactful things.

Fishing her teeth from their bath of water, Lizzie put them in, smiled experimentally and slid out of bed. She liked her rooms. The two windows, facing in different directions, gave her on one side a view of the gates, the church and the top of the High Street, and on the other a good slice of the garden and the sea. She teetered across in feathered mules to take a look at the day. No one was about in the village. She tried the garden side. What she saw there interested her very much indeed. In the shadow of a mass of hydrangea bushes, Stella Worth was in animated conversation with Wally Spratt, who smiled his fat smile, shaking his head at her, refusing something. He sat down on a garden chair and beckoned to her. At first she hesitated, then, shrugging her shoulders, she hitched up her skirt and clambered across his lap. Rhythmic movements agitated the hydrangeas. Browning pink flowerheads bounced and nodded as Wally's astonished face, appearing oddly over Stella's shoulder, contorted and his body heaved with a violent jerk that upset the chair and deposited them both among the bushes. Righted after a scramble, he slapped something into Stella's outstretched palm and limped away. He wasn't an athletic man.

Stella picked a few dead leaves from her hair, sat down on the vacant chair and appeared to nod off. You had to give her credit, thought Lizzie Greengrass; who would imagine that she had that much energy left at her age? She grinned to herself, remembering that Mrs Spratt was a large unexcitable woman, never seen without her knitting. Probably the needles clicked on in rhythm while Wally exercised his marital rights. He had just been granted a revelation.

Keeping her shop near Portsmouth docks had given Lizzie a phlegmatic outlook on human behaviour and she had learned to hold her tongue and mind her own business.

But exactly what Wally Spratt was up to now was, she felt, decidedly her business. He was not due to start work until nine o'clock and Stella had no right to be in the garden at all before the main gates were opened and the day officially began. The previous owners of The Glebe had treasured Wally. Odd, since he was not, in his person, an attractive man, nor a tireless and loyal worker. Interesting, perhaps, to know what his rôle had been. At that point in her musings, a maid brought in the tea-tray. 'Hallo, dear, all right? Would you like the telly on?'

'No thanks,' said Lizzie Greengrass. 'It's getting a bit sameish. I'll listen to the Queen when she gets around to saying anything and maybe I'll go up to town for the funeral.' She had only just thought of this. Bird would try to talk her out of it, but if she could get a couple of others to go with her it would be something to tell her two grandchildren, if they ever managed to turn into human beings. With the parents they had it was likely to be a struggle. She said, 'You could run me a bath, if you don't mind. Plenty of bubbles, please. I can get in and out on my own.'

'You sure? Ring the bell if you get stuck.'

Lying back in the comforting water she considered whether she should tell Bird about

the unexpected activities of Spratt, but came
to no decision.

★   ★   ★

Morning drinks were being served in the
conservatory. Miles, heavy-eyed with weeping, asked for hot milk with plenty of sugar.
'I'm like a lost child, Connie. Grief can be as
destructive as shame, don't you think?' He
was wearing a black sweater with a roll neck
that showed up the fairness of his skin and his
scant, apricot-grey hair. Clerical sobriety sat
well on him, making him seem quite pretty,
though of indeterminate sex. 'This awful
happening has changed everything. I feel that
I shall never be able to work on my book
again. Perhaps I should try to write a
valedictory piece for *Gay Times*.'

Connie bit into a chocolate Hobnob. She
imagined the piece in Miles's ponderous
style. ('Was it not that witty exemplar, Noël
Coward, who quipped, etc. etc.') She
regarded him gently and said, 'Try to
remember that you are grieving for a stranger
and moderate your feelings. They will pass
and so will the shock. Making yourself puffy
and pale is no help at all.'

'I adored her, all the gays did. She was so
brilliant and compassionate about AIDS. And

131

then the wicked, wicked truth about her marriage! A young girl out of the schoolroom, can you believe the disgust and the absolute need to be loved?'

Stella Worth, lacklustre, possibly from her encounter with Wally Spratt, lay on a garden lounger just outside the open door, smoking one cigarette after another and looking both ill and old. Her demand for a simply huge gin had been ignored. To Connie, the disillusioned weariness of the unfocused eyes suggested some deeper, more mysterious disturbance than drink. 'Disgust?' Her voice rang out with a dreadful clarity. 'I have experienced it in every degree. Parasites, disease, abuse. Marriage is bloody!'

Miles gave her a spiteful glare. 'You should know; you've been through it often enough.'

The care assistant drew a garden table close to her, put a large ashtray at her left hand and poured a cup of black coffee. Stella swore and dropped a cigarette into the cup. 'The triumph of hope over experience. Never again. I'd rather be crucified.' Connie did not miss Hereward's grunt of relief as he retired behind his newspaper.

Miles pressed on. 'A young life cut off points up the wisdom of cherishing every day, Connie. I've wasted so much time on self-pity and regrets and my novel may never now be finished. I do have one or two contacts in television. Perhaps I might try for a new career, character parts, you know, one of the soaps. What do you think?'

'Bloody good luck to you, dear,' said Stella. 'Put yourself about a bit, seduce a few casting directors. None of them have any balls these days. Just your type. Boys will be girls!' She sniggered, and for a moment or two, achieved complete and repressive silence. 'Oh, sorry, a *faux pas*.' She got up with a stagger. Recovering her balance she said with enormous dignity, 'Kindly get stuffed, the lot of you!' and wandered out across the terrace.

'Is that woman becoming daily more unhinged?' asked Miles, deeply upset; 'or is it just that at close quarters one notices more how ghastly she is?'

Lizzie Greengrass, as though she were comforting a forlorn sailor in her shop, patted his hands and fed him a number of unanswerable questions as a diversion from his misery. Would the Queen return from Balmoral today, did he think? Would she care enough to speak to the nation, order a state funeral, allow the flag on the palace to fly at half-mast? How did *he* feel with thousands of accusing eyes fixed on him?

'Damned fed-up like me, I should think,' said Charlie Bean. 'He's up to his neck in it, never mind the others. She couldn't have done him a worse turn if she'd tried, getting herself killed. There's a limit to power. Letting a disappointed woman go careering around like a loose cannon was downright arrogant. They should have treated her with a bit more caution.' He spooned sugar into his coffee cup. 'It's all something and nothing anyway. The human race is doomed. Polluted air, polluted water, poisoned soil, radioactive fall-out, low sperm counts; we'll be dying in our thousands soon and men will be impotent.'

'Not all bad news, then,' said Lizzie, drawing a scowl.

Out on the lawn, a thin woman, dressed in brief shorts and a singlet, materialized like an elderly sprite and began to exercise with verve, finishing her programme with three somersaults. 'Ought she to be doing that at her age?' Constance asked Miles.

'You haven't met Bunty, of course.'

'I believe that I may have met her foot,' she said, recognizing the bare leg and the boot.

'Except when she's out of doors, it's quite rare to see all of her at once. She's always the one half-hidden in photographs,' Miles said. 'And not a ready communicator. For seventy-nine she's quite extraordinarily fit. Do you remember Prunella Stack and the

Women's League of Health and Beauty, years ago in the thirties?'

'Just about. One of my aunts belonged. She died rather young, so did Miss Stack, I believe. Not the best of advertisements.'

'Old Bunty swears by it, that and Sloan's. Bird has to keep an eye on her exercising or she would be at it all morning.'

Charlie commented, 'She's not altogether shy. For years she spent her holidays in a nudist camp. When the fit takes her she pushes some of her snaps under our doors. I suppose we're intended to push them back when we've enjoyed them. That's what I do. At my age there's a limit to the entertainment value of male and female tits and bums.'

Lizzie smiled at him. 'It's a way of life to her, poor dear. In the war she joined ENSA, boosting the morale of the troops with a kind of circus act, trapeze, tumbling, low-wire, that sort of thing.'

Stella, her mood improving, put her head round the door. 'I did a bit of circus work myself before I went legit. Tough, but fun. You never quite lose the agility.'

Morosely ignoring her, Hereward said, 'As if those damned photographs weren't enough, she sings; morning, noon and night, she sings.'

Looking at him now, Connie wondered

135

about his state when he first came to The Glebe. To her he appeared to have faded rather than aged, accepting the purposelessness of his days like a penitential but comfortable robe. No token remained to him of those brilliant days of sun and pleasure. If Stella, the eternal hellhag, prowled his frontiers, she did not manage to pierce the defences.

Bird appeared, crossing the grass from the nursing wing to speak to Bunty. Hereward's gaze followed her, clinging with trust. Whatever went on in his mind, whether he loved or did not love, she must seem to him a protective angel. Bunty, now on her back, cycling violently with lean muscular shanks, subsided and allowed Bird to help her to her feet. They came inside on a waft of lavender and liniment. After she had been settled in a corner with her Benger's, Bunty whispered, 'Do we know yet when the funeral's to be?'

Lizzie nodded. 'Saturday, they expect.'

Then Bunty made what for her, Connie afterwards recognized, was a long speech. 'I shall take flowers, I shall go up for the funeral and take flowers. She wasn't just a mother, but a daughter and a sister. And then there's the young man, Doddy.'

'Not Doddy, love, Dodi. Foreign. Anybody else for the funeral?' asked Lizzie. 'Bird, could you lay on the little coach so that we can all go?'

Charlie snorted. 'You're daft. You'll never get near in the coach. And we were supposed to be using it for a trip to the Isle of Wight on Friday with the village OAPs.'

'That's had to be postponed,' Bird said, 'but Charlie's right. London will be impossibly crowded and there'll be nowhere to park. You'll get worn out and miss your meals. That reminds me, did you eat your prunes this morning, Bunty? We don't want you constipated again.'

Bunty pointed her boots, bent her knees one at a time and became positively chatty. 'Prunes? I've forgotten. I lost a lover in the war. It was painful. Who's that?'

Attention sharpened pleasurably as a young man came into view, carrying a full watering can as though it were a paper bag. He wore only a pair of ragged shorts. His feet were bare. The light of the sun polished his brown skin and glinted from a small gold ring in his left ear. On the far side of the garden by the bushes where lately she had given Wally a memory to treasure, Stella Worth stood and gaped. Miles made a sharp movement, quickly controlled, glanced at Connie and then away. In a neutral voice he said, 'He has a Spanish look, from a Velasquez or an El

Greco perhaps, don't you think, Bird?'

'Ched? I wouldn't know. He's the new undergardener, starting today. Rita Parry sent him to me — some sort of relation.'

Ched carefully poured water at the roots of a row of late raspberry canes, set down his can and stretched. Over his chest and rib cage the muscles moved like silk and he closed his eyes, lifting his face towards the sun with a smile. At the unselfconscious freedom of his movements Miles paled suddenly and made a faint moaning sound under his breath. He turned suddenly from the window and hurried away.

No one knew better than Connie how hard Miles had struggled for quietness of mind and now she had seen him struck with love at first sight. The passage of time had not dimmed her memory of the sudden shock, like a charge of electricity, that awakened every sense and tightened the nerves to breaking point. An awful, humiliating experience! With the young Miles she had felt compelled to follow him about, longed to touch him, just about prevented herself from begging him to love her. In short, she had dangerously lost her reason. The arrival of the boy in the garden dismayed her. Over the years, her passion for Miles had been replaced by an unsentimental, almost sisterly affection. His hurts distressed her also. She paused outside the door of his room and knocked lightly. He did not answer.

Feeling that she had already had as much chattering company as she could bear in one morning, Connie set off down the drive. Her holiday in the country, intended for the laying of her own ghosts and the broadening of her life, had begun to irritate her. No fate had summoned her to Dorset. Of all times this was the least appropriate, since she could not join in the excessive mourning, being capable only of compassion for an unnecessary death. She took herself to task with brisk self-command. Things were not, of course, normal at The Glebe, or in England itself, and when the English began to behave against their natures a certain ancestral extravagance, in earlier times fed and satisfied by public executions, was liable to creep in.

Vaguely, Connie hoped to get a close look at Bird's daughter, but no life stirred in the lodge cottage. She crossed the narrow road and went into the church. A visitors' book, flanked by vases of flowers, lay open on a table just inside the door, inviting tributes to Princess Diana. She glanced at the last few. In a flowing, elegant hand, Miles had covered half a page with a poem that Connie, annoyingly since she hated to be out-quoted, only half recognized. A very minor '90s poet, she thought. Quite apt in its way. Typical of Miles to find it. An anonymous individualist had written, 'Goodbye, Di. Men are dirty rotten curs. They always bugger up your life.' No doubt the vicar would tactfully censor that one. The rest were touching, but predictable: 'Queen of our hearts', 'people's princess', 'we loved you', and so on.

Saint Winifred's side-chapel was tiny and rather older than the rest of the church. On the walls a covering of decayed distemper flaked away, revealing traces of a brief history of the saint in pictures. Connie examined them with amused appreciation. Wear and tear caused Prince Cradoc, Saint Winifred's rejected suitor, to appear in patches, wearing a puzzled expression and looking too debilitated to wield the enormous sword he aimed at a few spots of blue and white. Next in sequence lay the virgin saint herself, in two parts, thoroughly dead. Connie noted that although her neck had been cleanly severed, her long fair plaits were undisturbed; not a blood drop, not a hair out of place, a tribute to Anglo-Saxon hairdressing. Then along came (presumably) Saint Beuno in vague outline to fit the pieces together. Expressionless despite the unusual turn of events, Saint Winifred was on her feet again and a neat, symmetrical fountain sprang up; a holy and miraculous well that predated Lourdes by many centuries.

The paintings gave no sense at all of her sister's presence, though Winifred would certainly have been touched by them. But Connie sat on, not praying, not knowing what to pray for. She had no wants or needs. Knowledge was all that she most valued, and learning had been the one pure and abiding pleasure of her life. Gradually the peace got through to her. She lapsed into unconnected thought, hoping that Miles was not about to be made miserable again simply because he could not, any more than the rest of mankind, subdue his desires and loves. Ched, the faun in the garden, had an innocent unawareness that was both his allure and his protection.

And Stella Worth? She, too, had stared at the boy. The woman seemed detached in mind from her own disintegration. Something there was seriously wrong. Again, after so many years, the uneasy sense of threat returned, a premonition of catastrophe, ridiculous to a logical mind. She crossed her ankles on a hassock and closed her eyes.

'Only saints can die twice, so they say,' croaked an elderly voice behind her. 'I'm none so sure. Your sister married Parstock!'

Calmly, though she was startled, Connie turned her head. 'Ah, you were often about in Swan House woods, picking plants. I don't know your name or where you come from.'

'Rita Parry, of no place in particular. Your sister was kind; she found me some woollens one cold winter and gave me leave to take a little fruit from her garden in season. I was sad when she died so sudden.'

So this was Ched's kinswoman, who had known Bird's mother and was said to be a witch. Was she, after all, the one who had called them, Miles, Hereward, Stella, herself, together? Surely the mention of Winifred's death, delivered in a faintly portentous tone, was intended to convey a message of sorts. Connie had not yet managed to talk to Miles. He would be in no shape for calm discussion of Swan House in 1970 until his emotions were resolved. It was not, she supposed, impossible that this old woman knew something of the activities in the house when Winifred had become ill. Approaching the subject with caution, she said, 'It was strange and unexpected. Pneumonia I could understand, but gastro-enteritis and an undetermined source of infection?'

'Not common. One of those forever in and out might have carried it.'

'Who would have been there in winter, I

wonder? It didn't occur to me to ask.' If her manner was casual and indifferent, Connie waited keenly for the answer.

But Rita seemed disinclined to give anything away. The shadows in the church drew around her until she almost disappeared into the scabrous patchwork of the old paintings. 'Names escape me nowadays. They say I see things that aren't there. Perhaps I do, perhaps I don't, but I know I'm too old to be living rough, either overhot or overcold, scratching about for a meal. I was the only friend Mrs Dawlish had and I thought Bird might take me in.' She gave a gusty, rum-scented sigh. 'A bit of a bed in an outhouse, a plate of bread and cheese. It's not a lot.'

Belatedly Connie understood that a question hung in the air; what help can I expect from you if I tell what I know? 'Subtleties are wasted on me,' she said amiably. 'I'm a plain woman and I prefer plain speaking.'

'Good enough if your words have a use. A reminder here or there, a hint that I'm ready to settle. Bird thinks I never can. Would I make a gypsy camp in her grounds?'

'Who knows? And in return?'

'You did well to come here. I can help you all to find what you seek,' she said, 'and when I'm safe home, I will.' She stood up, drew her several cardigans around her and disappeared among the visitors in the nave.

A curious encounter, though Connie had little faith that it would end her quest for the truth. She turned back to her study of the saint. Comforting to live in a time when death for the virtuous could so easily be undone, but what happened to the swaggering Prince Cradoc? Nothing, one supposed. Then as now, Princes of Wales, poor deluded creatures, expected to do much as they pleased without hurtful criticism. And why not, if they stopped short of murder? Any huckster felt entitled to ply strangers with impertinent questionnaires and meddle with lives. Reviving the old-fashioned virtue of privacy might relieve the world in general and this spinster in particular of a great deal of tedium. These reflections rapidly restored her to good humour.

8

Thursday began quietly. Council inspectors were due to visit that day and Bird was ready for them. Miles Alban had stopped weeping, the Queen had spoken, funeral arrangements were in hand for Saturday, the Union Jack would fly at half-mast above Buckingham Palace. Now the Princess could be sent properly to her rest.

Bird did not share Connie's discontent with the lost week. She felt that time had paused, adding days to all their lives in which anything might happen, good or evil. A gentle light surrounded her. 'You are extremely beautiful today,' said Tom Markham, who drove the coaches. 'And every day. Why don't you come to London with us on Saturday? Take a break for a change.'

'I was rather wishing that you would talk them out of it. Their nerve amazes me. Bunty's keen, but so erratic, ready to follow any piper's tune and get lost. Even the wheelchair-bound want to go. I've had to refuse them, I can't spare nurses to look after everyone. Later we can take them to Althorp, perhaps.'

'Don't worry about Bunty, I'll keep her on a lead,' Tom said. 'It would make the day if you came too, Bird, but I can't cancel. Some of the village pensioners say that they don't mind missing the Isle of Wight trip that they've paid for if they can go to the funeral instead.'

'Then there's no need to mention it to the inspectors. They *will* behave as though the old are essentially less intelligent than they are and I won't have my residents patronized. Unless the doctor intervenes, the fit have a right to make their own decisions.'

He smiled placidly. 'But you still worry? A good reason for coming along to supervise.'

Briefly she was tempted. There were too many better reasons why she ought not. Hereward could not face a long day out, her ninety-nine year-old was within five weeks of his telegram from the Queen and frail enough now to need perpetual care; and there was Stella, always there was Stella, promising to destroy the calm with her own peculiar brand of unbalance. She shook her head. 'Some of the nurses are keen to go with you and I shall have to fill in for them.'

Under the generalship of Lizzie Greengrass, The Glebers were on their best behaviour for the council's inspection. Bunty had obligingly postponed her callisthenics in favour of an erratic and unorthodox croquet game with Charlie Bean. They talked as they swung mallets. Neither had any grasp of the rules of play, nor took the slightest notice of what the other said. Charlie, in plus-fours and checked cap, reminisced about golfing triumphs of the past: Bunty described in detail her war work with ENSA.

On the way to her morning round with the sick and bedridden, Bird stopped in the shadow of a small open gazebo, noticing the slight tiredness of the green foliage, heralding autumn. By the rhododendrons, the focus of her occasional night-time unease, Wally Spratt leaned on a hoe. He bent his head as though he were at prayer. Slowly he began to topple forward, recovering with a start from a brief doze. Exasperated, Bird watched him prod languidly at the soil for a moment, then slide behind the high bushes. She considered following him. One day she might find an unassailable reason for dismissing him, though with the inspectors due this was scarcely the time. Hereward, inseparable now from his walking-stick, limped towards her. He began to speak. His words trailed away, interrupted by the urgent voice of Lizzie Greengrass, calling for help from the direction of the shell grotto. Bird reacted immediately. 'Stay there, Hereward. Better sit down,' she said, and ran.

Stella, in high exhilaration, leaned with her full weight against the restraining arms of the shorter, stockier Lizzie, jabbering wildly and steadily pushing her over. One foot was entangled in the handle of her straw basket. A broken bottle seeped gin into the grass border. Bird reached them as Stella collapsed like an empty sack. They caught her before she hit the ground. Her grey pallor had an alarming appearance of death; only occasional convulsive movements showed that she was still alive.

'I need Dr Early as soon as he can get here and a couple of nurses or porters *now*,' Bird said. 'The nursing wing's closest. Hurry, Lizzie.'

'I'll get my puff back in a minute.' Exuding hostility, Lizzie smoothed her crumpled ribbons and glared at the recumbent Stella. 'Why couldn't the wretched woman collapse in her own home? You're not going to take her in, I hope: she sounded dead drunk the stuff she was saying and I draw the line at filth. Why don't I give you a hand and we'll lock her in that grotto until the inspectors have gone?'

'She's really ill. By the look of her she could die at any minute.'

'Good riddance then. It'd be her own fault.

Lord knows what she thought she was about at her time of life.' Lizzie bowled away in moderate haste, leaving Bird to make what she could of this censorious remark. Hereward still sat on a seat by the path. As the stretcher went past he glanced once at the strapped-in, corpse-like figure of Stella, then turned a bleak profile to the small procession and looked out on the sea. The women who had loved him, Bird thought, had disappointed him. In her susceptible heart she felt a piercing regret that she would never again find in him the god she had lost. Heaven had no more gifts.

★ ★ ★

Gus Early was out on calls though not far from The Glebe, when his bleeper sounded. For Hannah he had worked a miraculous cure. A touch of usefulness and independence added substance to her meagre emotional diet of self-hatred. The old impulsiveness, that so far had brought her nothing but trouble, returned at full blast. Her deep-frozen libido thawed. The memory of her husband's deficiencies and the shame of divorce, with its accompanying fog of disillusion and melancholy, receded, leaving her voraciously alive. Hannah, both elated

149

and dismayed by her sudden hunger, wanted Gus now, at once. She had no idea of how to get him. In imagination, his naked body, smelling wholesomely of disinfectant, pressed urgently against hers, raising her to heights of pleasure never before attained. She cursed her own clumsiness with relationships.

And there were other barriers. Doctors were constrained by professional ethics and she was both his employee and his patient. Her grandmother's repressive love, followed by a freakish, impulsive marriage, had not taught her subtlety, nor the art of conveying that she was available. If she desired him, and she certainly did, she would have to show herself worth the risk to his career. And he might already have a girlfriend or a fiancée, unencumbered by goats and a small son.

Gus had condemned goat's milk. 'It isn't necessary for a strong and healthy boy like Joshua. You'll simply turn him into a fat kid.' But the goats still posed problems. Wally Spratt had told her that he knew of a farm that would take them, and offered to transport them himself in his truck for twenty-five pounds. It was tempting. Hannah examined the beaming insincerity of his smile and the latent social worker in her rose to the surface. Not her goats, however stroppy and troublesome. There was a dog-food factory no more than ten miles away and it was a fair guess that Wally knew his way there blindfold. She turned him down.

At the end of Wednesday morning surgery, she locked the outer door and returned to the consulting-room to file the records. Although her thoughts were busy and content enough, except for the goats, her frustration showed. A small frown of concentration and the downward curve of her mouth conveyed total misery. Gus sat in front of the new computer. 'Is that the lot? Good. You don't look happy; what's wrong?'

'Nothing at all. I'm fine. I have a dismal face.'

'Rather beautiful, I thought. If you can spare a minute before you go, come and have a look at this damned machine. It's died on me. It won't do anything at all.'

'Move over, let me try; it's simple really.' Hannah took his place. 'Oh, it's frozen.' She flipped the main switch off, then on again. 'There.' She turned her head towards him and smiled, lighting herself up like a sudden whoosh of fireworks.

An expression of bemusement appeared on Gus's face. 'I thought you weren't pleased to be working here,' he said to the back of her head; 'are you pleased?'

'Oh yes, I am, hugely, enormously.' She

swung round, embraced his knees and burst into tears. 'It's the goats,' she wailed. 'I need a good home for them, a place that's willing to collect as I don't have transport, and I can't find one.'

He helped her to her feet and pressed her head against his shoulder. 'You'd better come up here and weep. Damp trousers take a lot of explaining. Is that all that's upsetting you, the goats?'

Once her loneliness and misery surfaced, there was no way of stemming the tide. 'This is the wrong way to do it,' she wailed. 'It's me. I'm dull and boring and plain and sex-starved. Each time I walk in here I want you more and I've only known you three days. It's disgusting. Now you'll sack me and I don't blame you.'

'Well, well.' Gus patted her on the back. 'There, there. You're very forthright. I'm at a loss.' Instead of pushing her away from him, he kissed her neck. 'I seem to be on the path to disgrace, and very pleasant it is too. No, please don't look at me like that or I shall be telling you that your eyes are drowned pools or some such nonsense.'

'You're truly not angry? You're not going to sack me? You don't hate me?' Hannah blazed into life all over again.

'Flattery isn't a reason for hatred. My

knees have gone weak.'

'Perhaps you'd better sit down on the couch,' said Hannah. 'The blinds are drawn.'

'Absolutely not,' he said, putting her away from him. 'Don't, please, rush us both into a furtive affair. You're worth better. Or am I completely misreading the situation.'

Humilation deepened Hannah's pallor. 'No, Gus, you're not. I'm behaving badly. I've never had much subtlety and I know you can't possibly find me attractive. I'll go home now and send my resignation.'

'Do slow down, woman; I don't want you to resign. I know it ought to be your line, but this is so sudden. I am sworn to abstain from all seductions and I need time.'

'I suppose I'm trying to seduce you, not you me, so that's all right. You're in the clear.'

'Mere sophistry, and I don't like it when you're bitter. Shall we both calm down and talk about goats? Why don't you borrow your mother's car and drive around the farms?'

Hannah mopped her eyes and tried not to hear the phantom voice of her grandmother telling her that she had made herself cheap to no purpose. 'I don't approve of private motor cars. They're elitest and killing all hope of equality.'

'All these principles! You need to bend them a little, if only for Joshua's sake. He's mad on cars and dying to go to that vintage motor place at Beaulieu.'

'How do you know? I didn't. He never said a word to me.'

'We had a long talk when I was over at the school. He's a bright little beggar, good company, and I fancy he knows your feelings. I half-promised to speak to you about taking him and a couple of his friends over some time.' He gave her a doubtful look. 'As you feel so strongly, I imagine you wouldn't care to come with us. There are other attractions, I believe.'

'Well, perhaps it won't hurt just once,' Hannah muttered, both touched by Joshua's patience with her and faintly aggrieved at this evidence of conspiracy. 'I don't want Josh to forget what his feet are for or to be dependent on machines.'

'Very worthy. Now, these blasted animals. I saw an advertisement for goat's milk, cheese, yoghurt, the whole range of healthful nourishment, in the New Forest. Late surgery tomorrow morning. Can you be ready to go by half-past eight? I'll run you there. If they can't take your two they'll be bound to know of someone who can. Mine's a working vehicle so you needn't feel pangs of conscience.'

Goatless, at last, thought Hannah, so

brimming over with relief that she hugged him extravagantly. 'I won't, Gus, I'm a fool. That's wonderful.' Seduction and rejection temporarily slipped her mind until he kissed her.

'I'm pitifully starved of female affection and the sad thing is that by tomorrow you'll have noticed what a dull fellow I am and recovered your wits. You smell delicious too. What is it?'

'Carbolic soap, I expect, and by tomorrow I shall be ashamed of behaving badly and then behave even worse. Would it be too sudden to ask for a home visit when we get back from the Forest? You could bring your bleeper.'

'Oh lord,' said Gus, 'oh lord.'

★ ★ ★

In Hannah's bedroom the bleeper bleeped in vain the first time, since Gus was imprisoned by her arms and busy. They lay still, relaxed, until the call came again. Hannah stretched out a lazy hand and passed him the telephone, examining his naked body minutely, touching him here and there as he spoke. 'Behave,' he said; 'no, not you Marian, an unruly patient. The Glebe? Any details? Sudden collapse, right;

I'll be there in five minutes.' And to Hannah, 'Don't move yet, I want to look at you while I'm dressing. You're amazingly beautiful.'

'I'm amazingly content.'

'Are you sure?' He spoke seriously. 'We've known each other hardly any time at all and before I lay my career on the line and my heart at your feet, I need to see where we're going. Is this a one-off with no future? Loneliness on your part, a very natural attraction on mine?'

'Can't we wait and see? I haven't met a man I wanted so badly for several years, but if marriage taught me nothing else, it taught me not to confuse sex with love. You lead, and I'll follow. Any time you fancy, I shall be here.' She raised her eyebrows. 'How surprised you look. You're a very, very attractive man and you never talk about football or reek of beer. Now hurry up. We'll have loads of time later.'

'Oh good,' said Gus. 'No, please don't smile like that; it does disgraceful things to me.'

* * *

'I didn't imagine you could get here so promptly,' Bird said. 'You can't guess how grateful I am. This would happen when the

156

council inspectors will be here at any minute.'

Gus smiled. 'Mrs Marsh is trying to dispose of her goats and as she doesn't have a car I took her to a place in the Forest that will give them a home. Luckily we had just got back. Where's the patient?'

Stella, conscious now, but confused and feverishly talkative, thrashed around in her jaunty underwear on a bed in the isolation unit. The nurses had folded her tights neatly down to her ankles. Under the heavy make-up, her face was collapsed into a crumpled mask. As the doctor bent over her she grasped him with shaky hands and tried to kiss him. 'Friendly old soul, isn't she?' he said, moving back out of reach. 'Have much trouble with her?'

'Some. She isn't a resident,' Bird explained, 'only a very unwelcome visitor. I thought at first that she might have an infection, though perhaps it seems more like poisoning.'

Stella's rich voice intervened. 'Either come back here, darling, or piss off.' The effort seemed to exhaust her and she lay still, glaring malevolently at the ceiling.

While the doctor examined her, Bird had an opportunity to study him. He was, after all, Hannah's employer and ready, it seemed, to help her in other ways; in short, a young man able to thaw permafrost and with pleasant, if undistinguished, looks. Glancing up suddenly, he caught her staring at him and grinned, seeming not to mind. His examination was careful and thorough. 'She's taken a hefty drug overdose, almost certainly cocaine, by injection. How long has she been like this?'

'She first collapsed about half an hour ago. She's more often drunk than sober, but not usually ill or raving.'

'Tricky. Then all I can do for now is to give barbiturates.' He filled a syringe and injected into a flaccid arm. 'This should calm her down long enough not to scandalize the inspectors, and to ward off any more convulsions. A nurse must be with her all the time. If she shows signs of cardiac failure, ring me at once. I'll call back this evening in any case. From what I can see, I doubt whether she was an addict. The stuff's about, but where did she get it in Wynfred Abbas?'

A deep anger overtook Bird. A feeling that she had at some stage walked into a simple trap nagged away at the back of her mind. At the trial of the last owners, morphia and cocaine had both been mentioned, to relieve, they said, sanctimonious to the last, the pain and suffering of their dear old people. Where the massive quantities came from was never discovered. She believed now that she knew and her spirits sank even further.

'You realize,' Gus said, very gently, 'that I shall have to make a report to the police? It will be troublesome. As Mrs Worth isn't a resident you are not strictly responsible. I had better arrange for her to be moved to a hospital.'

'How I would love to be rid of her, but I feel responsible. She lives alone. Someone will have to keep an eye on her until she's safe.' He seemed surprised at her concern and she added hastily, 'It's not care for her, but for The Glebe itself. You see, I think I may know who supplied the drug, but unless she gives the police a name, I certainly couldn't prove it, not yet.' A telephone rang; the inspectors had arrived. Despondently she walked to the door. 'If I'm right, they'll do their damnedest to close me down.'

'No chance of that without good evidence. Perhaps we can head them off at the pass. If it's convenient to you to accompany me, I can do my rounds now. We care, therefore we might as well be seen to care, don't you think?'

This is, thought Bird, an extraordinarily nice, humorous man, and very probably a good doctor. The softening of her daughter's unpromisingly censorious nature began to seem less of a miracle. Impulsively she said, 'You've done Joshua a great favour, ridding him of goats. I hope Hannah appreciates your help.'

'Oh, she does, I promise you.' Gus Early glanced at her with every appearance of contentment.

* * *

When Stella Worth had been carried away, Lizzie Greengrass indulged in one of her thinks. Her view of the world was realistic rather than hard-boiled, and intelligent to a point just short of cynicism. Also she had a fierce sense of justice and a deep curiosity. Having seen Stella's condition for herself, it did not take a great mind to guess at the nature of the traffic between her and Wally Spratt, or to make other connections. Under the old management, Wally had been the universal provider, the one that got away. The situation began to take on a threatening air. Lizzie looked thoughtfully at the matter of ridding her small world of him. Life at The Glebe pleased her and she wanted no well-meaning interference that would drive her out. It might have helped to tell Bird at once of the early morning grapplings, though what she could have done about it was anybody's guess. Stella's sex life was hardly her problem.

In a mood to exercise, Lizzie elected for a stroll through the grounds. The magical boy, Ched, worked among the roses. He straightened as she approached, smiled, and in a soft voice said, 'Good morning, Aunt,' holding out to her an unfurling bud.

Charmed, Lizzie pinned the flower among her ribbons, thanked him and walked on. It was a long time since she had heard that polite Romany way of speaking to an elder. No scavenging traveller would use it. They had no tradition and no pride, only a determination to do nothing and live off the labours of others. Pitying the true gypsies, she detested travellers. She wondered where Ched's family most often camped and whether they had been forced on to one of the council's permanent sites so alien to their life-style. Gypsies saw and heard much. They said little. What he, or Rita Parry might have noticed in and around the gardens of The Glebe teased her curiosity.

Away from the house, the grounds were at that moment quiet and empty. The peace was absolute. Lizzie Greengrass passed the spot where Stella had collapsed, climbed up the mossy steps of the gazebo and down the other side. Glimpses of the sea appeared and disappeared among a tangle of bushes. Sighing with pleasure, she made for a rustic revolving summerhouse that no longer revolved, but faced permanently west into a nettlebed. There she took off her shoes and gently massaged her hot feet. A few yards behind the summerhouse stood the shell grotto and there all pretence of cultivation ended. She had walked far enough. Her eyes closed.

A scraping of metal on metal woke her. Craning her neck, she saw the door of the grotto open wide enough to admit the stout form of Wally Spratt, then close again. On stockinged feet, Lizzie crept to the back of the summerhouse, cursing silently the fierceness of the nettles that stung her legs and toes, finding a vantage point behind an elder tree from which she had a direct view of the grotto. After a moment Spratt emerged. Before the door swung to, she noticed a row of small polythene sacks resting against the wall. He locked the door. Removing the key, he went whistling towards the gates as the inspection team arrived. Odd, thought Lizzie Greengrass. She recalled that because the grotto was dangerous and the residents discouraged from entering it without supervision, the only key hung in Bird's office. Rubbing one foot against the other to ease the pain of the nettle stings, she found a few dock leaves to put down her stockings. Then she went in search of Charlie Bean. On her way, she glanced in to the office and saw that Bird's key was on its hook. Wally Spratt's must be a duplicate.

★ ★ ★

'Wally Spratt and Stella Worth?' Charlie said, looking sick. 'I wish you hadn't told me that. It's enough to give me nightmares. The world's a midden. The sooner the human race becomes extinct the better.'

Lizzie examined him and smiled. 'You're a bit down, just now, my lad. So all right, nobody measures up to your standards of behaviour; that isn't our business: The Glebe is.'

He brooded, clasping his bony knees. 'It's certainly our business when those who used to set standards let us down. Look at the royal family. I've always admired them. If they had troubles they handled them discreetly instead of trumpeting them to the world on television and making blasted idiots of themselves.'

'Isn't that our fault? We bow and scrape and let them think they're above criticism. They're still human, aren't they?'

'They've no right to be,' said Charlie unreasonably, 'not if they want to be fawned on by me.'

Lizzie did not point out that the royal family was totally unaware of his existence and would scarcely miss the homage of one cantankerous old citizen. His England, and hers, had changed too much ever again to be the slow, repressive country they had been born into. 'You can admire the Queen and the Queen Mother. They're as much out of their depth as you are. Once we've sorted out Wally, you can get on with mapping out the destruction of mankind. That'll cheer you up.'

'It's not a joke, it's scientific fact.'

'Do you want to hear the rest about Stella Worth, or do you not?'

'Just get on with it.' Lizzie Greengrass got on with it. At the end of her recital, Charlie said, 'They never did find out where those drugs came from. Somehow or other we need to get a look in the grotto. Plastic sacks could mean anything. He might just be stocking up on compost for all we know. Then we'd better have a chat with the boy and his old grannie, or whatever she is.'

'If Stella's staying a while, we could try her as well.'

'Drunk or sober, I've never heard her talk a word of sense. And where's Bird going to put her so she won't drive other patients up the wall?'

'If it were up to me I'd get shut of her, but

then I'm not Bird. One of the bungalows behind the nursing wing is empty. She could go in there until someone can persuade Bird to get the police in.'

The lunch gong sounded. Attacking her roast chicken with appetite, Lizzie said, 'It's not quite over yet, is it, Charlie? I'm looking forward to a bit of action. We've been too comfortable just lately and getting lazy.'

'Speak for yourself. I'm all for peace and quiet.'

'No you're not. You get bored with too much female company. Why don't you invite that friend of yours from Liverpool down here when a vacancy comes along? He's a man with a sense of adventure.'

'Getting a lump bitten out of my leg by a shark isn't my idea of adventure. Showing off to some Australian girl young enough to be his granddaughter, the old fool. Anyway, he's already in a home. He might not want to move.'

'You could suggest it.' Lizzie tutted under her breath and asked for a large portion of sherry trifle. It struck her as she poured on extra cream that contentment carried too far takes every scrap of amusement out of life. Miles Alban went on long holidays and Bunty joined clubs, whether they interested her or not. She and Charlie did nothing much. She said, 'Come to the funeral with us. We can have a picnic in the park and watch the crowds and get Tom Markham to stop off at a pub for a drink and a bite of supper coming back. And when we've got Wally Spratt seen to we can make a few plans.'

Alarm sent his eyebrows shooting halfway up his bald head. 'Plans for what?'

'I'll get my hip done and take up golf, perhaps. We can play together.'

Charlie inspected her shelf-like bosom dispassionately. 'You're the wrong shape for golf. Over that lot, you won't be able to see the ball when it's right in front of you.'

'Then I'll diet, or buy one of those sports bras that hold everything in. And we can take a holiday — not some tame place like the Isle of Wight — Disneyland or Bangkok; or we can run the London Marathon, or do bungee jumping, something different.'

'Lizzie,' he said, 'you're cracked. Bungee jumping, dear lord! And Spratt won't be as easy to nail as you imagine. If your ideas are right he's been getting away with it for years.'

'All the more reason for putting a stop to it.' She gave him a bland smile as she helped herself to a piece of Stilton and a handful of water biscuits, but her small black eyes shone like particularly obstreperous boot buttons. As one tough nut to another, she meant to bother the life out of the mysterious Rita Parry, who appeared to know everything. Enigmatic was she? Liked to be in control of secrets? With Wally, that could be a dangerous game to play. She could use a partner, whether she wanted one or not.

9

With Bird, Connie stood beside Stella's bed, examining her with a critical and unkindly eye, feeling pleased that she was likely to survive long enough to be questioned. The uninvited guest made an occasional popping sound with her lips, otherwise she slept peacefully.

'Unconsciousness suits her,' said Connie, who had not slept well at all. 'Like this she's quite tolerable, though even her silence gives an odd impression of noise and rumpus. She always believed that she would get Hereward. It's an idea she ought to give up.' She studied the old face, as though by tracing its lines and crevices she could make a precise judgement of Stella's capacity for unbalanced action. It had certainly not been her moving around the grounds in the night. But someone had been. Each time Connie had fallen into a doze, she had awakened to an impression of stealthy and hurried movement.

Bird said, 'I can't understand why she kept marrying other men instead of waiting. Wasn't it rather like Box and Cox? When he was free, she wasn't.'

'Illogical to us. She was a well-known actress and it was part of her image to be desired. A raft of discarded husbands made good publicity. Unrequited love, on the other hand, equated with unattractiveness and failure. Of course she was lovely then and, would you believe, naive about men? She made some awful mistakes, never smelling a rat until she had married it! God knows how much she spent buying off husbands.'

Bird nodded. 'A let-down to an over-inflated ego!'

'And do you think that ego is dangerous to others? Capable of maiming or killing to acquire the desired object? I wish I knew.'

'You know more about her than I do, but I would certainly judge her to be capable of any impulse. She seems never to think at all before she acts. In spite of taking drugs enough to kill a horse, I suspect that she isn't truly hooked; it simply seemed like a good idea at the time!'

'An instinctive talent for drama.' Connie wanted to get on to the subject of Hereward and her sister, but Bird's reluctance to discuss Stella's amours was plain. She tried another tack. 'Speaking of desired objects, would you consider allowing Rita Parry to have this bungalow when Stella's gone? She has a hankering to die in what she regards as the bosom of her family — you, presumably, and that unsettlingly beautiful boy.' Hastily she added, 'I can see that the house is out of the question.'

She had chosen a bad time. Bird had not waited for Gus Early to act. Her suspicions of Wally Spratt had become a near certainty; the drug that Stella had taken had been obtained on her property, and who else was capable of supplying it but the detestable Wally? After the council team had duly inspected, pronounced themselves satisfied, and wolfed a sumptuous lunch, she had spoken to the police herself, naming no names. They were astute enough to draw their own conclusions. 'We can talk about Rita another time, if you don't mind, Connie, when the doctor has declared Stella out of danger.'

Not for the first time, Connie found herself angry and puzzled over Stella, and over Hereward, who had brought her into their lives, trailing her behind him like a sick dog, faithful to the death. She hated the muddle in which she had embroiled herself. With another present and prominent death to mourn, she could not hope to interest anyone in her past griefs. Why on earth had she exhumed an old sorrow and not simply taken up life where she had left it, going on instead of back and leaving all questions unasked?

Winifred had long been dead. Her bones rested peacefully and did not cry out for vengeance.

She thought of Rye as it would be now, swarming with tourists. Soon the strangers would be packed away for the winter while neighbours met, gardens were tended, little treats arranged; and in her house, tranquillity, and new books to be read, as gales screeched across the rooftops and every gully and gutter ran with rain. Ought she to abandon her small act of rebellion for the safe and dull? Old fool, she thought crossly, and reminded herself to buy a red plastic bucket and to order a radio and a television set when she was ready to return.

In the garden, she found Miles watching Ched dig potatoes for the kitchen. His expression was carefully guarded, though his hands were tightly clasped and he had bitten his nails, which had been growing nicely, to the quick. Before Connie sat down beside him she hesitated for a second. His body trembled slightly and she feared that he was locked in an erotic fantasy from which he did not want to be released. He spoke first, but reluctantly and with unusual firmness. 'Don't scold me, Connie, please. You know what I'm going through. I've never fooled around with boys and never wanted to. Perfection is simply not fair.'

'I'm in no position to scold over love. You won't approach him, you'll simply suffer, and that's not good enough for you, my dear, not nearly good enough. Do you want to stay here, or will you walk with me as far as the church? I'm feeling restive.'

With a last look back at Ched, Miles got to his feet. 'What deters me isn't virtue, but fear of disgust politely concealed, and the inevitable rebuff. So why not church? I've never been hugely religious, though I've hung on to my faith. Now I'm in danger of losing it.' Unshaven, his thinning hair blown up and about by the wind, he cut a faintly ridiculous figure and knew it. 'Until now, I've always felt that God made me as I am for a purpose, expecting me to do my best with it. And I have tried. Just look at what's left of a life, Connie; a comical old clown, come suddenly to a place of ashes and dry bones, a Golgotha if you like. If only I had your strength and detachment.'

He slipped an arm through hers. Although Connie did not much care for casual contacts, she did not move away from him, but drew him closer to her side, thinking — strength and detachment, balls! Who is strong or detached in the throes of an unfulfilled passion? By self-imposed retirement and solitude, Miles had extended his solitary penance far, far too long. He needed a reminder of his humanity and her own. She said in a calming tone, 'Few people with an eye to beauty could see that young man and not feel a desire to possess, to touch. In the Swan House days, you had much the same power, Miles, and the same unconsciousness of your effect on others.'

'*I* had? You're not serious? Do you imagine I can't see how plain I am? My looks can never have matched his.'

'Thirty years will change Ched too, of course. You were the most glorious, golden creature I had ever seen and how I burned for you! Hopelessly and helplessly; a form of midsummer madness. You would have fainted with fright had I done to you what came to mind!' He stopped dead and drew his arm away. Connie smiled. 'Don't be alarmed, I ran away and worked like a demon. That cured me quite quickly and I promise that I've never lusted after you since.'

At first Miles looked so stunned that she wondered whether it had been a mistake to confess. Then a pleased expression livened his face. 'Glorious and golden? What a charming thing to say, Connie, even if it isn't entirely true. Perhaps I should run away too, though I have no work to be my salvation.' He took her arm again and together, like a pair of elderly invalids, they ambled into the church, stepping carefully to avoid trampling the flowers heaped almost to their feet. The scents were too sweet and strong. A photograph of Princess Diana now hung above the table with the book of remembrance. Miles became silent. He sat down in a pew facing the pierced and painted rood screen, leaned forward and propped his chin on his hands. A tear or two ran down his cheeks.

Connie's store of compassion was running low. She left him to God and went into Saint Winifred's chapel, hoping that Rita Parry would be there, but it was empty. The wall-paintings mouldered quietly away in peace without regard to the secular dead. Connie thought of her sister, of miracles, of Miles, of her father who would have wanted to have the paintings restored and protected. Was Saint Winifred's resurrection a folk tale with no foundation in fact at all? Certainly it was no mean conjuring trick to unite nerves, bone and blood-vessels, matching exactly the head to the body. Quite dreadful to have a crooked saint. Here Connie stopped short, disapproving of her own frivolity.

The sooner Saturday came, the better she

would like it. It seemed that some inhibiting force, a kind of spell, had seized the people and that everyone waited, suspending life until the funeral that would bury an icon. People spoke, but said little. She shook off a creeping inertia and returned to Miles, who stood in front of the photograph. He said, 'The sick and the unconsidered poor have lost a great-hearted friend. Who is there now prepared to embrace the diseased or hold a damaged child like a mother?'

And there lies the true loss, Connie thought; not the loveliness, the youth, the beauty, all of which would have faded, but the compassion, the forgetting of rank and self. Others of importance lent their names to charitable causes, Diana gave herself. And so did many people of course, good people who received no adulation and precious little reward. 'There's you, Miles,' she said.

He choked slightly on an indrawn breath. 'Are you mocking me? Is this a joke? If so, it's in extremely poor taste.'

Considering that the idea had only just come into her head, Connie saw that it really was quite a workable one. 'Mockery? Of course not. Who better than you? You are independent, with unsatisfied aspirations, and you understand despair. Bird would support you as hard as she could and so would I. You have The Glebe as a permanent home and my house remains open to you when you need to be closer to London. A kind heart ought not to be wasted.'

'But my book, what would happen to my book?'

'If you will forgive me for saying so, your plot has an air of artificiality because you retired so early and so thoroughly from the world. Contacts, carrying on the good work, will give you much more to write about.'

Absentmindedly he stroked his bristly chin, making a faint, annoying rasping sound. 'But my awkwardness and diffidence; people would simply laugh at me, wouldn't they, however much I wanted to help?'

'If there's love enough, who will laugh? Not the injured and the dying.'

'Suffering has always frightened me, and wounds and blood turn my stomach. It's a terrifying commitment to make. If I volunteer and they don't turn me down, I might make a mess of it, and yet for her I could dare anything. But oh blast, I did so much want to be a writer and see my novel in print.' His prim shell was cracking already. Once launched, he would make a gentle and generous helper and be helped in turn. And with luck, Connie thought a trifle unkindly, the poor man will never again have time to put pen to paper or to undergo more agonies of rejection. Miles said, throwing himself into his new role, 'Just look at me, I must shave; or perhaps I should grow a beard to give myself more gravitas.'

Exhausted by her exercise in arranging lives, she ushered him steadily to the door, 'Shave, please do. An unsuccessful beard is simply an irritant.' He drifted off on his own charitable cloud, and none the worse for it if his determination lasted. Needing an antidote to such high aspiration, she set off alone down the High Street to buy the ugliest souvenir of Wynfred Abbas that she could find. Something musical in plastic, perhaps, with shells. It could stand on the drawing-room mantelpiece, a vulgar, discordant note among her father's treasures! And what would that prove? Not a damn thing.

In this disordered frame of mind, Connie almost missed seeing Rita Parry. The old lady crept out of a narrow alleyway between the Duke's Head and Madam Dulcie, Lady's Fashions. At its furthermost limits the alley widened into a small courtyard of beaten earth, containing four derelict cottages. One of these, the least decrepit, was Rita's home. The rest suffered from her habit of using their fencing, sheds and privy doors to keep her fire going. Connie stopped in her tracks.

'Hallo Mrs Parry, I was hoping to see you in the church, just for a chat. Is there somewhere we could get a cup of tea? Or perhaps you could manage something to eat.' As she spoke it occurred to her that the village, a dead end with no beach to speak of, did not attract the tourist trade or boast a Copper Kettle or a Jane's Pantry. Catering stopped short at Fred's Diner (Sandwiches to Order).

It didn't matter. Rita nodded graciously and turned right for the Duke's Head. 'A drop of rum would go down nicely since you offer. And I wouldn't say no to a pasty. The days are drawing in and it gets chilly of a night when the grey ones come in off the sea.'

Grey ones? Don't ask, thought Connie, if we have to be mystic, I'll go along with it. At least the pub, probably once a Victorian country beer-house, contained nothing in the least supernatural, nothing of any interest at all. She inspected the labels on the sherry bottles. 'I wouldn't,' said Rita, 'not sherry. Play safe with the scrumpy; it's local and it's good.' The landlord had never been tempted to launch into catering on the grand scale. He kept a jar of pickled onions and another of sour green gherkins on the counter, presumably to help down the plastic-wrapped pies. The meat in Rita's pasty, eaten in silence, was as grey as (presumably) the grey ones from the sea. She seemed not to mind and asked for another. Connie added a second rum. If it did nothing else, it might help to neutralize any stray unwholesomeness in the food.

As Rita showed no inclination to initiate conversation, Connie said, 'You understand what will happen if Bird takes you into The Glebe? She will have to get your birth certificate and register you with the Social Services so that you can claim a pension and benefits. You can no longer remain anonymous and free.'

'Freedom's a thing of the spirit. Soon I'll die and be free again. They tell me she's got Mrs Worth on her hands.'

They, in this instance, meaning Ched, of course. 'An overdose of drugs, the silly woman. Dangerous, not only for Bird but for the survival of The Glebe. She needs your help, information that I believe you can supply.' Rita glanced at her, giving nothing away. 'When Mrs Worth goes, there's a bungalow, private, but with the same care that's offered to other residents. How long is it, I wonder, since you last had a decent meal?'

She shrugged. 'If I have things to tell, they're for her alone. My life isn't for picking apart. She must make what use of them she can. What's happening now?'

'The police will be there around noon. As soon as they're satisfied, Bird will get rid of Mrs Worth, though I expect a delay until the unfortunate Princess Diana is seen to be mourned and honoured.'

'In death, if not in life,' Rita said, as though condemning the tardiness of human kindness. 'This afternoon I'll visit the boy. Then we'll see about your needs, lady. When all's settled.'

She stood up and shuffled to the door without farewell. Connie sat on for a while, finishing her cider and thinking of families and the past. In the summer of 1970, she could not have guessed that the shy, elusive and unconsidered child who passed so quickly through their lives would one day become significant to them all. Bird brooded them like stray cygnets, a kind and beautiful woman who appeared to be unaware of the sadness of her past. Connie felt no guilt at preaching to Miles the satisfaction of a life of service to others. He would be found by friends. She did not, however, think it nearly enough for Bird.

★　★　★

Dr Early's last patient of the morning was Mrs Wally Spratt, with her knitting. Hannah locked the outer door behind her, eased her into Gus's surgery and managed after a slight struggle to get her seated in the largest chair. Much of her overflowed in all directions. She sweated heavily. 'I've come for me white bottle, Doctor,' she said, fanning herself with her knitting pattern. 'For wind,' she added helpfully. A ball of heather mixture wool escaped from her bag. Hannah retrieved it and would have held on to it except that Mrs Spratt snatched it away from her.

Gus motioned Hannah to stay. 'Just get your breath back, Mrs Spratt, then I'll examine you.'

'Old doctor didn't do no examining. He just gave me a white bottle, private. Fifty pee.'

'You're carrying a lot of weight. Do you have any other problems, palpitations, faintness, chest pains, sore places anywhere?'

'All them off and on, Doctor. It's the wind gets me down.'

He assessed the size of the couch and the mass that confronted him. 'I don't think we've much hope of getting you up there, do you? If you lean back, Hannah will undo your blouse and support your head while I check your heart and your blood pressure. Don't look so alarmed, I shan't hurt you.'

It was not an easy examination. Mrs Spratt, bereft of her white bottle, made no secret of

181

her disappointment. 'Old doctor could tell what were wrong with me without all this fiddle-faddle. He were one of us like.' Reluctantly she allowed Hannah to ease her arms out of the long sleeves. Her almost supernaturally white flesh was marred by a scattering of purple, mauve and yellow bruises the size of large fingers.

Gus frowned. 'You seem to have been hurting yourself, or someone else has. What happened?'

She spoke too quickly. 'I bruise easy. It's my size, really, bumping into door-handles and things.' As soon as he released her she grabbed for her blouse, stabbing Hannah, who wrestled to help her, with a knitting needle. 'Leave be, will you, girl? I'll see to my own buttons, thanks.'

'You're not a well woman and all that excess weight is a strain on the heart,' Gus said. 'I'll give you a diet sheet now and you can get this made up at the chemist. There's only emergency surgery tomorrow, but pop in with a specimen. I'd like the hospital to check for diabetes.' He handed her a small bottle.

'Specimen? You mean wee in that little thing? Some hope! And I'm not going to no hospital; my Wally goes spare if his dinner isn't on the table when he gets in.' She shivered and her soft cushions of flesh rippled

182

sympathetically. 'It's more than I dare do to ask what's going on. He's cruel. When he smiles the way he does I get really scared.' With these revelations Mrs Spratt melted sadly into a rain of tears. 'Some marriage! He's never home. What's the fat sod up to when he's out all hours, I'd like to know?' She sniffed and mopped her eyes. 'My mother used to say, take no notice; they always come home to die. That's a treat to look forward to, I don't think. I don't know how your mum puts up with him.'

Hannah, inclined to smile but made compassionate by her love for Gus, put an arm across the pillowy shoulders. 'If Wally bullies you, or tries to interfere with your treatment, you're to let us know at once and the doctor will do something about it, won't you, Doctor?' Gus nodded so approvingly that she blushed. 'My mother will sack him at once if she finds out that he hurts you.'

'I hope she does,' said Mrs Spratt unexpectedly. 'Time he got a proper job where he can't take advantage. Scrawny old women in big hats knocking at my front door and paying him money! It's like on the TV, James Bond and Russian spies and that. I'd never be surprised to find the p'lice down on him.'

Nor would Hannah or any other person in

the village. Dismissing the thought of Wally turning out to be even mildly interesting to international criminals, she went over the diet sheet and explained how to get a urine sample into an inadequate receptacle. 'If you don't have a chamber-pot, I'm sure you've got a bucket. First flow is what the doctor needs, as soon as you get up in the morning.'

'Disgusting,' said Mrs Spratt. 'I never mixed myself in with anything medical. I won't tell Spratt what you said about the sack. He'll overreach himself one of these days.'

On her way home, having filed the records and been asked out to dinner by Gus, Hannah saw that a small crowd was gathered at the Spratt's front gate, inspecting both the bottle and the diet sheet. The centre of this interest waved regally. Smiling, Hannah said, 'Don't forget the sample.' Instead of failing to notice her, several ladies smiled back. She felt inordinately pleased. If I never again give an opinion, she thought, or sit on a committee, or judge so much as a rock cake, it seems possible that one day I might be accepted, even liked.

10

Bunty began her day early on Friday morning, flitting around, bare as a winter tree, to slip a few of her holiday snaps under neighbouring doors. They were becoming a little dog-eared with use. Under the shower (cold), she sang 'Bless This House', waking Hereward. He banged on the wall with his walking-stick. She did not notice. Once dressed, she sat down and wrote an abusive letter to her sister who, some sixty years before, had stolen her young man. These letters were never posted. Bunty did not know where her sister was, nor whether she was still alive. They had not met since before the war. Writing down those things she might have said, had she thought of them in time, freed her spirit.

Lizzie Greengrass, who had spent a restless but interesting night, saw her offerings arrive and examined them for any items of note. She had seen them several times before. Two were so badly out of focus that she could not decide whether she was looking at a gigantic bottom or a close-up of assorted fruit. The third always made her wince. Cricket in association with elderly, unboxed nakedness was surely a dangerous game. The lady spectators were laughing. Perhaps at the men or at each other, since they all looked equally ridiculous. None of them was Bunty, who retained a distinctive charm beyond her age and oddness. Vaguely speculating about her girlhood and the hopes and disappointments that had driven her to a super-fit but solitary old age, Lizzie returned to flicking through a pile of travel brochures in the hope of finding a holiday that might tempt Charlie back to life. They all appeared much of a muchness. To judge from the coloured illustrations, every blessed place in Europe, other than England, was an identical composition of sea, blue skies and palm trees. Lizzie did not much care for scenery, nor for plodding around art galleries or historic buildings. Secretly she yearned for undiscovered places. Package tours had put paid to mystery, leaving little in the way of trail-blazing or exotic pleasures. Perhaps a 'themed break', studying wild-life, diving on wrecks or reefs, surfing, ski jumping, might be diverting. She could not envisage Charlie embracing any of those things, and his views on the danger lurking in foreign food would probably lead to an international incident. She wished, just a little, that they were young again. Getting old was not for the faint-hearted, damning adventure and offering metal joints, rheumatism rubs, pills to make you go and pills to stop you going. In a huff, she dropped the brochures into the wastepaper basket.

On her way to the bathroom, she checked from her windows that nothing nefarious was afoot. Someone or something had been moving around in the night. Out in the street, by the gates, shadows had wavered in the weak lamplight and been swallowed up by the deeper darkness of the graveyard. This was commonplace rather than sinister. Dogs were banned from fouling God's little acre, but the idle often used it rather than face the steep ascent to the fields beyond the village. Courting couples also found the gravestones handy. Lizzie emerged from her bath, strongly scented with earth-friendly essences and pink as the dawn, before trotting along to Bunty's room to return the photographs.

'What in God's name have you put on yourself?' asked Charlie Bean when she joined him later in the breakfast room. 'You smell like a blasted compost heap.'

Lizzie did not deign to answer. She knew that he was not a jolly morning person. Trying to hurry him over his breakfast made him crotchety for the rest of the day. For a thin man, he could certainly put away a fair quantity of assorted groceries and it took an iron self-control not to urge him to get on with it before it was lunchtime. 'Finished?' she asked eventually. He poured another cup of tea in stubborn silence. 'Well, don't be all day. You'll find me under the big yew-tree near the gates. Then we'll get busy.'

★ ★ ★

Debating with himself, Charlie Bean wondered whether he could sneak away without Lizzie spotting him. He had hoped that she would forget overnight her crackpot notion of playing at detectives, and leave it to the professionals. He planned a quiet day. A chap in the Duke's Head had offered to take him out on a fishing trip while the fair weather lasted. The mackerel were running and the tide was right. Also there wouldn't be a pack of women around, giving him orders and wanting him to do things. Out on the water, he might get a chance to assess the degree of pollution in the sea and make a guess about the probable safety of the redundant nuclear research establishment at Winfrith. His statistics notebooks were filling up nicely. If he slacked, he might easily miss the one vital piece of information that would prove that human extinction had begun and that no amount of buggering about with safe aerosols or organic carrots was going to stop it.

He was out of luck. Knowing the weakness of men and their skill at evasion, Lizzie's uncompromising eyes were on him as he left the house. She waved, her arms flailing like windmills. 'Trying to give yourself a stroke, are you?' he asked crossly. 'What is it now?'

'You know what it is. We've got to get a look inside that grotto and I don't want Spratt creeping up behind me and giving me a crack over the head with a spade.'

'Well don't do it then,' he said. 'I thought you were going to tell Bird what's been happening. It's her business, isn't it? She'd love an excuse to get rid of Spratt. Can't you let things rest just for one day?'

'She needs reasons, not excuses, and I don't want her worried over nothing. We're going to look proper fools if those sacks are full of manure.' She stood up and settled her bosom, which was inclined to escape its confinement. 'For heaven's sake, Charlie, what's got into you? If we'd let people push us around we'd be enjoying eternal rest over in the cemetery, with a stone to weigh us down.'

'You're going to look a fool, not me. This time it's not our affair. I've got better things to do, if you haven't.'

'I keep forgetting what an old man you are. Never mind. You just wrap up warm and take care of yourself. I'll go on my own.'

A flush of annoyance flowed over Charlie's bald scalp. Reason was wasted on women and on Lizzie most of all. 'Don't you mother me,' he said. 'I'm as strong as I ever was and you know it.'

'Then stop arguing. All you've got to do is sit here and watch that gate while I do the rest. If Wally turns up, warn me. That's not going to overtax you, is it?'

'Not unless you're going to start dreaming up other things to waste my time. I've got plans.'

Lizzie said with hauteur, 'You're not the only one. I'm going to be late for the hairdresser, thanks to you. Sit down, keep quiet and for God's sake, don't drop off and miss anything.' Charlie opened his mouth to speak, but she was already several yards away and moving fast.

★　★　★

Collecting the key from Bird's office was easy, Lizzie found with some disapproval. Hereward Parstock had caused this upset, worming his way in and lumbering them with Stella Worth and a tangle of relationships. A

190

juiceless husk of a man with nothing left to give to a woman, in her opinion, and not nearly good enough for Bird, though he tried to claim a lot of her time. The rusting iron key in her pocket banged painfully against her sore leg. She decided that sometimes Charlie was right; women could be fools and men took advantage of it.

Getting into the grotto caused her more of an effort than she had anticipated. The door squealed and stuck halfway. A stone had wedged itself under the wood and refused to budge. She managed to squeeze through, bringing down a snow of distemper with every movement. No sacks stood where she had seen them. Someone, Spratt of course, had moved them, and not so much as a footprint disturbed the swept dust. This was a horrible place. The sour smell of rot and mould and urine turned her stomach and without reason Lizzie felt very afraid. She forced herself to explore further, past the contorted lump that, from the safety of the doorway, reminded her of Harold Wilson. Shreds of paper and plastic had collected round an empty wine bottle at its base. Beyond, where she had never before penetrated, lay a path of beaten earth and an opening covered by a grating. Lizzie shook it. It moved under her hands, but there was no latch and no sign that it was intended to open. Simply a dead end then. Leaning forward, she saw only a few feet of overhang and, beyond, the sea. The grating shifted again, more sharply with her full weight. Shivering, she turned and fled from her fear, followed by whispering echoes. Bird was right, this was a dangerous place. Another whisper slid along the walls. 'If you're in there, come on out,' Charlie hissed. 'He's in the High Street, nearly at the gates.'

'Right. Give me a hand, will you?' He grabbed her arm and pulled her forcibly through the gap, brushing plaster and cobwebs from her hair and shoulders as she turned the key. When Wally Spratt came in sight they were idling along the path, dishevelled, but harmless. He shot a suspicious look at Lizzie's white face. She managed to nod to him and when they were out of earshot said, meek now, and biddable, 'You were right, Charlie, I shouldn't have gone in there. It's foul and it's empty. Aren't you going to say, I told you so?'

He sniffed at such childishness. 'Why would he bother to move the sacks, I wonder? That's suspicious in itself. You look a mess. Better sit down and tidy yourself up a bit.'

'Never mind. I'm off to the hairdresser. I

can get a cup of coffee there and have a bit of a think.'

'Thank God.' Charlie loped away to his researches without a farewell.

★ ★ ★

When first the doctor and then the police arrived, Rita Parry was sitting in a deckchair at the doorway of the potting-shed, watching Ched work. He kept the place very clean and tidy. She thought of another shed, scarcely visited and littered with broken furniture, old vermin traps, unlabelled jars that might hold anything, rusting tins of pest killer and rat bane. At Swan House in sharp weather she had sometimes borrowed a corner of that shed for a night or two. Who noticed a bundle of rags, wrapped snugly in canvas torn from the ruin of a hammock? Who was there to notice? Or to be noticed?

Profoundly pleased with herself, Rita nodded her head like a jointed china mandarin. Her thoughts followed no rational train. She rummaged around in the ragbag of her mind and came up with an assortment of scraps. In this jumble were observations and folk-lore, voices speaking high and low, visions and dreams past and present. To be a watcher and a listener had put power into her hands and she enjoyed it.

The sun eased her old bones nicely. Out of habit, she placed people. In the Duke's Head, with half her attention on Connie Lovibond, she had learned of Charlie Bean's fishing trip. Lizzie Greengrass, tripping along to Cut And Dyed, had seen her in her alleyway and paused. After studying her closely without a smile, she said as though she wanted to say something quite different, 'Good morning, Mrs Parry; it's a nice day.' On the lawn outside the conservatory, Bunty exercised pointlessly. Adrift on the slow soft rhythms of the morning, Rita became as invisible as a blade of grass, except to Wally Spratt, who wandered restlessly between the shrubbery and the sea. The two cars of officialdom were parked outside the nursing wing. Behind that block of brick and stone stood, according to Connie Lovibond, the bungalows. Rita decided on a little excursion.

In a row of six, the one she wanted was not hard to find. Through the open bedroom window came the voice of Stella Worth, analysing with enjoyable frankness the characters of her husbands. A nurse moved to and fro. 'I don't think you ought to be dwelling on these things, Mrs Worth,' she said. 'It's not good for you. You're getting confused between them, aren't you? Didn't you say that it was number two who was — er — diseased, or was he the one who poisoned the champagne rather than be divorced?' An object thudded against the wall. 'Please don't throw shoes at me. Try to sit still and drink some water. Perhaps a counsellor could help you sort out what really happened.'

'They're my sodding husbands, aren't they? I don't need help, what I need is the teeniest gin and tonic. On second thoughts, forget the tonic; just ice and lemon. My skin's crawling. You ought to get this place fumigated. It's full of fleas.'

'That's your condition. No alcohol for a while. Don't you remember how you came to collapse like that?'

Stella grew peevish. 'I don't have a condition, only one hell of a hangover. So what's new? Where's my bag got to? Find it for me, there's a lambikins. We'll split a nice bottle and I'll give you the dirt on our leading stars of stage and screen, then I'll go for a swim.'

Rita detected a triumphant note in the nurse's voice. 'Swim you will not. Do you want to drown?'

'The sea is the only good thing about this dreary hole. It's bright and clean and kind. Out there, I can forget the bloody awfulness of people.'

Of all natural forces, Rita feared only the sea. The power of Stella's swimming seemed to her something almost supernatural. That tough withered body cut a clean path through the roughest tides, heading fast for the green distance. The gods scattered their gifts in a random fashion. Rita would have given half her life to be at home in water.

'This is a nice little village,' said the nurse, who was a local girl.

'Oh shut up, will you, and bring me my bag.'

'You dropped it when you fell. The bottles broke.'

'*All* of them? Shit, I'll have to go down to the village for more. Pass me my hat.' At the sound of a scuffle, Rita felt that it was time for her to intervene. She rapped on the door and walked in. 'What do you want?' asked Stella. 'Who are you?' asked the nurse.

'Just a nice, friendly social visit, ladies. Nurse, you're flustered. Rest a spell and get your breath back while Mrs Worth and I have a chat. We know each other of old.'

'No we don't,' said Stella. 'The woman's seeing things. Why would I want to talk to some mad old bat with delusions? Give her a quid and throw her out.'

The nurse raised her eyebrows. Rita smiled. 'I see all kinds of things, it's true. We could talk about Swan House, for instance, or sheds, or summerhouses, or tins and boxes. And, of course, the spirits of friends no longer with us.'

'Isn't that rather morbid for a sick woman? Mrs Worth is supposed to be kept quiet and comfortable until the pol — , I mean the visitors, have gone.'

Stella did not react at all. She rubbed her arms then pulled the blanket up to her chin. 'Christ, I'm cold,' she complained. 'I want my clothes.'

'They were in a state. I told you, we've sent them to the laundry and given you a dressing-gown. Put that on.'

'She's very good at not remembering what she prefers to forget,' said Rita, with a degree of satisfaction, confirming to herself a conclusion she had reached earlier. Stella Worth wiped away uncomfortable memories, absolving herself of guilt. 'It's the only explanation.'

'For what? She remembers drink and men, and now swimming.'

'Never mind for what.' Rita wandered from the bedroom into the sitting-room. 'Snug place. Don't take what she says about anything as gospel truth. To her the past is a lost world with only a single landmark.'

'I don't understand,' the nurse said. But

Rita opened the door and moved on as she had done all her life. This time, though, was different. She expected to return.

★   ★   ★

As the police car pulled away from The Glebe, the plain-clothes Inspector smiled at a pair of old people lying side by side outside the nursing wing. 'I like to see a quiet couple enjoying the sunshine,' he said to his sergeant. 'Still together after years, till death does them part, you might say; just like my mum and dad. It's not too common nowadays.'

The sergeant grunted. His parents had divorced when he was nineteen and he found The Glebe a creepy kind of place. Pretty young nurses looking after old scarecrows who would be better off dead; it didn't seem right. 'That's like the creature from the black lagoon, the one that took the drugs,' he said. 'Boozed out of her skull and just about knows her own name. I bet she got the stuff down in Bournemouth, never here.'

'You don't know much, lad, you're too young to remember what went on a few years back: there were rumours of dope up here then, before we managed to get enough on the last owners to send them down. We have all sorts round and about; black magic, grave robbers, scum who mutilate animals, half-brain arsonists. That's the country nowadays. Got a fag on you, by any chance?' The sergeant obliged reluctantly. 'Mrs Dawlish is working on an idea or two. Not that she'll accuse anyone without being sure; a nice woman.' They had both enjoyed a sumptuous lunch and the inspector beamed, glad of an excuse to come back again. 'Not much point in trying to interview the residents until after Lady Di's funeral tomorrow, but we'll have to talk to some of them later, and the staff she's put names to.'

'And do a search. We'll need to search, won't we?'

'If there was anything dodgy here when we drove in those gates, I'd lay odds it's gone by now. There'll be watching eyes in a small village like this. The stuff shouldn't be hard to track down.'

'Could we get the dog-handlers in? I like it when we have the dogs.'

'Relax,' said the inspector. 'Let's see our princess nicely buried first. We don't want to spoil the occasion for anyone. She was a real lady, an English aristocrat, and it's a shame she ever got mixed up with royals and dodgy foreigners.'

'Isn't that a bit of a rascist remark, sir?'

Bland of expression, the inspector shook his head. 'Classist, if you like. There's no rules about that as far as I know. All that glitters is not gold, as some old fart once mentioned. I like to see respect given where it's due. You keep that in mind and we'll always get along.'

★ ★ ★

Stella Worth's failure to recall even taking cocaine, let alone who had given it to her, came as a disappointment to Bird. Her hopes had been thoroughly dashed. Spratt was not, after all, to be got rid of easily. A faint, weary depression settled over her. She wished that Gus Early would hurry up and drink his coffee so that she could finish her chores and be alone. He was, he mentioned, expecting a telephone call. When the phone rang she left him to answer it. After a brief exchange, he handed her the receiver. 'Hannah wants to speak to you,' he said, smiling.

'Hallo, Mother, Gus says the police have gone and that it's all right for now. Listen, dear, he's taking me out to dinner at a really posh place in the Forest. Hallo, are you still there?'

Dear? Hannah had called her dear? 'Yes, of course.'

'We're bound to be late. Can Josh stay the night with you? He says, please, it'll be brill if you say yes.'

Bird's depression flew away on black wings, leaving her young and light as air. Joshua had been since his birth a part of her punishment. No lies surrounded him; he was legitimate and she took enormous pride in him. Not that it would have mattered had he been conceived under a hedge. She loved him. Their rare, 'accidental' meetings Bird carefully arranged. To her the saddest part was that Joshua understood that these encounters must not be mentioned and that their affection for each other was a secret. Hannah's possessiveness would not easily have admitted other loves than her own. And suddenly this opening of a door. 'Yes, oh yes, I'd love to have him. I'll have a bed put in my room for him.'

Hannah laughed. 'He'll beg for chips for his supper. Not too many, please, and no Coke at bedtime; milk, weak tea or fruit juice. Put Gus back on, will you?'

He said, 'You're a dear good girl and I love you. Now I'm going to hang up and administer first aid.' A pause, then, 'A patient with long-standing trouble of the heart. Your mother's in shock.'

201

Bird was. She felt as though only the ceiling kept her from floating free of earth. 'You and Hannah, it's very quick, isn't it? Are you sure about each other?' she asked, and smiled.

'Now I know where she gets that sudden, unnerving radiance. I'm very sure. Do you mind? There'll be a lot of Josh-sitting to come.'

'I can't believe this is really happening. I was never allowed to have Hannah to myself — I expect she told you — and I was the worst and most useless of mothers. Now I can feel forgiven.'

'You women,' Gus said gently, 'what a fuss you make of a simple thing like living. In case you're bothered about it, I know that nothing can be kept a secret in this small village; we shall be married when Hannah's divorce is final. She doesn't know it yet, but tonight she will. Would you like me to call you mother?'

Bird opened her arms to him. They executed a few polka steps, cannoned into a filing cabinet and laughed like idiots. She had not been invited to the first disastrous wedding. Next time would surely be different. For a second she was tempted to tell Gus that Hannah had a living father, but she dared not. Her daughter's indoctrination had been thorough. Neither Hereward nor any other Parstock belonged in this moment. Pure happiness was a secret enjoyment, easily spoiled, and such happiness did not come often.

11

In Cut And Dyed, Denny's hair salon, the inevitable photograph of Princess Diana hung in a space between the washbasins. The smoke from a coloured candle quarrelled with the usual scent of shampoo. The 'girl', balancing a pair of huge breasts above tiny bunioned feet, stowed Lizzie Greengrass in a chair, then took up a broom and swept hair into corners. While she was waiting, Lizzie thought her thoughts. They did not get her much further with her efforts at detection though she decided on her next move and relaxed in the flow of Denny's chatter. He was presently spraying lacquer on the intimidating hair of a lady in the next chair. Sitting down she was almost as tall as he was standing up. Even her voice held a note of sinewy aggression. 'You trying to turn me into a fire-ball or something, spraying that stuff on me with a candle burning?' Denny looked as though he wouldn't much mind, but he pinched out the flame. She sniffed. 'I don't know what's got into people, splashing money around on royals who own half the country anyway. The fancy florists are raking in the cash. Is this how it's going to be every time someone like her gets killed, flowers and candles and grizzling? Really!'

Under his breath, Denny muttered, 'Well, they won't do it for you, duckie, that's for sure.' Lizzie grinned. He renewed his attack, pleating up an iron-hard wave that threatened to stray, and lapsing into his French mode. 'Zo,' he said aloud, parodying a self-congratulatory gesture around his handiwork. 'Would Madame care to see the back?'

'Is that the best you can do? I wanted it more bouffant.'

'Bouffant I don't do, not nowadays; bouffant is old time, even for you. You asked for tight waves; you've got tight waves.'

'Don't flap around me and put on airs, you fool. I wanted bouffant *and* tight waves.'

'Miss Marple crossed with Dusty Springfield? Get a life, dear! You don't lend yourself to the exotic. Sorry not to oblige, I'm sure.'

'Well, I'm not paying a penny more than I did last time. There's five pounds and that's plenty. I shan't be coming here again.' She stalked out, throwing back the door with reckless disregard for its hinges.

'Missing you *already* — you old cow!' fluted Denny to her departing back, none too quietly. 'Now we can have a cosy chat, Lizzie. I've made up my mind to get rid of customers

I don't like, and she always gets on my tits: ugly as sin and never satisfied. I could do with a few more like you.'

He hovered affectionately over her. Denny was a wicked young man, whose wickedness Lizzie enjoyed, though she preferred not to trust him. 'How do I know what you say about me when my back's turned?'

'Ooh, I thought we were friends.' He smiled at her in the mirror, pleased with himself. 'One more to go, a ponced-up Fleet Street crime writer. He says! Not that I believe a word, bringing his six strands of hair to me as if he was doing me a favour and showing off his bits of cuttings. 'Where's your byline?' I asked him. He didn't know what to say, and he had the nerve to give me a ten-pence tip. I gave it back and said he must need it more than I did. That man could bore and scrounge for England.'

'I don't know him, do I?'

'I shouldn't think so, dear. There's a wife who's after him for maintenance and he dodges around a bit. You'll be going up for the funeral, I hope. I've got my place on the coach booked and I'm bringing extra packs of tissues for everyone. I feel it's going to be that kind of a day. Now, what's the news from your end?'

'Nothing much,' Lizzie said, exercising caution.

'Come on, dear. I saw you had the police in. How can I keep up my reputation as the local gossip if you don't tell me things?'

'I don't want you spreading scandal about The Glebe. All that's happened is that we've got lumbered with Mrs Worth. You know the one. She was taken ill a bit suddenly in our grounds and Bird called the police just in case there's been any funny business.'

'Don't tell me someone's tried to do her in?' Denny sounded delighted and less than sympathetic. 'That hair of hers is a crime in itself. It's as dry as a chip. I don't know who does it for her, but black dye's never going to look natural.'

Hair was always a safe subject. 'What goes on in that cottage of hers is a mystery,' Lizzie said. 'I expect she does it herself when she thinks about it, which by the look of her isn't very often. And I don't think she ever takes off her make-up, just puts on another layer now and then. Of course, she used to be on the stage and I expect it's habit.'

'Vanity dies hard,' said Denny. 'I'd say she was raving mad. Hair like soot and straw and she goes in swimming without a cap; forgets her cossie, too, half the time. Not a sight I'd want to see without dark glasses. How about a cup of coffee? I've trained the girl to make it properly, but she'll never be a stylist, not with those knockers in the way.'

Lizzie, similarly overburdened, accepted coffee without comment, and dodging further questions about The Glebe, emerged refreshed on to the High Street. As she neared the gate, the ten-minute lunch gong sounded. She hesitated, then turned right into the churchyard. She was not alone. At times like these, she thought, wars and disasters and deaths, the church really came into its own and drew the people in. Stragglers wandered among the gravestones as if their lives had no purpose other than to wait for tomorrow's funeral. She passed on, around the church to the oldest burials in the parish. There she found Rita Parry. 'We're looking for the same thing, maybe,' Lizzie said, examining a table tomb of monstrous size with a speculative eye.

'There's both smugglers and excisemen got buried here after they'd killed each other. These are Spratts.' According to the inscription, squeezed into a spare corner at the base, the last Spratt to be interred there was one William Thos. Walter, 'died in pursuit of his trade and cleansed of his sins, Oct. 20th 1815'. Later and lesser Spratts were modestly ranged alongside in poorer accommodation.

'It's a lot of stone,' said Lizzie, wondering how many bottles of brandy it had taken to persuade the parson to cleanse the late William's sins; 'and with smuggling you have to think about its uses. A boat into the cove, a dash up the High Street ahead of the excise, a place to dump the contraband and an innocent face to show when they caught up?'

Rita nodded and grinned. 'Until the night when William Thos. Walter didn't run fast enough.'

'Mrs Parry, I'm probably telling you what you already know, but there's some interesting packages missing from that grotto in our grounds and I'd like to track them down. A wily bird like our Wally would use whatever safe hiding-place came to hand. He'll know the family history.'

'Aye, he would. Old habits die hard and ghosts don't reck much to heavy weights. If they did, I'd say they'd been shifting that top stone. There's a long scrape here in the green mould and another round the back.'

Inspecting the ground after the manner of Sherlock Holmes, whom she admired, Lizzie noticed trampled weeds (recently crushed) and damp earth churned up by boots possibly trying for purchase. Some chips here and there in the stone might have been made by a crowbar. As she had never seen let alone used one, it would be necessary to get a man's opinion. She said, 'Two old women are never going to lift that kind of weight, not without help, and anything in there will soon be moved out. We ought to tell Bird now and get a watch kept.'

'No hurry, it's off her land and I've a bargain to strike. The police can do the heavy work. You'll be up to London tomorrow, no doubt. He'll be waiting for that, when the village is half-empty.' Lizzie's frustrated air seemed to amuse Rita. 'Trust me,' she said, 'Wally Spratt imagines he's always one jump ahead of the law. Jail doesn't frighten him, but I do. He believes I'm a witch.'

There was a fairly close physical resemblance. Everyone is frightened of something, and a small-time crook like Wally could be forgiven for reading supernatural powers into Mrs Parry's carefully manipulated store of facts and the knowingness of her eyes. Lizzie took this as her dismissal. While she hesitated, the second gong sounded. She felt decidedly peckish. With a last regretful look at the tomb, she made off at a fast trot for a late, but substantial lunch. A police car left as she arrived. Matron waved it off at the door, with a sigh. 'Disappointing in a way,' she said. 'Not a trace of third degree or police bullying, but what appetites. Dear me.'

210

Drinking cider with Rita had almost diverted Connie Lovibond from her first errand, the search for an antidote to her late father's artistic perfection. Then she spotted precisely what she had in mind in a small crowded window of the newsagent's and general store. It, too, was perfect in its way. Excavated from its newspaper wrapping, it stood proudly on the table in her sitting-room, reflected again in the polished surface. At its birth it had clearly been a small cheap mirror. The artist's hand had encrusted it with seashells painted in a variety of cheerful colours. Above, a row of Dorset views was surmounted by a red plastic horseshoe announcing, DORSET, to avoid confusion. (Sadly, Wynfred Abbas, being mainly feature-less in the matter of points of interest, failed even to rate a picture.) A musical black and white Friesian cow formed the base of the piece. Connie hoped that, when wound, it might moo. But no, it tinkled out, very slowly, 'The Anniversary Waltz', causing the whole hideous structure to tremble in a musical palsy.

She surveyed it happily and thought she would show it to Miles. A touch of vulgarity was just the thing to dislodge him from his aesthetic cloud. She found him in his room, writing furiously. 'Do you mind, Connie dear, if I press on?' he said. 'I'm writing out everything that troubles me, Ched, my career, the novel, Princess Di, your suggestion; it's a kind of life-exercise to help me get myself together.' She left before he could ask her to read it.

After trying vainly for an afternoon nap, she again went out into the grounds and headed for the nursing wing. Hereward wandered along the path ahead of her, stopping now and then to look at the sea. Since her arrival at The Glebe, he had neither avoided her nor sought her out. The inconvenient tragedy that had set the royal family by the ears and brought the principal players to the brink of dislike and hostility, passed him by without notice. He seemed to wait, inert and unexpectant. Occasional spurts of irritation, as with Bunty's singing, reminded her of Winifred's remark about the Parstock temper; for the rest he remained courteous, especially with Bunty herself, for whom he had a fondness. 'It's extravagantly beautiful here,' he said as she caught him up. 'Winifred would have loved it, don't you think?'

How long since he had voluntarily spoken her name, Connie wondered? His air of detached resignation put him firmly in his age-group now, removing him from the golden years and distancing him utterly from Bird. 'I'm sure she would, Hereward.'

'We truly liked each other. Life has never been the same, missing her all the interminable years. What *did* happen, Connie? You don't believe that it was a natural death, do you? Isn't that why you came here?'

'In part, yes it was, though I hoped for nothing much. That old woman, Rita Parry, pretends to know things. Certainly she enjoys being enigmatic, but is she informed? If what I think is wrong, then my thoughts are monstrous and unforgivable.'

'And I am culpable,' he said. 'Where are you going?'

'To see Bird, if she isn't busy. Stella must be sent packing before she infects this place with her particular brand of poison. Come with me, Hereward. She's well out of the way and watched by three nurses, so you won't run into her.'

He shook his head, flushing so deeply that Connie, fearing he might be about to have a heart attack, put a hand on his arm to steady him. After a moment he smiled at her with all the old generosity. 'This will sound fanciful, but Bird has laid an enchanter's hand on this place, a protection against all demons. Love is a damned tenacious thing, though its face changes. I need very much to speak to her alone, to unburden my conscience. It's that I fear. There are moments when loving-kindness is simply not enough and if she should hate me — well.' Nervously he began to excavate the gravel with his stick. 'The moment never offers and time is growing short, I think.'

Connie thought so too, and that all his life he had been much too dependent upon the love of women. Briskly she said, 'You should know by now that Bird's incapable of hatred.' She led him along, scheming to find the two of them some quietness together. As usual, it seemed to be Stella Worth who made peace and privacy impossible. Definitely she must go. Not simply from The Glebe, but from Wynfred Abbas and out of Hereward's life altogether.

The amount of activity in the nursing wing surprised Connie, who had found it on her rare visits a hushed place. People dawdled to and fro, competing loudly to relate their symptoms, dropping sticks, comparing ban-dages, complaining to the physiotherapist in attendance, wanting something, wanting nothing other than an audience. In the large dayroom, an amateur mime group struggled to entertain. Their small audience ignored the white faces and gloves, talking among themselves. A pair of old men who looked as though they might be brothers got up. They clumped out noisily, moving towards the blare of a television set in the room next door. 'Mimes, dear God,' muttered Hereward. 'Is there *no* escape?'

The nursing auxiliary said, 'They're so keen to help, poor dears, but really a sing-song would be better, something cheerful to join in with. Are you looking for Bird? She's in the clinic, supervising the medicines.'

'Is it all right for us to go in?'

'Knock first. She won't be much longer; it's her evening off. Her young grandson is staying the night with her.'

So far away in time was Hereward's affair with Bird, that Connie could have forgotten that this child was his grandson also. She felt the sudden tremor that betrayed his agitation. 'We'd better not wait,' he said.

He was already panicky. She took a firm grasp of his arm before he could leave. 'We'll just say hallo, and find out what's happening about Stella. You have to weather these small shocks, Hereward, my dear, if you are ever to manage a sensible conversation with Bird.'

'She'll think I'm trying to butt in; it will remind her.'

'Do you suppose she ever forgets?' said Connie, becoming cross with him. 'Don't behave like an ass, please. Just nod and smile. You do know how to smile, don't you?'

Hereward did smile. 'Sometimes you sound remarkably like your sister.'

And Bird, dropping pills and pouring medicines into little plastic cups, was quite untroubled by his arrival. Happiness radiated from her. 'Isn't it a thrill?' she said. 'I so rarely have the chance to see Joshua. And Gus Early's in love with poor Hannah. He wants to marry her when the divorce is through. Tonight's the night when he's going to ask her, so if she gets highminded or political and messes things up I shall despair of her.'

'Splendid,' said Hereward, not forgetting to smile. 'Perhaps tomorrow you can tell me all about it, Bird. In the meantime, Connie has some questions.'

'What's happening to Stella? Is there any chance of getting rid of her soon?'

'Quite soon, I think; why?'

Again there was to be no opportunity for conversation. It was scarcely possible for Connie to explain just yet the tacit bargain she had made with Rita Parry, the need for a meeting with her, the price exacted in the form of the bungalow. 'Like Hereward, I feel that it must all wait until tomorrow. Assuming that you won't be off to London for the funeral.'

Bird shook her head. 'Several of the nurses are eager to go and I hate to stop them. The coach leaves at half past six in the morning and I shall have Josh until after breakfast. In any case, someone has to stay.'

A nurse came in, grinning. 'Mrs Worth is going to effingwell sue us for stealing her effing clothes. Thought you'd like to know.' She picked up a tray of the plastic cups and rattled away with them.

Hereward said a courteous farewell, plucked at Connie's sleeve and limped from the room, leaving her to follow.

She did not go immediately. 'The young seem to fall in love at the drop of a hat nowadays. Very unlike the long courtships of my youth.'

'Hannah has always been immediate and so have I,' Bird said. 'It got us both into trouble once, but we don't make the same mistake twice.'

'Was Hereward such a mistake? Surely without your mother's interference all would have been well? There was devotion enough.'

In silence, Bird checked her list of medicines, closed and locked the drugs cabinet. 'Can you believe that I'm nervous of being alone with him? His sadness and frailty appal me. He's still mine, you see. I lost him once and I can scarcely bear to lose him again.'

In the course of ordering her own life into a neat routine, Connie had decided that living could never be tidy. From birth to death it was a mess. Banish emotion and it rebounded to hit you between the eyes. 'Talk to him, please,' she said. 'He has never seen Hannah or his grandchild, and I feel that he deserves to, just once. I shall drag him down to the card-room this evening and sit him where he can get a view of the hall. We can play bezique or snap, anything. Those two are what you share and they may give you something to discuss.'

The card-room, previously a waiting-room, had a large, fixed glass panel, installed so that visitors could be inspected before being received. Bird did not argue. 'Has anyone ever told you, Connie, that you're an interfering busybody?'

'Many times, but not so politely,' she said, smiling. 'It's what spinsters are for.' Hurrying to catch up with Hereward, she noticed Rita, watching or dozing in the doorway of the tool shed. How very much at home she looked. And why not? This was a place where love obstinately persisted and the solitary were drawn in to shelter under the presiding wing. Connie shook her head. It was possible to love too generously and too much.

★   ★   ★

Hannah arrived as the residents began to amble down to the television lounge to watch the six o'clock news. Gus stayed in the car while she brought Joshua into the house. Clutching her hand, he danced up the steps, chattering without drawing breath. She bent towards him, captivated. Her mass of hair had been subdued to sit in a smooth, pale coronet around her head. Like the looks she so deplored, her deep-green velvet gown with its high-standing, stiffened collar possessed a timeless elegance that conformed to no modern fashion. Brightly lit by the hall chandelier, she was alien and utterly beautiful. Wondering how, out of her ordinariness, she had produced such a child, Bird thought tritely that her plain, unhappy little duckling was on the way to becoming the swan of swans.

Hereward had kept to their bargain and sat obscurely at a remote table behind the glass panel. He had elected to dine in his room. She knew that he would not pretend affection for a grandchild he did not know, nor would he spoil her time with Joshua. The boy did not link them. They were joined by a thread more tenuous, stretched thin by the passage of the years, yet not broken. Such ties, thought Bird, never quite break. Yet she was not sorry for Connie's interference. Now was the moment when Hereward should see his creation, sparking with vitality and absolutely transformed by love.

Joshua brought her back to earth. 'Mum looks nice, doesn't she,' he said. 'I'm supposed to be in bed by nine o'clock. If I don't play up, Gus is going to take me to see a lot of cars.'

'Just behave yourself, then,' Hannah said, kissing him. And to Bird, 'He had his tea at four so he ought not to be hungry yet. You won't let your residents spoil him with sweets, will you? I'll collect him in the morning.'

'How very lovely you are, Hannah, and that's not just a mother's fond eye. Josh and I won't be dining with the others. Tom Markham's coming to make a last check on tomorrow's arrangements, so it will be a light supper and an early night. Have the best of evenings and look after Gus.'

'Look after Gus? Really, Mother. Believe me, he's more than capable of looking after himself. And me.'

'He kisses Mum a lot,' Josh said casually,

'and they're going to an extra-special place to have their dinners.' Hannah, let down by the small spy in her house, blushed and dimmed the chandelier with her smile. 'I've got something to whisper when I've had my supper, Gran.'

'You dare!' Hannah gave his hand a shake. 'If there's anything to be told, I want to tell it myself.'

The boy seemed set to argue, but there was a sudden scuffle on the landing. With a muted, 'Whoopee', Bunty came flying backwards down the polished banister to land neatly at their feet.

Lizzie Greengrass craned over to watch her progress. 'One of these days you'll break your neck, you bad girl,' she said. 'There's such a thing as carrying exercise too far.'

'No there isn't. I've been wanting to do that for ages. Now I have.'

Descending with awful dignity, Lizzie shooed the delinquent towards the lounge. 'Good evening everyone. Fit or unfit, Bunty, you're too old for such tricks. Come along, or we shall miss the news.'

'That's cool!' Josh moved forward. 'Can I try?'

'No, you cannot,' said Hannah, startled and faintly disapproving. 'Gran will see that you don't. And before you think of coaxing

Gus, he'll say no as well.' She kissed the top of his head and was gone.

On this prized evening with her grandson, Bird discovered with sadness how little she knew about the entertaining of a small child. Tom Markham proved a godsend. He talked cars until even Joshua's passion was satisfied. Then he proposed games. 'Happy Families, please,' said Josh. Bird had never played that or any other children's game and had to be taught. She thanked heaven that it was simple. Joshua won without any help on her part, and if Tom cheated, it was skilfully. Together they put him to bed and stayed until he fell asleep.

'A nice boy,' Tom said and hesitated. 'Do you sometimes feel lonely here? At night, when you're on duty, or when your old darlings are asleep? It's a lot for a woman to handle on her own.'

'Is it? I haven't thought of it, at least, not until lately, since the princess was killed, poor girl. Even Stella Worth seems to take it personally, as though it were her own life lost. Emotions all over the place! Of course, it may simply be that The Glebe is haunted by its past.'

'You know damned well that whatever happens here is by some human agency. There ought to be a reliable man on the premises at night.'

'You're not applying for another job?' asked Bird anxiously. 'I can pay you more for driving if the money isn't enough. Please don't leave.'

Tom laughed. 'Don't you have any vanity, girl? This isn't about money. What I'm trying to find out is whether you like me at all. My ex-wife preferred a double-glazing salesman, so naturally I'm not altogether certain of my charms.'

'Of course I like you, in fact I'm fond of you; and I depend on you. Why?'

'That'll do for now. If you haven't noticed that I'm inclined to be in love with you, you're the only person in The Glebe who hasn't.' He caught her very firmly round the waist and kissed her goodnight. She couldn't afterwards recall whether she had managed to kiss him back. Dear me, she thought, it's been so long that I've almost forgotten how it's done and that is definitely pathetic. In the small bed next to hers, Joshua clutched a battered toy rabbit, breathing quietly. She stretched out. A sudden blazing heat rushed over her. Was she, after so many sensible years, burning for Tom Markham? Certainly she liked him, she liked him a lot. So much so that she hadn't troubled to look out of the window for night prowlers or double-check that the outside doors were locked. But love? She was too tired to analyse her emotions. Tomorrow she would think about it all. When the commotion in the village started, she was already in the first deep sleep of the night. Josh stirred and smiled, but did not wake.

12

The landlord of the Duke's Head, at rest beside his wife and the safe that contained the day's takings, was the first to notice the blaze. His dark room under the eaves danced in a splendour of golden light. Beside him, her back turned, his lightly breathing consort smiled in her sleep. 'Wake up and get your big arse out of there, Mavis,' he shrilled. 'We're on fire.'

'Aah, it's you. I was dreaming.' She was a calm woman and on principle never believed a word that her husband said without checking for herself. Majestically, she slid out of bed and crossed to the window. From the derelict cottages behind and close to the inn, flames rose in the air above waves of blue evil-smelling smoke. Too close for comfort. She watched disdainfully as her husband scrabbled in the unlocked safe. 'There's no more than twenty pounds in there. Calm down and put some trousers on if you're going outside. It's not us, it's the cottages.'

Wynfred Abbas did not, of course, boast a fire station and the villagers, inured to neglect, turned out to haul their one ancient handpump up the hill and along the narrow passageway. Its usefulness was limited since the tank was dry. At ground level, the rolling, stinking fumes were enough to choke a horse. When the constable, still struggling to do up his trousers, pushed his way through the crowd, buckets were already passing hand to hand from the well that had once served the houses. He had telephoned for the fire brigade, but without much hope. A sensible man, he blew his whistle. Everyone froze.

'You'll make it worse slinging on water,' he said, staring at the impressive tower of flame. 'Leave it to burn itself out and get on damping down the other cottages. I'll get the pump working.'

'That old dosser woman'll be done to a turn be now,' said a voice from the shadows. 'She'll not come out of that.'

The constable swung round. 'You mean someone's inside there? Why the devil didn't you say so before?'

'Thought everyone knew that,' said the landlord. 'Place is too far gone to do anything. She'll have knocked a candle over, happen.'

'And happen not.' The constable sniffed the air. 'I'll have a report to make and I don't like this, not one bit. The back's not too bad. I'm going to have a look.' He stripped off his shirt, dipped it in a water bucket, tied it over his nose and mouth, and disappeared through a gap between the cottages. The walls of the lean-to scullery still stood, but the roof was gone and it was empty.

The first false dawn light was in the sky, the fire was almost out and the brigade sifting through the hot embers, when he found Rita Parry. A dark trail led from the cottage to the privy. She lay half inside, face down, savagely battered about the head and body and to all appearances dead.

★   ★   ★

At around three o'clock, Bird surfaced and lay for a few moments with her eyes closed, thinking of Tom Markham. How many eternities had passed since a man had kissed her, properly, with passion? Her mind had forgotten the comfort of it, but her body had responded with a surging warmth that subdued her customary anxiety. For once she had not thought of Hereward at all.

Beside her, Joshua slept the intense sleep of the very young. A thick smell of smoke, as though someone was illicitly burning oil, drifted through the open window, and light flickered behind the High Street. She got up and closed the sash. With tomorrow's early start, staying in bed was pointless. Tom had relieved her anxieties about the London journey but, wide awake now, she decided to make a last round of the venturers in case of any late emergency. She put on her dressing-gown, plain navy-blue and dull. Nowadays, all her clothes were dull, and she wondered what on earth Tom saw in her that made him think he loved her.

Moving silently, Bird stopped briefly at the bedroom doors. Lizzie snored with vigorous satisfaction. She had overcome Charlie Bean's determination not to join the coach party by booking his seat and, while he was weary from his fishing trip, ruthlessly battering down his objections. Charlie himself was silent. He did not stir when Bird looked in at him. Bunty talked animatedly in her sleep, freed from whatever hindrance made it not worth her while to bother much with speech when she was awake. Outside Hereward's room Bird paused, noticing that his light was still burning. Had the evening's glimpse of his daughter and grandson distressed him, she wondered, and did he feel slighted that he had not been allowed to meet his own flesh and blood? She knocked gently and went in.

★ ★ ★

Hereward was not in bed, but lying in a reclining chair that he used by day, facing the window. The curtains were not drawn. In the clear night he had been lying in darkness looking out at the vastness of the stars hanging in infinite space, when uneasy speculations began to disturb his comfort. Why were they there? Why? Scientists and astronomers explained how, but never why. Half alarmed, he switched on the lamp beside him and poured himself a glass of scotch. Reflected light shut out the sky. Bird's knock relieved him of objective thought, which he had always avoided.

'Not asleep yet?' she asked unnecessarily.

'There was a din from the village earlier. Lord knows what was going on. Draw the curtains, please, and sit down a while.' He wanted her to stay. They seldom had private conversations now. She extended to him the same care as she did to everyone in the house, while making it clear that the sick came first.

Until he had been idiot enough to allow himself to be deflected by star-gazing, the evening had been satisfactory. To pretend instant love for his child and grandchild was a hypocrisy he could not manage out of the small store of emotion left to him. They were strangers. His curiosity satisfied, he was content that they should remain so. The Dorset Parstocks, producing only one child in each generation, were uninterested in creating dynasties. Fortunately Hannah, in looks a mixture of her grandmother and his mother, could not by any stretch of coincidence or imagination be recognizable as his. The boy, good-looking in a blunt fashion, favoured another line. Hereward had already relegated them to the back of his mind and now wanted conviviality. Ignoring Bird's retreat towards the door, he said, 'Do have a drink.'

'No thank you. I'm only checking that everyone is well, especially today's travellers.'

'Devil take the travellers,' he said. 'Stay a while. Since I came here we've never spent time together. I'm as far from you as I've ever been. Surely there need not be coldness between us?'

'I mustn't stay.' She looked down at him with passive neutrality, but stayed just the same.

'That's better. I'm pleased that you don't want to go off to London with the rest. It's extraordinarily excessive. People are camping out on pavements and in the parks, drawn by a compulsion that I simply can not understand. The girl was a charmer, of course, and much maligned.'

'You knew her?'

'Met her at one of Stella's first nights, then again at charity events. She was pushed by that shabby marriage on to a dangerous path, trusting too much and sold out every time. The Hewitt fellow — I'm not the only bounder in the world!' He knew that indirectly he was apologizing for himself, but he pressed on, anxious that she should not go. 'What could have come of her latest affair? Yet another betrayal. Inevitably one feels that death has spared her a worse end. It says little for the natures of men, don't you think?'

Bird raised her eyebrows enquiringly. He admired their even arches and the lucent blue of her eyes. She would be as lovely in old age as she had been in youth. 'How can I know? I haven't enough experience to generalize.'

'Is that true? In case you have ever doubted, I adored you then and adore you still. Had you not left me, I could never have left you, for good or ill, whatever disaster I brought down on us.'

She began to fidget. 'Disaster? That's a strong term for quite an ordinary situation. I find it difficult to follow you, Hereward, unless there was something that I was never told. Now I must get back. Joshua might wake up and be frightened.'

'We'll talk about it tomorrow, after

breakfast. I don't want to have you hating me again. What I want to hear now is that you loved me once, that it was real until I destroyed it.'

'Mm.' There was more to come. He waited, impatient to be comforted. Bird bent over him. 'Come along, my poor dear, I'll help you into bed. Would you like me to send up another hot drink?' He shook his head and went on waiting. She put an arm around him and lifted him. The warmth of her body seemed to send fresh blood running through his veins, lightly and without threat. Then unexpectedly she kissed his cheek. 'You know it,' she said; 'you know I loved you with every part of me. For a long time I believed that you would arrive and rescue me from disgrace, but you made no sign. I thought I might die of love, but I didn't, I went on living and in the end I stopped wanting you.' Bird tidied the usual night-time clutter, tablets, a cup of Bovril, untouched and now cold, a carafe of water, a clock with a silent tick and the hand-control for the television set, folded the bedclothes neatly across him and put the bell cord close to hand. 'There's a purpose in you coming here, after all. Until now you were never really mine. At last, in a totally different way, you are.'

'Until death parts us permanently, yes. Not

much left to enjoy and not for long, but perhaps that was always the gift the gods intended, a happy death where I choose to be. May I kiss you goodnight?' She bent and lightly brushed her lips against his, then perched at the end of the bed. 'You'll be able to put out the light when you're ready. I've never hated you, Hereward. I simply stopped thinking about you. Hospitals are noisy places, and so busy. I thought far more of the wasted years, and what I had missed by not going to university. The idea of research, looking for facts and meanings, alone and peaceful, appealed to me very much.'

'You ought to have married — someone with a decent brain who would have helped you. I was always an empty-headed fool. Not good enough.'

Bird neither contradicted him, nor did she offer confidences. She picked up the cup of Bovril and left him.

★ ★ ★

Surfacing from a light doze, Connie Lovibond, whose temper was strained and whose ears were exceptionally sharp, heard Hereward's door open and close. She guessed that Bird also was wakeful, though it was early.

Tom Markham's organization of the mourning party could hardly be faulted, yet Bird would not be easy until she had her swans safely home again.

Content at the prospect of a day without Miles, Connie had not hurried to bed, waiting until silence settled down on the early risers before launching on her evening routine. With her hair in blue plastic rollers and a thick layer of moisturising cream on her rather dry skin, she slid between the sheets. Once her pillows were exactly right, she selected a novel. The distant shouting from somewhere outside barely penetrated her consciousness. She felt uncommonly secure and at ease. The sense of a summoning, that she had dismissed as ridiculous, had brought her to this place at precisely the right time. Steeped though she was in the creation of mysteries, Rita Parry was neither mad nor a witch, simply aggravatingly determined to extract the last drop of interest out of life. And Rita held the key. There was, after all, no reason why she should not simply have asked Bird to take her in. Had she done so, Connie would have learned nothing.

For Miles to burst in on her with barely a knock and insist on reading to her his latest literary work, *Elegy On The Death Of Diana, Princess Of Wales*, seriously annoyed her. He had stayed often enough at her house in Rye to know that this time was sacrosanct. 'I wrote it in white heat, Connie, and it needs polishing. I'm not too happy about rhyming lover with brother, for example, but I do so much want you to hear it.'

'Oh God,' she groaned, aware that she looked a fright, and trying surreptitiously to massage in the face cream. But Miles was not looking at her or even listening. His poem was very long and where a word did not please him, he stopped, made an alteration or two, then went back to the beginning of the verse and read it again. And again. Despair set in before he had finished. Closing her eyes, Connie tried to lose herself in beautiful images of mountain streams and leaping salmon. Behind closed lids, she could see still Miles's round face and thinning hair; all she could hear was his unnatural poetry-reader's voice.

'There, that's it,' he said at last. (Surely dawn must be breaking by now!) 'I thought of publishing. What do you think? A perfectly honest opinion, of course.'

However keen her enthusiasm for the muses might be in the morning, Connie's honest opinion at so late an hour was that all amateur poets should have a compulsory lobotomy and their writing hands cut off.

Miles, of course, wanted praise, not criticism. She said, 'It requires thought; no doubt it can be polished, as you say. You must excuse me from a detailed analysis, Miles. I really am rather weary.'

'Oh dear, I saw light under your door and got carried away.' His face sagged with disappointment, then brightened. 'I forgot about your evening ritual. Poetry is best read to oneself, I suppose. I'll leave it here with you until the morning, shall I?'

'We shan't be meeting in the morning,' she said doggedly, 'and I may well be asleep when you get back from London. You'll have time to work on it.' (Or to forget it.)

'Perhaps you're right. The funeral may inspire changes. Tell me, Connie, is that cream you use any good for sensitive skin? Does it reduce lines?'

In a tone so repressive that Miles collected the many pages of his elegy and got to his feet, she said, 'I have absolutely no idea. Now goodnight.' Sweet peace returned. Connie picked up her book, but she could not recapture her interest. Making friends with Bird and meeting poor Hereward again had pleased her and neutralized the pains of that faraway summer, yet holidays really did not suit her at all. She looked forward to certainty, to arranging, perhaps, a small memorial to Winifred. Then she would tackle the task of selling her father's pictures and filling the spaces with her own ordinary things.

And somehow Miles must be firmly discouraged from writing poetry. Judged against the awful effusions that would be published in local newspapers throughout the land, his elegy was by no means as bad as she had expected. The emotion was genuine enough, and astoundingly indiscreet. That was a flaw. Like Charlie Bean, Connie deplored the current fashion for scratching one's sores in public. It was certain that if Miles managed to get the poem into print, the Queen would never be giving him a knighthood!

★　★　★

The opening and closing of his door wakened Charlie from a light doze. He did not stir. Bird or one of the nurses always checked in the night in case of illness. Usually he fell asleep again immediately, but he remembered with shame for his weakness that somehow he had been bludgeoned into joining the funeral coach, carrying what Bunty persisted in calling a floral tribute. His loyalty to his Queen and country was as great as any man's. It made him uncomfortable to see the gradual dissolution of respect for hereditary heads of state because of the antics of their young. It was all of a piece with Charlie's consolation, the headlong rush of mankind towards extinction. Nothing, happy or sad, lasted forever. It was right that the folly of overpopulating the earth and greedily robbing it of those elements that sustained life, should bring down on man an appropriate punishment. And, he thought, we live too long; I have lived too long. What use am I? Yet idiot scientists misused their skills by inventing unnatural ways of producing yet more children without futures; and now cloning, the ultimate obscenity.

Considering these things, Charlie felt soothed. His melancholy thoughts were a barrier to softer feelings. They could not, however, always be kept at bay. In his youth he had fallen in and out of love, never committing himself to marriage, and his secret tenderness for Lizzie Greengrass deeply embarrassed him. What a laughing-stock he would be if ever it became public knowledge. He did not ask who would laugh. All his family and friends were dead or lost in the tangle of the years, except for his old friend up in Liverpool, and he never laughed at attachments to women. By his own account he still led a full and exciting sex-life. Frowning in the darkness, Charlie thought that it might be an idea to get him to The Glebe so that he could explain how it could be done with dignity. While he pondered on the strangeness of women and their passion to organize men, Lizzie began to float about in his head, dragging with her the Queen, Princess Diana and Bird. They merged into one, separated, smiled, scowled and nagged at him. Charlie slept.

★   ★   ★

Her rounds finished, Bird stood beside Joshua's bed, loving and admiring him. He was at the very best age for little boys, seeing as yet no reason to be ashamed of clinging to those he loved, talkative, confiding, full of wonder. She felt that he was her recompense. A few words in the night, a kiss without urgency or passion, had proved to her the endurance of the heart and the truth of her one love affair. Altered by separation, yes, yet the ghost of emotion had remained throughout her life and Hereward's. When next she lost him she would possess him forever. On the whole she felt glad to have resisted the temptation to tell him that she might still marry. It was not in her nature to appear to triumph over a sick man.

It occurred to her that she wanted Tom Markham and might have done so almost from the day she met him. She no longer recognized sudden emotions. Probably she was too old for sex, and Hannah would find her shocking and ridiculous. With that uncomfortable thought, she tucked the covers around her grandson, wondering whether the evening had brought him a prospective new father or whether Hannah had been idiot enough to turn Gus down. Surely it was high time that the Dawlish women learned how to be happy.

★　★　★

Back sooner in Wynfred Abbas than they had expected to investigate the assault and the subsequent fire, the CID inspector and his sergeant, prowled at dawn around the ash-bed that had once been Rita Parry's home. The local constable, weary-eyed and blackened by smoke, silently stood guard. 'Arson,' said the sergeant happily for the fifth or sixth time. 'Just smell that petrol. He must have used gallons of it. Villages are poxy holes; screwing each other senseless all night and ripping off tourists by day.' He did not notice the constable's expression of deep offence.

'How d'you know it was a he?' The inspector, too, looked at him without favour.

'You're not about to tell me the old granny hit herself over the head and then tried to fry herself, I hope.'

'I'm not trying to tell you a damned thing until I've got more facts, except that I believe this ties in somehow with that Glebe business. Mrs Dawlish is a nice woman, not wanting to speak ill, but she'll have to put a name to who's bothering her. And don't look so happy; we can't call at this hour, it's too early.' The constable coughed to draw attention to himself. 'You, son, what time does that diner place open? One thing I do know, I'm bloody hungry.'

'It'll be open now, sir. Fred's doing the sandwiches for the funeral outing.'

'Right. You come along with me, then. We'll get you cleaned up and have a bite of breakfast, then you can tell me what goes on around these parts.' His sergeant made a move towards the alley. 'Not you, my lad, not until forensic gets here. We don't want anyone tampering with the evidence, do we?' He smiled a malicious smile. 'I'll bring you back a bacon butty and a mug of tea if you're good.'

Directing an evil look at their departing

backs, his colleague fished in his pocket and found a Mars bar. The chocolate had begun to melt. Biting into it, he sat down on a crumbling wall and glared at the unhelpful ashes as though by concentration they would give up their secrets to him. His stomach gave a protesting rumble that sounded like thunder in the unnatural silence. Of all places on earth, this village was the arsehole of the world; being alone in it gave him the creeps. Now and then ash settled with a rustling sigh, startling him. Presently he yawned and dozed off.

13

Tom Markham leaned against the side of his coach, waiting for his elderly cargo and wishing that he had not decided to give up smoking. The first cigarette of the morning was always the best. He took immense pride in the coach, cherishing the deep blue paintwork with the name of The Glebe elegantly written in gold. Inside it was fitted especially to give leg-room and carried only twenty people and four wheelchairs. He allowed himself to daydream of marrying Bird. All the residents knew that he loved her and that in spite of his flaming red hair he had an even temper and an amiable disposition. They pitied him for having wasted time on a shrew who not only ran off with another man, but came back the next day with a van and emptied the house of furniture. Tom's eyes creased at the corners with secret amusement. In the spare peace of the rooms not a single trace of his ex-wife's presence remained. Let the double-glazing salesman have the benefit of her barbed-wire tongue and rasping nature; poor devil, he would have his work cut out to satisfy her rapacious demands for sex and more sex, not to mention money. Persuaded at first that he had loved her, Tom had quickly discovered that his bride directed his life and his performance with all the sensitivity of a Nazi general. She was not an affectionate woman. Bird's sheer loving-kindness touched him almost to tears.

It was nearly six o'clock and promising to be a beautiful sunny day. In the church, the bell-ringers began a brief practice run of the knell they would be tolling later in the day. A woman in a nightgown burst from the next-door cottage. She ran through the churchyard and began hammering violently at the locked door. 'Shut up, you beasts!' she screamed. 'It's too early. Call yourselves Christians? I can't sleep for your horrible noise.' The ringers boomed on. Defeated, she turned on Tom. 'What are you looking at? It's the same every time somebody dies, never mind princesses. You'd go mad too if you had to live here, fires and murders all night, then getting shook out of your bed, and the poor cat running up the curtains. I'm going to sue.' He nodded peaceably. With a long drive in front of him he could have done with more sleep himself. It was a pity to have turned out to fight the fire and then been able to do nothing, except perhaps to stop it from spreading. He hoped that the news had not yet reached Bird. The old lady picked out of the ruins had been a friend of hers from the past, as he remembered.

Down the High Street, outside the community centre, the Over-Sixties Club was gathering and its members began to straggle up the hill, stopping and starting and ducking their heads like a bevy of farmyard hens. The flowers and plastic balloons they carried gave an air of jollity to the procession. Tom opened the boot. The Glebe hamper was already in place and two folded wheelchairs for emergencies. Happily Bird had ordered and chosen the tributary offerings herself and made sure that they were small. He was going to have none too much space.

At that moment she ran down the front steps and grasped his arm. From the anguish in her face he knew that news of the fire had reached The Glebe and devastated her. 'Tom, the cleaners say that Rita was killed last night, burnt to death. It can't be true, can it?'

He thought how much he would like to pick her up bodily, put her in the coach and drive off with her into the blue where he could always protect her. 'Now, my dear heart, it's bad, but not that bad. I was there. She was battered, not burned, poor soul, and still breathing when the ambulance picked her up. Got a fight on her hands, they said.'

'What shall I do? I ought to go to her but I can't leave here, today of all days.'

'The police are in the village this morning. You can have a talk with them later. Come inside for now. I don't know where they took her, probably Poole or Bournemouth. I'll ring round the hospitals. You can speak to them yourself.'

'They won't tell me much,' Bird said eventually, replacing the receiver, 'but she's still alive. No visitors, not even family. There's a policewoman with her. It's my fault. I should have told the inspector; I should have helped more.' She wiped away tears as the lift began a descent. 'Oh dear, the others are on their way. I wish they weren't going. Supposing one of them gets ill. Are you sure you'll get them to the palace in time?'

'No problem. I'm picking up a mate in Hammersmith who used to be a taxi driver. He knows all the back ways and he's done me a list of toilets too. If the police don't try to stop us and we get off in good time, we'll be there by half nine, ten at the latest. You mustn't worry so much.'

'I just want you here with me, Tom,' she said passionately, warming his heart. 'Without you I should simply give up.' As she turned back to the house he thought, I love you, Bird Dawlish, and I don't want to leave you behind, alone with all this mess. The jaunt to London was going to try his patience as much as hers.

★ ★ ★

From the marble balustrade at the top of the steps, Bird watched her swans amble towards the coach. The outside staff had been given the day off, yet a sombre-faced Ched was already at work in the garden, turning soil with savage intensity. Hereward, in his dressing-gown, sat alone in the sun-lounge. He looked, thought Bird, with a painful wrench somewhere in the region of her heart, almost young under the soft, half-shaded light. The plants had recently been watered. Little pools lay on the red and buff tiles, two orange trees in tubs gave off a sharp, delicious scent and the air felt fresh and cool. He beckoned to her. 'Come in and sit down, my dear,' he said gently; 'here beside me.'

'Let me just see everyone off first, then I have to take Joshua home. It's very early still. Have you had breakfast? Can I get you coffee or a pot of tea?'

'Nothing. I was awake when the others began moving about and I thought I might as well get up.' Suddenly he straightened and peered past her, moving his chair to get a better view. 'Great suffering martyrs, what's this?'

Bird swung round. Down the path and heading fast for the coach came Stella Worth, off to the funeral, jauntily swinging her empty straw bag. She wore the large hat with the roses and a pair of black trainer shoes. In all other respects, she was completely naked. A pennant of green toilet paper trapped between her buttocks fluttered prettily as she walked. 'I have to concede,' said Hereward judiciously, 'that she still moves like an actress.'

This detachment angered Bird. She gave him a single withering glance. 'You brought her here, damn you,' she muttered, snatched the blanket from his lap and ran. Staff and convalescents on sticks and crutches laboured along in Stella's wake, uttering faint distracted cries like the calling of birds. At the sound of pursuit, Stella speeded up, breaking into a creditable trot. Over the years Wynfred Abbas had reared a phlegmatic population, untroubled by the occasional oddity thrown up by inbreeding. The Over-Sixties Club watched with silent interest. Denny of Cut And Dyed leaned on the shoulder of Lizzie Greengrass and went into quiet shrieks of laughter.

'Hey there,' Stella called to Tom, waving the basket, 'wait for me, darling.' But Ched got to her first. He mentioned that it was a fine, bright morning, lady, and how was she and did she have everything she needed for the day?

For the attention of an attractive young man, Stella skidded to a stop. 'Have a cigarette, dear boy,' she offered as Bird reached them, feeling for a non-existent pocket. She looked down. 'Dear Christ, I forgot, they pinched my clothes? It's a diabolical liberty.'

Bird threw the blanket around her. 'You had an accident and they got spoiled, remember? Come back to bed for now. If you let Sister have your house key, she'll get fresh ones for you.'

Help was on the way as coats, macs and more blankets arrived from the house. Ched neatly retrieved the toilet paper and dropped it into the incinerator. Stella's hat sat rakishly over one eye. The other, watching Bird's face, betrayed an unexpected and startling mockery. 'No, I don't remember and I'm damned if I'll stay here with that thieving horse-faced nurse buggering me about. Get this stuff off me. I'll sue you, just see if I don't.'

The slyness of Stella's regard killed pity. Mad or simply bad? Bird held on to her anger. 'Be quiet,' she said; 'there's trouble enough in this place without your idiocies. The police will be here and asking questions soon. Go home, if you want, but they'll find you and get the truth out of you.' Stella gaped and allowed a tear to creep slowly down her face. 'And you can just stop that. You're by no means as crazy as you pretend.'

She pushed her head forward tortoise-like from under the carapace of clothes and grinned winningly at Ched. 'Don't go away, darling; loved our chat. I'll be back in a jiffy.'

He gave her a soft, bland smile that did not disguise the anxiety in his eyes. 'I'm so sorry about this,' Bird said, 'and about poor Rita. Why not go home now?'

'It's better to work. Later we'll visit if they let us. We are her people after all.'

There was no reproach in his voice, only resignation. Hating her own failure to understand and protect, she led Stella, her brightness dimmed, back to the bungalow and locked her in. The trainers thudded once or twice against the door. Then the bedsprings creaked and vibrated. She rested from her labours.

'I'm sorry,' the duty nurse said. 'I only turned my back for a minute. She got herself in a state after the old woman burst in on her yesterday, but she's been quiet enough since.'

'What old woman?'

'The one that got killed last night. Talking nonsense about sheds and swan houses and all sorts. I couldn't make out what she was on about.'

Now what on earth had Rita Parry to do with Stella Worth? Bird wondered, not troubling to explain that she was still alive. If she died now her secrets and mysteries would die with her. And that, perhaps, had been her assailant's idea.

★　★　★

With no more exciting distractions to be had, the coach party crowded to the open door. Tom collected the Glebers at the front. 'No need to push, ladies and gentlemen. You just line up nicely and you'll all get on.' An underdeveloped youth, dressed in stained black plastic with a rash of zips, eeled around the shopping baskets and broad backsides, questing like a hungry dog. He dragged a plump girl in his wake. 'Here you go, Trace.'

Tom blocked his way with a freckled arm. 'Get to the back, you two. You're not pensioners.'

'My hubby can't come, no more can his sister,' explained Mrs Fred of the Diner and Takeaway, 'he's opened up to do the packed lunches and now the police are in, wanting breakfast. The sausage special goes a bomb. I paid for three tickets, so I brought our Eric instead to get him out of the way.' ('Zeke, Auntie,' said our Eric.) She ignored this interruption. 'He's my sister's daughter's boyfriend, that's Tracey here, and a Spratt on his mother's side — full of daft ideas. Shut him up if he gets above himself.'

'Why do you want to be called Zeke?' asked Tom, giving a hand to Lizzie Greengrass.

'Ever heard of an eco-warrior called Eric? I hate the Spratts; they got no social conscience. And you can stop glaring at me like that, Auntie; I saw him watching the old'un in the cemetery. It'd be just like him to try to do her in and burn the evidence.' For a second, Lizzie froze with one foot in mid-air, then she moved very slowly along the coach and found her seat. Charlie Bean followed. Tom also was deeply interested in this exchange.

'Will you shut up, you fool, before someone fetches you a blinder?' Mrs Fred glared so fiercely that Eric subsided. 'You can't go saying things like that without a shred of reason. We're having a day out, aren't we? Be grateful and stop arguing with your elders and betters or you can go on home.'

'Respect!' Eric said, raising a hand.

'Yer can't learn the young nothing. Which notwithstanding, he's got as much right as all of us so why're you letting them from The Glebe get on first?'

'Because it's their coach and they don't need to take you if they don't want to. You can always have your money back. Any more questions?'

Denny headed the village queue, pressed hard by the woman behind. 'No need to squirm about, dear, you'll make me drop my flask,' he said turning to look at her. From under her coat, a tail appeared. 'Have you got a dog in there?' As if in answer, a shaggy head struggled free and pounced on him, licking his face with loving thoroughness. Denny screeched. 'Take it away! I'm not going to London with that thing; I'm allergic and it's weeing all down your front.'

'What's the matter with you, you daft beggar? She's only small and she gets overexcited.' Tom put out an arm and stopped her. 'Hands off me, Tom Markham. I can't leave my poor girlie at home all day just because *he* don't like animals. Poncing around, making out he's a pansy when everyone knows he's knocking off Madam Dulcie!'

'That doesn't make me a bad person.' Denny simpered sweetly. 'Ask Arlene from the mini-market where Dulcie's husband spends *his* playtime. Sex is a great tonic; her hair's never looked so good. You ought to try it some time.' He delved into a plastic bag and handed her a packet of tissues. 'Here, wipe yourself down with these. I wish I'd brought some air freshener; you're going to smell to high heaven by the time we get to London.' He passed on down the aisle, dispensing tissues as he went.

'I can't allow dogs, madam,' said Tom, passing the animal to a care assistant, who ran with it to the house, mentioned that the animal had a bladder problem and suggested bedding it down in the garage. Running back, she settled herself comfortably in a front seat reserved for her.

Troubled by her conscience, Lizzie, sucked thoughtfully on a mint. She did not respond when Charlie, recovered from his sense of weakness, mentioned that he was quite pleased that she had persuaded him to go to London. Time passed. The rest of the pensioners jostled for window seats.

Last aboard was Eric, his hair greased into spikes, plastic creaking and metal tinkling, to take his seat beside Tracey. He stretched his legs across the aisle on to another and turned on a Walkman. A rhythmic hissing seeped from his ears. Peeved again, Charlie advanced on him, kicked his legs down and pulled off the headphones. The Walkman fell to the floor and expired. 'Someone's got to sit there and they don't want the muck off your boots. They don't want that idiot din either. Tom, are we going on this blasted junket, or are we not? At this rate we'll be there by bedtime, *if* we're lucky.'

'Respect, man,' murmured Eric, staring wonderingly at his abused toy and rubbing his ears. Tracey sniggered. 'Shut it, Trace, or I'll give you a thick 'un.'

A nurse said, 'We're waiting for Florrie from the bungalows. She's just soaking her feet. Someone will fetch her along in a minute or two.'

'What's she soaking her feet now for? We haven't been anywhere yet. If she doesn't get a move on she'll have nothing to soak her feet for.'

Suddenly Lizzie stood up. 'Now what's wrong?' asked Charlie.

'Get off, quickly. We can't go.'

'What, after all that nagging? I'm going if you're not.'

'Keep your voice down and let me out. I've got to talk to Bird. It's important.'

'Oh God,' groaned Charlie, 'other people's business again, I suppose? You're a nosy, impossible old woman.'

Tom said, 'Keep your hair on, Bird's here and so is Florrie. If you make it quick, I'll wait for you.' He took off his cap, smiled at his love and helped up the stray with a hand on her substantial rear.

*   *   *

'It's about Rita and the churchyard,' began Lizzie quietly, and proceeded to recount their conversation by the Spratt family grave. 'We may have been seen, overheard even. There's a lad on the coach with Fred's wife. His name's Eric. He knows something, I'm sure, but she shut him up when he tried to talk about it. I must tell the police.'

Bird deliberated. There was no way of knowing when the police would call or where they and Wally Spratt were now. Charlie stared at her, the anxiety in his eyes reflecting her own. She acknowledged it with a slight nod. Lizzie, in possession of too much information, seemed to have no sense at all of her own possible danger. Away from Wynfred Abbas she would be safe. 'It seems a pity to miss the funeral. I can mention it to the inspector, and after all you'll be back here by early evening.'

'Quite right,' said Charlie, firmly steering Lizzie by the arm. 'The princess may have made no difference in the end, but she tried to change things and got sneered at for her pains. I don't like that. Now come on, we'll give her her due. Wally Spratt will keep.'

Tom shut the coach door behind them, started the engine, travelled a few yards then stopped and reversed to the front door. One of the escorts helped down an elderly lady from the village and rushed her inside. 'Lavatory,' she said tersely. 'They forget to go before they come out.' At last, and only twenty minutes late, the party was on its way.

A rare tranquillity settled over The Glebe. In the huge empty kitchen, Bird and the duty nurses made toast and tea. Joshua was watching cartoons with Connie Lovibond, and Stella Worth was, for the moment, secure. She could not be kept a prisoner for much longer. It was clear that she would have to leave that day, but Gus's authority would be needed. Nevertheless, Bird relaxed. The river of life ran fast around her, picking up men and women to struggle like insects, then stranding them at will. A dreamy sense of fate moving inevitably towards some completion, good or bad, washed over her. She could not have avoided loving Hereward any more than Princess Diana could have resisted the pressure that drove her to a headlong rush for happiness and death. 'Life's a crow's march,' said the staff-nurse suddenly; 'no sense, no reason. The girl did what they wanted, gave them two sons to stave off the republican camp. After that they had no use for her. And I've no use for any of them; I'm a socialist, me. I'd vote for a republic any day.'

The youngest probationer looked stricken. 'But I love the royals. The Queen's speech is my favourite bit of Christmas, and she was as upset about Princess Di as we are.'

'If you say so, dear, though words are cheap enough. I didn't notice the word, love, in what she said, nor affection. But you just stick to your guns and don't be put off by me. I've seen the damage families do to one another. It makes you cynical about husbands and wives and mothers and their sons.'

'I'm videoing the funeral, just in case,' said the probationer. 'Awful to be the only one in the country to miss it. I'd best clear away in here as chef's off.'

Bird heard Joshua chattering in the hall and left her to it. He insisted on kissing Connie goodbye, which seemed to gratify her, and swung on his grandmother's hand as she walked him home. 'I watched all the cartoon things,' he said. 'Connie won't let me call her Auntie Connie. She says it might comport-omise her position as a trendy young swinger to have a nephew my age. I think she was making a joke. She's quite old really. Do you think she was making a joke?'

'I'm sure she was, Josh.'

'That's good. Gran, can I slide down your stairs one day like that lady, when Mum's not around?'

'She worries about you hurting yourself. You're the only boy she has. When you're older, perhaps she won't mind so much.'

Joshua gave her a sidelong look. 'If she marries Gus she might have other little boys — or girls.' He clapped a small palm over his mouth in exaggerated dismay. 'Oh dearie me, I wasn't supposed to tell you about that. Now I'll be in trouble, I expect.'

Bird squeezed his hand. 'Not this time. Gus told me about it himself. He's a nice man.'

'Brill,' said Joshua. 'Only drippy kids don't have fathers.'

This harsh judgement deserved a lecture as Bird well knew, but Hannah was the social worker. It was one for her to sort out.

★ ★ ★

Gus, bare-chested and bare-footed, opened the door to them, picked up Josh and swung him around. 'She's fallen into my trap,' he said in a dramatic stage whisper. 'She can't escape me now!' He smiled at Bird. 'I suppose I ought to be slipping out of a window to spare your daughter's shame, but I'm not dressed for it. Hannah's still in bed and I'm a happy man. Do you mind?'

Joshua went thundering up the stairs, chattering as he went. Bird said, 'I'd think you a bit of a wet if you confined yourself to hand kissing. Hannah had just about forgotten how to be a woman. She needs to be pounced on and reminded as often and as thoroughly as possible.'

Gus inspected her with deep interest. 'Sometimes I wonder about your youth, Bird Dawlish. And what about now? You're by no means old and decrepit. If any man has the courage to ignore that cool exterior and pounce on *you*, I feel he might have rather an enviable experience.'

'Stranger things have happened, though any man who wanted me would have to take my old swans too. Unless they close me down, I'm here until I need looking after myself. Which reminds me — Stella Worth.'

Gus listened to her account of Stella's all-too public appearance and shook his head. 'It could be senility or even the onset of Alzheimer's, complicated by alcohol and drugs. I need help, a specialist. I'll try to get her to a private hospital today, but if she won't go, I can't force her.'

'And I really can't keep her. She's such a disturbing presence and I won't have the sick upset.' Bird hesitated. 'Is she truly mad? Obsessed certainly, but it doesn't do to forget that she's an actress.'

'So she is,' he said softly. 'Obsession is agonizing to watch. Could it be that she honestly loves Parstock and has no idea of how to handle her disappointment?' Bird did not comment. 'Well, find her some clothes, my dear, anything, an old hospital gown. If she wants to go home for now, let her. I hate to have anyone sectioned, but if I must then I will.'

To clothe Stella's nakedness in a maroon crimplene dress, unearthed from jumble collected for The Glebe's annual fete, took the efforts of three nurses. Her vociferous and colourful refusal to be passed on to any hospital echoed across the sea and unnerved a night fisherman pulling his boat ashore. Gus and Bird took her back to her cottage. The smell inside made Gus gag and throw open a window, fighting for a clean breath. Braving the squalor and stumbling over empty bottles and discarded plastic bags, they managed to get her upstairs. Stella sank happily down on to bed sheets that had needed changing some weeks before and closed her eyes. 'Home, sweet home,' she murmured. 'Now sod off, dear. I'm tired. See you in the morning.'

'Let me change those bedclothes for you,' Bird offered.

'I'm sick of you, Nest. You can sod off too.'

Gus looked down on his patient, trying to find some trace of the frequently mentioned loveliness. Nothing remained but a gaunt, sick old woman. The filth of the place seemed to cling in a greasy pall to his clothes and skin. He felt a vast longing to be with Hannah and to bury his face in her mass of clean-smelling hair. After taking Bird back to The Glebe, he paused at the lodge, then drove on and spent a long time in the shower. There were times when he did not enjoy his work.

14

In a state between sleeping and waking, Hereward dreamed that Stella Worth floated past his bedroom window, naive and open as a flower. He had never known her like that. It was a description a friend had given him of her early youth, when she had performed in circuses and carnivals and not yet taken to marrying God-awful men who cheated and robbed her. Before his sleep-filled eyes, she changed and became hideous and threatening. Her naked body smothered him. An almighty blow to his chest wakened him thoroughly. Struggling for breath, he discovered that he was still in the conservatory and that it was still Saturday. I feel ill and empty, he complained silently to himself, self-pitying and out of temper. Last night Bird was loving, or did I dream that, too? Oh where is she? At that moment she arrived, carrying a tray with silver covers. 'Where have you been? You're always leaving me and it's comfortless without my blanket. What time is it anyway?' he asked irritably.

'Almost nine. I've brought your breakfast: scrambled egg, smoked salmon, toast, coffee.

Juice if you want it. And you forgot to take your medication.' She took a car-rug from another chair and straightened it over his knees, watching while he swallowed his pills.

Suddenly ravenous, he attacked the food with appetite. 'Did Stella truly walk past with no clothes on, or did I dream it?'

'She's in a poor state. Someone gave her a drug, a large dose, and it seems to have disturbed her mind quite seriously. Gus Early and I drove her home. He feels she should be sectioned for a while under the Mental Health Act.'

'Don't look at me as though it were my fault. It's not, even though you blame me. Why must she follow me around all the time?'

She frowned, anxious for him. 'I wish you wouldn't read expressions on my face that aren't there. I imagine that she follows you because she loves you.'

'And that doctor, is there something going on between you?'

'For heaven's sake, he's engaged to our daughter. Had you forgotten?'

Hereward *had* forgotten. His mind and his body were giving up and he wasn't altogether sorry. A man grew tired of dragging around a burden of flesh that gave no pleasure, obeyed no commands and simply did what it chose. But first the moment of death must be passed. Pain, perhaps, and a last choking breath before the heart stopped. He had never been a thinker or a man for abstracts, nor did he bother God with demands and supplications. As far as he knew, God, if he existed, had no interest in him. It was a fair arrangement. Then he had begun to look up at the sky from his window or walking through the garden at night and been shaken by the terrifying prospect of infinite space and unnumbered worlds. Worse, he had become haunted by a question. It was all very well to have universes explained, but why were they there? Why? Why should anything or anybody exist at all? Scientists had exploded the creation myth. They explored stars and planets and came up with theories to explain how, but not why. If there were no creator there should be no space, no gases, no fish or insects or reptiles, nothing to evolve from. So the tormenting question remained. Why?

He could not confess his fear to Bird. His hands shook nervously as he picked up the coffee-cup. She put her fingers lightly on his wrist to take his pulse, but he enclosed them with his own. 'Sit down. I want to talk to you.' Bird tried to free her hand but he clung on. 'Don't walk out on me again. It's important.'

'Can you just give me an hour? Half the staff have gone to the funeral and I must see that the bed-patients are comfortable. Connie is on her — '

'To the devil with Connie and the bed-patients. I won't give you another minute. I've waited long enough and I need to tell you about your father.'

'Sorry, Hereward, I must go. I never knew him anyway. He died soon after I was born.'

She was almost out of the door when he roared after her, 'In the name of Heaven, woman, will you come back here and just listen to me for a change. I'm not talking about Arnold Dawlish; he had nothing to do with you. You aren't his daughter, you're my grandfather's child! Dammit, you're my aunt!' The effect was more than he hoped for. Bird stopped dead, turned and walked back to him. 'Now will you please sit down and let me speak?'

She sat as Connie appeared in the doorway. 'I did try to tell you that Connie was on her way here, but you wouldn't listen,' she said.

'And I suppose she heard?' Hereward sagged and the too-ready tears rose to his eyes. Dragging a handkerchief from his pocket, he blew his nose vigorously.

'You poor man, you were very loud and I have excellent hearing,' said Connie. 'I never quite believed in the violent chastity of Mrs Dawlish. All that praying presupposes guilt. I imagine she was beautiful once.'

The look that Hereward turned on her was both anguished and resentful. He had planned to tell Bird why he had deserted her with love and gentleness, not like an overbearing bully. The situation could not now be retrieved. For a moment he was utterly lost, and drowning in weariness. 'There are photographs,' he muttered. 'She was educated, well-bred too. I couldn't persuade Bird that she had catalogued my grandfather's library. That's when it happened.'

'But wasn't he a widower then?'

'Grandfather adored his wife, the original Bird. Her death devastated him. He never tried to replace her, though he wasn't past wanting other women. With Mrs Dawlish it took patience and a promise of marriage.'

Suddenly Bird, almost forgotten, spoke. The scorn in her voice made him flush. 'That sounds familiar. Presumably he didn't die or anything convenient like that? Just dumped her like a true Parstock?'

He turned to her then and managed to regain his grip on her hand, wanting to protest that he had none of his grandfather's coldness and calculation, that he had suffered all his life by losing her. Weak, disconsolate words arranged themselves in his mind. I won't whine, he thought savagely. But the wretched tears came back, running down his face and dripping on to their linked fingers. 'I imagine he felt a traitor to my grandmother's memory or something of the kind, so yes, when she told him she was pregnant, he dumped her, as you put it. Worse, he paid Arnold Dawlish to marry her and threatened to sack him if he refused. What could the man do? He was coming up to sixty and knew that he would never get another job. He didn't want a wife, but he agreed.'

'Nice one,' said Connie with sardonic appreciation. 'And in the fifties it didn't do to be pregnant without a husband, so Bird's mother accepted the practical solution. Defiant to name her daughter after the dead wife. I begin to be the slightest bit sympathetic towards her, though destroying her own life and the child's with extremes of hatred and pride was wicked to say the least.'

'I'm so very sorry, my dearest,' Hereward said to Bird, whose face was contorting oddly as though she struggled to suppress tears. 'Please don't cry. Above all things I wanted to marry you, but I couldn't burden you with incest. Your mother would have betrayed us at once.'

'My poor Hereward.' Bird began to laugh, the last reaction he had expected. 'Your aunt? Is that it? Didn't it occur to you that in betraying us my mother would also have needed to betray herself? After all those years of secrecy? She would never have done it and she must have been the only one alive who knew.'

★ ★ ★

They both stared at her, Connie with amusement, Hereward shocked. 'You would have stayed with me? But it's a crime. Do women have no conscience whatsoever?'

'Not where love is concerned,' Bird said. 'How often do you suppose such accidents happen nowadays, with artificial insemination and adoptions and people sleeping around so much? They never find out. You weren't so lucky.'

At last he began to relax, leaning back against the cushions and regarding her with the kind of curiosity he had never shown before. 'I don't understand. Hannah must never know, surely?'

Connie smiled. 'Don't be silly, Hereward, of course she mustn't. I need hardly assure you that she'll hear nothing from either of us. Bird, if you have things to do you might as

269

well run along. I'll help Hereward upstairs to dress. He can watch the funeral with you.'

'I'll thank you not to treat me as though I were an idiot, Connie. I'm perfectly able to dress myself. And why on earth should I want to watch the funeral? It's an exercise in damage limitation with a pop star thrown in to symbolize democracy. Not even a new song at that; rehashed nonsense written for an American film star. Damned tasteless!'

Obstinately Bird declined to agree with him. 'Not to ordinary people. They loved her and they are the ones who count today. Anyway, it's quite a nice song.'

Relief at the off-loading of his burden overcame true anger. 'All this emotion, it's beyond reason.'

'Men have never been much good at disinterested love,' Connie said. 'Women on the whole have a stronger sense of justice and this is their chance of putting down princes.'

Still Hereward appeared to be puzzled, but he did not pursue the subject. To Bird's relief, he at last released her hand. She shook it to get the blood back into her numb fingers. 'I suspect,' he said, 'that I've missed a wonderful life and I dare say it serves me right. At least I knew that you had money enough to live comfortably.'

'What money?'

'My solicitors were instructed to pay your mother whatever she asked for you and the child of course.'

'And I saw none of it. After Hannah was born, I thought I had to make a living to keep us both. Denying me university was my mother's idea of proper punishment, I suppose. No wonder she died rich.'

'And frustrated, I imagine, piling up the money, watching it multiply,' said Connie. 'Hannah had blotted her copybook, so in the end she had to leave it to you. Don't look so upset, Hereward. Hence The Glebe, your present home.'

'But it was my only means of showing that I wasn't indifferent, that I — oh damn it, what an awful woman, what a mess.' With a despondent air, he stood up. 'Come along, Connie, I feel badly in need of a drink.'

Bird became a nurse again. 'Only one, Hereward, please. It's a buffet lunch today and if you intend to stay in your room, I'll choose yours for you. Do make sure that you eat it all.'

The sensible words belied her glowing mood. On this dreadful day, with Rita lying injured in hospital, with Lizzie perhaps in danger, with Stella Worth an unshakeable penance, a shred of magic lurked. She left behind the tired, goose-footed nurse's plod and almost ran, swinging her arms like a girl. Hereward *had* loved her. Her steady, sensible heart rejoiced. Month upon month, tormented and shamed, she had wrestled with an unappeasable hunger for a man who clearly cared nothing for her; and that was how her mother had finally exacted vengeance. Then Bird had not cried. Now her eyes began to ache pleasantly with retrospective tears to find that she was not the unloveable simpleton she had believed herself to be. Life had its recompenses. Her mother had hated her Parstock daughter, but she had loved Hannah and lost her. And, late though it was, Hereward had come home to her to die. She thought with a smile, I'm another reprehensible Parstock and I don't care.

'What's so funny?' asked the auxiliary in charge as Bird flew up the steps of the nursing wing.

'The world, people, me. Come along, let's do the rounds.' Television sets were on in most of the rooms. The ninety-nine-year-old held an animated conversation with his wife, who had died five years before.

'She must have been a quiet sort of woman,' said the care assistant. 'He doesn't seem to notice that she never answers him back.'

'Perhaps she does and we can't hear her.'

Bird bent over and kissed his cheek. He smiled sweetly and thanked her for putting up with her tiresome old husband. 'Will you have chicken soup for lunch?'

'Plenty of sherry in it, please, my dear. You remember how I like sherry in it?'

'Of course,' said Bird, feeling that she had been given a prize. A single mild regret stirred. It would have been interesting to know whether she would have made a good scientist. She suspected that fate and old Mr Parstock's hush money had pushed her into her proper destiny, relieving her loneliness and giving her contentment. She glanced at her watch; half past eleven and almost time to begin serving the makeshift lunch. The television in the lounge showed an alien London without traffic, full of silent people in summer clothes, moving gravely among flowers. Bird was reassured about the safety of her residents. Nothing there could threaten them. For this one day, in that one place, violence was temporarily suspended.

★ ★ ★

After Hereward's revelation and Bird's unexpected response, Connie experienced an acute sense of irritation with what used to be called the way of the world. People, including herself, were such muddlers. They should not confess for the good of their own souls or probe into the past as she was doing. Better by far to forget Swan House completely. In Rye she might easily have escaped much of the week's commotion.

'It's extraordinary,' Connie remarked aloud. She had lived in three reigns, not counting that of Edward VIII, another prince who had seriously misjudged the nature of women and the supposed power of the monarchy. No royal birth, coronation, wedding or funeral had produced such a spectacle. A glance at the television screen showed her that any reasoned analysis of the power of Princess Diana to attract devotion was likely to be fruitless. In a sense, those who mourned so extravagantly had loved the girl to death. It concerned her more that her own search for answers might in the end come to nothing. Stella had lost her grip on reality altogether if her exhibition that morning was anything to go by, and, should old Rita die, whatever she knew would die with her.

Vengeance had never been in Connie's mind. Patience was the great avenger, punishing appropriately and thoroughly in its own good time. She simply needed to know. To curb her restlessness, she installed herself in the writing-room and began to list her father's pictures. Many of them she had forgotten. Those she remembered were likely to fetch a fortune for her and the State. The thought depressed her. She could think of nothing at all to do with the money, except to give it away. She drew the line at random good works. Unrewarding at best, given the reluctance of those helped to embrace civilization, positively harmful if you were seen as a soft touch. When Bird looked in at her she was absorbed in dividing her inheritance between likely charities.

'A buffet lunch today, Connie, I hope you don't mind. It will give the staff — and me — a chance to watch the funeral. Will you join us?'

'Vanity forbids. I'm not an unduly senti-mental woman, but only a heart of stone can see the pathos and not weep. Red eyes on top of my dishevelled looks age me by a hundred years.'

'We're all about to make fools of ourselves and I want you to persuade Hereward. He's too much alone.'

'Perhaps then, though I planned to watch in my room and not for long. Will we ever, do you suppose, get back to conversation rather than mere speculation and tittle-tattle?' She studied Bird closely. 'Would you truly have married Hereward, knowing?'

After a brief hesitation, she answered honestly. 'It's a strange thing, Connie, until today I had no perception of who I was or where I belonged. And I certainly didn't know what I was capable of. Right and wrong were only words. I loved him enough to do anything he asked of me.'

'You know, I wonder more and more about the virtue of an embittered woman like your mother, obsessed with prayer and sin. Her acceptance of the evangelist is an aberration, unless they — could they have been lovers?'

Bird pulled a face compounded of disgust and disbelief. 'I refuse even to think about the grubby creature in that context. On balance I shall be very glad when this day is over and I can get back to scrubbing commodes and counting sterile dressings.'

★ ★ ★

No onlookers cluttered up the scene of the fire. Wynfred Abbas had forgotten yesterday's news and transferred its interest to London. Reinforcements for the inspector and his sergeant had, however, arrived in the shape of two uniformed constables. Neither was in a sunny mood. Both had admired the princess and were shattered by her death; both had expected to be off-duty in time to see her taken to her rest. The inspector did not listen to their protests. 'You'll get a chance to watch the service and have a good snivel when it comes time. We can watch together and share hankies.' He left the younger to watch the crime scene and went with the other and his sergeant in search of petrol sales. The one garage, a single-storeyed wooden shack tacked on to a Victorian cottage that had seen better days, was closed. 'Round the back,' he said.

The only response to their knocking was a voice that shouted, 'We're closed. Can't you bloody-well read?'

'I'll break the door down, shall I, sir?' asked the sergeant, eagerly squaring his shoulders.

The constable leaned indifferently against a rotting post, divorcing himself from whatever was to happen next until the inspector kicked his ankles. 'Stand up and look useful before you bring the whole damned porch down on us.' He knocked again, but with more insistence. 'This is the police. Open up there, we want a word.'

The door opened a crack and an unshaven face appeared. 'You buggers would. What is it this time?'

'Petrol,' said the sergeant. 'We want to know if you've sold a few gallon cans lately.'

A whole man emerged into the open. 'Who's pulling your strings, then, sunshine? This is a garage. Petrol's what I sell, OK?'

Not entirely displeased by this affront to his junior, the inspector pushed his way inside and showed his identification. 'That'll do, son. I dare say that if I look hard enough I can find some offence you're committing in this rat-hole, so the sooner I get sensible answers, the sooner you can get back to your television. The fire at the old cottages last night was started with petrol, a lot of petrol, and I want names.'

It took time for the owner to assure them that he had never put a foot wrong in all his life and that all his customers were honest, law-abiding people. He used his own cans and charged a two pound deposit on them. But eventually the police emerged with four leads. A farmer upalong sometimes bought a few cans when his delivery was late, as did a couple of other customers who drove a lot and were scared of running out on the road. The fourth, and the most interesting to the inspector, worked as gardener up at The Glebe and needed it for mowing and such. Name of Wally Spratt.

★　★　★

A rousing welcome at the Spratt household was not to be expected, so the inspector was not put out by the long wait before the door opened. 'We want to speak to your husband, madam,' the sergeant said in his sternest manner. 'At once, if you please. The constable here, will guard the door.'

It was somehow not his day. 'Guard what you like, you've come to the wrong place. He ain't been home all night.'

'You sure? Trying to protect him won't do any good, you know, or lying to the police.'

'Don't call me a liar, *if* you don't mind; there's nothing gets my goat quicker. And why should I protect him? He can stay away forever if he wants, horrible nuisance. I'm sure I don't want to see him again, and before you ask, I don't know where he is, neither. He doesn't tell me anything about his comings and goings, thank the Lord.'

Mrs Spratt had gone early to the surgery with her specimen, leaving it on the doorstep, wrapped in a plastic bag and labelled, 'All the best, A Spratt'. On her return home, she had made arrangements for the day. Having enjoyed a mild revenge against his sergeant, who was inclined to mock at the old-fashioned methods of older policemen, the inspector surveyed her preparations complacently. A bowl of fruit, a plastic-wrapped chicken sandwich from Fred's, a jug of orange juice and another of water stood on a table beside a large sagging armchair facing the television set. A complicated piece of knitting, stuck with needles, lay on a stool beside the chair. Lunch for one and no sign that Wally was invited. 'I'm very sorry to intrude, my dear,' he began.

'I should just think you are, today of all days.'

'Alas, crime waits for no one. May we just take a look around. You are fully entitled to refuse since I don't have a warrant, but it may save disturbing you again later.'

Mrs Spratt preceded them into the kitchen and put a kettle on the gas. 'Look where you want. He kept most of his stuff in the outhouse. I'm going to fill meself a flask of tea, then I'm settling down. Princess Di meant a lot to me. I'll see her to her grave, poor girl, if a thousand police try to stop me.'

Under a bench in the outhouse stood a gallon can half full of petrol, but no empty cans. A search, however, produced several items of interest. A locked suitcase, breached by the sergeant with a handy screwdriver, contained a bizarre assortment of porno-graphic photographs and magazines, designed to erect the limpest of deviants. 'Some of this has got to be illegal,' he said, sweating lightly.

'We'd better impound the lot.'

'Leave it where it is, son, including the stuff you just shoved in your pocket, and tackle that old freezer. I doubt that it's chained and padlocked to stop Mrs Spratt from helping herself to a packet of frozen peas.' The sergeant picked up bolt-cutters. 'Not like that. Dearie me, do use a bit of delicacy. A kid of ten could pick that lock so as no one would ever know it had been opened.'

Under a store of assorted foodstuffs, possibly, thought the inspector, purloined from The Glebe storerooms, they uncovered a box of syringes and two dozen pairs of ladies' silk knickers without gussets, together with a bundle of five pound notes. 'Too bad, nothing much he can't talk his way out of here, though the syringes are suggestive. A bit of a dirty tyke, but he'll just tell us the money's his life savings, which it may be.' Disappointed, he began to restore the food more or less as he had found it. Fate rewarded him for his neatness. Frozen fast to a leg of English lamb was a small plastic packet and inside, barely visible under the frost, a powder. 'If this turns out to be gravy browning,' he said, 'I'm going to be very, very cross, but I don't think so. Now for the elusive Wally. It's going on for lunchtime; we could try

281

The Glebe first, though I don't want to spoil the old dears' fun.'

On the way out, he risked asking Mrs Spratt's back where her husband might keep containers that he had no further use for.

'Don't know. In his old truck, maybe, ready to be got to the tip. Make sure you lock the front as you go out.'

'Can you, by any chance, give me the registration number and a brief description?'

'It's supposed to be white, but you can't hardly tell for dirt and rust. I don't properly remember the number; there's a D and an R and two ones in it.' She leaned forward and turned up the sound on the television. The sergeant cursed under his breath, but the inspector nodded contentedly and hurried him out of the door.

15

Soon after Gus Early left her, Stella Worth got out of bed, discarded the maroon crimplene and found instead a romantic affair in flowered chiffon. Nothing moved on the High Street. Needing a pick-me-up, she too set out in search of Wally Spratt. Before she reached his cottage the police emerged and the constable went off to Fred's Diner for his lunch. 'There's the old bird they think took drugs,' the sergeant said, as the car passed her: 'do you want me to bring her in?'

'Any time will do for her. Just keep an eye open your side for Spratt's truck. And stop at the pub, will you? I could use a beer and a chat with the landlord. He was one of the first on the scene last night.'

'I thought you were set on scrounging a bite at The Glebe and having a look round.'

'That'll have to wait till later,' the inspector said, ignoring the imputation of greed. 'On second thoughts, that's the one place Spratt won't be and we could do with having him in custody before we tackle the old folk.'

At the Duke's Head, the landlord was pleased to see them since they were his only customers. He served them beer and accepted one himself. 'No deliveries today so there's only yesterday's pies, but they're fresh out of the freezer. Or the missus'll make you up a sandwich if you'd rather.' Out of habit, he swiped a cloth over the perfectly dry bar. 'You'll be wanting to know about the fire, I expect.'

His story tumbled out: the fear for his premises, the slowness of his wife in getting herself dressed, being a big woman, the shock of them finding a corpse just over the wall from his yard. 'You didn't happen to hear or see anything before the fire started?' asked the inspector. 'Or notice who was on the scene when you got there?'

'Not before, no. Dead to the world, both of us. They was bringing the pump up the hill as I came out the door, so I let them get through. A waste of bleeding time, that were. Fire brigade were here before they got the tank filled. Some of the neighbours got busy with buckets and I think there was one or two useless buggers hanging around just gawping.'

The sergeant was about to speak, but a shake of the head and a heavy hand on his arm stopped him. 'Can I ask you to try to picture the scene as you first saw it and tell me if you can recollect who was present, but not engaged in fighting the fire.'

Unused to deep thought, the landlord furrowed his brow and seemed to fall into a light trance. His wife walked in, bearing her considerable bulk with easy pride, nodded, put a plate of sandwiches on the bar-counter, moved the pickled onion jar to stand beside it and got out some forks. She withdrew, though only as far as a vantage point behind the door to the kitchen, which she left open. The sergeant spent several minutes ineffectually chasing an onion around the jar. He gave up and bit deeply into a sandwich. It was princely; a thick layer of country ham spread with mustard, topped with ripe cheddar and tomato. 'Well then,' came her husband's undecided voice. A long silence followed. 'Well then, I saw old Eli; he walks on two sticks on account of being rheumatic and in his nineties. And Madam Dulcie's husband; he'll have been just coming home from seeing to one of his lady friends. Too wore out to lift a bucket, him; he'll die on the job, one of these days. There was others I didn't properly notice. One was a burly sort of chap that put me in mind of Wally Spratt, though I couldn't swear to him and I'm probably wrong anyway. Friday nights regular he goes down to Bournemouth round the clubs, seeing what he can pick up in the way of business.

Don't ask me what business 'cause I don't know. Buying and selling — anything and everything.'

'Thank you.' Having made a couple of unnecessary notes in his notebook (the inspector had an excellent memory), he directed his voice towards the kitchen door. 'No point in questioning your wife, I suppose.'

He shook his head slowly from side to side. 'Her wasn't there. Her'll have gone back to bed.'

The lady of the house appeared majestically in the doorway. 'No her didn't. A couple of pals of mine from the old-time dancing came out for a look at the fire. We stayed talking for a bit by the top of the alley.' The landlord tried to give her a warning look. She ignored it, but jerked her head in his general direction. 'He's scared stiff of getting on the wrong side of Wally, but I aren't. Firstly, he was there all right, grinning his evil face off. I saw him go on his way, the three of us did. Then we come in here and had a cup of tea.'

Radiance burnished the inspector's face. He approved of this large, plain, independent-minded woman. 'You did not, I suppose, happen to notice which way he went?'

'You supposes wrong, then. When he saw us, he shot across the street and went upalong towards the church. After that I don't know. Away from the flames it was pitchy dark. Can I do you some more sandwiches?'

'Indeed you can and if you will accept a drink with us, I should be honoured,' said the inspector, at his smoothest. 'If you weren't an attractive married lady and liable to excite jealousy among the gentlemen, I should certainly kiss you.'

She smiled. 'Feel free, my lover. I'll be back in a minute.' The landlord, having after years of marriage ceased to regard her as a sex object, seemed puzzled and deeply unhappy. 'You look mental with your mouth hanging open,' she said. 'Pour me a scotch and dry ginger. No ice.'

'Watch what you're saying, Mavis,' he muttered. 'It don't do to let people think you know all their business.' He locked the door, frustrating Stella Worth in her pursuit of comfort, and retired to the furthest corner of the bar. Without him, the party became convivial and informative. Wally Spratt, the universal provider, had, it emerged, a monopoly on cheap supplies of all kinds in Wynfred Abbas, down to the pies served at the Duke's Head. 'God alone knows what's in 'em,' Mavis said, with scorn. 'Fell off the back of a waste lorry is my guess and him there daresn't say he don't want any more in case

Wally tells on him for receiving and he loses his licence.'

'Do you know for sure that they're stolen goods?'

'Wally doesn't like people to know things about him for sure. I reckon that's why poor old Rita got bashed on the head. She used to hint about what went on in the past. It frightened him, whether she really knew anything bad or not.' She looked directly at the inspector. 'It is him you're looking for, isn't it?'

'We need him to assist in our enquiries, yes, but he and his pick-up seem to have vanished.'

'Eat up that last sandwich; you need your food,' said Mavis. 'He's not gone far. There's plenty of cuts and snickets behind the houses to park a truck in. After the coach went off to London I saw him drive down from the fields above the village. He didn't call in home and he wasn't long away. By the time I went out to shake the mats he was up by The Glebe gates on foot. I doubt he was going in.'

'Ah. We'd best get along, though, and have a word with Mrs Dawlish before the coach party gets home.' They thanked each other for what had proved to be an unexpectedly pleasant lunch and forgot to say goodbye to the landlord.

'This place certainly goes in for big women,' the sergeant commented as he drove up the hill.

'There's a lady who's comfortable with her size and her conscience.' The inspector shook his head sadly. 'Pity about the husband. A waste of space if ever I met one.' For a wistful moment he imagined Mavis moving confidently around his kitchen, dishing up meals to make the heart glad. His own wife was an erratic cook and her sandwiches lacked substance. But she had other talents and, on the whole, he loved her too much to pursue his disloyal thoughts.

★   ★   ★

Bird, with brisk help from Connie Lovibond, was serving tea at the nursing wing. After the funeral, emotional saturation point had been reached. The hearse and the attendant mourners had passed over a carpet of thrown flowers and the princess had reached her last and ancestral home. 'It's a revelation,' Connie said. 'I deplore excesses, yet one has to admire a nation that declares for fair play and against servility. It will never happen in quite this way again, not for pop-stars, politicians or princes.'

'Getting everyone to calm down enough to

sleep is a problem. I don't want them bothered if the police turn up.' Bird, grateful for Connie's effort to divert her, could not co-operate in conversation. Below her habitual optimism she struggled with a sense that, awful as things were, worse was to come. She had failed everyone. Rita, who in her erratic way had been more her mother than the woman who had reared her, might die through her mistakes and weaknesses. And, distrusting him, she ought never to have employed Wally Spratt. Worse, a misplaced sentiment had betrayed her into admitting Hereward Parstock to her precious haven, where he brought unwanted echoes of dead emotions. And yet, the morning's euphoria persisted. Events were moving on and somewhere ahead lay an ending and a new beginning. Preferring not to be told that they were contradictory and irrational, she kept these thoughts to herself.

'When does the London party get back?' asked Connie.

'Two or three hours yet.'

'Then you've time to come to my rooms for a glass of sherry. No, don't shake your head. I know you're distressed about Rita and feel that your work here is threatened, but don't make yourself responsible for the well-being of the whole world, if you please.

There's no point in worrying alone. You need an ally and I'm it.' She led the way upstairs.

'Rita,' said Bird faintly; 'I ought to phone the hospital again. If she dies I shall feel like her murderer.'

'That, my dear, is absolute twaddle. For heaven's sake don't say things like that to the police. They might not understand.' As though she had conjured them up, her house phone buzzed at that moment to announce their arrival. 'Show them up here,' she said.

From that moment, Bird noticed, Connie began to enjoy herself. Her offer of drinks was refused, though the inspector carefully explained that she was not suspected of anything nefarious, but that few wines and spirits sat well with the beer they had consumed at lunch. ' 'Whisky after beer makes you queer', as they say, and for all I know to the contrary it may be true.'

'Give us a break,' muttered the sergeant and seeing the eyes of his superior roll calculatingly in his direction, added aloud, 'We ought to speak to the er — the ladies separately, oughtn't we, sir?'

'This is my private room,' said Connie, with a malicious smile. 'Neither of us is leaving it at present. You must wring a confession out of us as best you can, young man. Fire away.'

'He isn't used to such hardened criminals,' said the inspector, blander than ever. 'Allow me. Perhaps you can tell me something about the injured lady Mrs Parry. What there is about her to cause so violent an assault on her person, for instance. By all reports she's harmless enough.'

The question was addressed to Connie and Bird made no attempt to answer. Rita must still be alive and the relief made her weak. 'Certainly I can,' said Connie. 'She's a loner, an old travelling woman grown tired of travelling. A picker-up of information, too, though whether she knows as much as she pretends to know has yet to be proved. Sees things, past and future, if you believe in second-sight.'

'Didn't see the assault coming, though, did she? Who might she have threatened with her information, do you know?' When Connie hesitated, he allowed his slow glance to travel round the room and winced when he encountered her musical souvenir of Dorset.

She smiled. 'Hideous, isn't it? A perfect antidote to good taste; I'm extremely fond of it for reasons that don't concern your enquiry. Mrs Parry likes to hint about her secrets. At a guess — I have no certain knowledge — I should say that Mrs Worth might see her as a threat and the gardener here, Wally Spratt, seems frightened of her. He thinks she's a witch.'

The sergeant, taking notes, sneered at his pen, but wrote it down. He turned his attention to Bird. 'What's the set-up here, then? It's your place. A proper little nest of criminals as far as I can see. And where's this person Greengrass you rang up about? We ought to be talking to her.'

However unwelcome a visitor at first, Connie had put heart into Bird, who said, 'I can't help your stupid suspicions. You'll have to wait like the rest of us until *Mrs* Greengrass returns from London, and if you propose to bully her I shall advise her not to talk to you at all.'

'Forgive him, Mrs Dawlish.' The inspector gave her the full benefit of his most charming smile. 'He's over-keen. His handcuffs are burning a hole in his pocket. What we need to know first of all is whether you've seen Wally Spratt today or have any idea of where he might be found. Mrs Greengrass may be a valuable witness. If you'd rather, we'll be happy to go now and come back and speak to her later.'

Lizzie's revelations that morning had made plain to Bird an uncomfortable truth. She was not told things. Her residents had schemes of their own and they protected her from unwelcome knowledge as diligently as she cared for their physical well-being. Heaven knew what perils they invited. 'Stay, please. You must ask permission of the residents before going into their private rooms, but look around the rest of the house and the grounds as much as you want; have supper with us. Harm enough has been done. I don't much care for the idea that Spratt is hanging around and we may all need protection.'

'You think he's our man, then?'

'I'm sure of it now,' said Bird. 'Supper at seven o'clock.'

He collected his sergeant, who seemed torn between a desire to stay and eagerness to look for clues, and said his thanks. Weary of hints and questions, Bird picked up the sherry bottle, raised her eyebrows at Connie, who nodded. They drank in companionable silence.

★ ★ ★

On the way to London there were frequent stops while the Over-Sixties piled out of the coach and queued for the lavatories. Irked, Lizzie, possessor of an iron bladder, said, 'They don't seem to feel that they've had a good day unless they've seen the inside of every toilet we come to.'

Miles Alban sank low in his seat. Time enough had not passed to let him forget that a public convenience had been the scene of his disgrace. He dreaded the occasion when he would have to use one. Unaware of the reason for his sudden nervousness, Bunty patted his hand. 'There's nothing to worry about. I'm sure you'll find your friends.' He smiled at her unusual animation. He was sure, too, knowing that even among crowds, Jeremy, who was shepherding a group from the hostel, would certainly not miss seeing him.

'We're a good mile from the Palace,' Tom said, as he parked. 'Anyone not up to walking that far?'

'We didn't come all this way to sit in the coach,' said Mrs Fred. 'Every trip we do there's a lot of traipsing around houses and gardens.'

There was no dissenting voice. 'Then stay together if you can, or make sure you know your way back. There's to be a television screen in the park and the service will be broadcast. We'll be leaving as soon as possible after they take the princess off to Althorp.' He watched Bunty fidgeting. Instead of her habitual shorts, she wore a grey and white dress that suited her, though she had not felt able to leave off her soft black boots. He hoped that she would not take it into her head to do her exercises on the royal grass. Lizzie took over. 'You come along with us, Bunty, when Tom's ready. We don't know London as well as you do, and I can use someone strong to lean on now and then; my hip's playing up a bit.'

'Isn't it lovely,' Bunty said; 'all the people. Lovely, lovely, lovely. Sad, but lovely. I wish she could know.'

'Better, perhaps, that she doesn't,' said Lizzie, firmly grasping her bony elbow as they set off through the slow-moving crowds. 'I'd be mad at missing things if it were me.' Unsmothered by fumes, the sea of flowers outside Buckingham Palace scented the air. Bunty clutched at Lizzie's arm and they waited.

A sound like a long rustling sigh came from the people as the coffin of the lost princess arrived at the gates of Buckingham Palace. Heads bowed. The royal ladies were helped into their carriages. The cortège set off. Diana's sons, with their father and uncle followed their dead young mother on foot. The sad day had begun.

★　★　★

Tom's passengers straggled back to their coach, having wept themselves into a state of calm satisfaction, though Mrs Fred craned her neck, watching Eric and Trace in deep conversation with Lizzie Greengrass. 'What's that boy up to?' she muttered to herself.

'Settle down, for heaven's sake,' said Denny. 'Do you imagine he's plotting to bomb the palace?'

'Of course not, you daft beggar. God knows what rubbish he's telling Lizzie. He don't know when to keep his mouth shut.'

'Giving away the secret recipe for Fred's sausage special, I expect, or that saucy night-club he's running in your back room.'

She was not amused. 'Get in here, Tracey, and the two of you sit in front of me,' she commanded, as Eric helped Lizzie into the coach.

'No, ta; we're going to sit at the back and have a talk about the funeral.'

'Do as you're told, will you! Who was it paid for your tickets?'

Tracey tossed her head. 'We're never goin' to hear the last of it, are we, Auntie? You got no business interfering with my Eric. Leave him alone and stop nagging.'

'Now then, Trace, that's well out of order,' said Eric. 'Give respect and take no notice; she's an old lady after all.' Mrs Fred's glare of displeasure deepened, until Bunty, finding her original place occupied, asked if she might sit beside her. The coach moved away. The Over-Sixties plunged into animated conversation.

'With luck we'll beat the traffic out of London,' said Tom. 'We'll be stopping at the M3 services. I hope you can all manage to hold out until then.'

An hour later, Lizzie extricated herself from the crush heading for the Ladies and pausing in the empty foyer decided to inspect the café food. She did not anticipate much of a treat. The tea, for which she yearned, would be awful and she doubted whether the restaurant had ever heard of a Chelsea bun. Through the open glass door she saw that the men were already in the queue. Denny's voice pierced the general chatter. 'That's a blueberry *cake*, dear. Why call it a muffin, when it's nothing of the sort? It may be American. I don't care if it comes from Outer Mongolia; you can't toast that and spread it with butter. Isn't there anything English? A round of bread, then; toasted. And strawberry jam.'

'Butter and jam by the till,' said a disembodied presence.

While Lizzie mulled over the relative merits of toast or cake, she felt someone tread on her heel and a groping hand. 'Don't make a noise, Grandma. Give us your handbag. I gotta knife.'

It occurred to her that she was being mugged, in public, in broad daylight, within yards of her friends. Seriously annoyed, she swung herself around. Her bag, well loaded with those extra things that she felt might be needed on a day out — manicure set, emergency ladder-stop for nylons, a small first-aid tin, refreshing face wipes and a box of assorted sweets — followed. It struck the youth a heavy blow just above a knee. He gasped and bent over. 'Was that what you wanted?' asked Lizzie.

'You've hurt me, you old cow. Me leg's gone numb.'

'Not as numb as the space where your brain ought to be.' Lizzie, who had in her day dealt firmly with gangs of bullet-headed trash intent on robbing her shop, felt deeply insulted by the pathetic inadequacy of her opponent. Before he could straighten up, she put a foot in his chest and pushed him over. He fell backwards, hitting his head on a stand advertising ice-cream sundaes. 'Tell your mother she wasted a day having you. She didn't do the world any favours either.'

'Too true,' said Eric, appearing with Trace like the United States cavalry. 'You all right, then? Not hurt? I'll duff the bugger up for you, if you like.'

'Thank you, Eric, but I don't think it will be necessary. I spy a security officer coming this way. Shall we go before we have to waste time making statements and signing forms?' Her assailant scrambled to his feet and ran. 'Now, come along, let me buy you both something to eat.'

'Where have you been?' asked Charlie. 'We've finished our tea.'

'You can just wait ten minutes while I have a cup and get Eric and Tracey some fish and chips to take away. No, Eric, don't bother explaining. Any Chelsea buns?'

'Only toast; stone cold and tough as boot soles,' said Denny.

'Then I'll save my appetite for supper.'

'They oughter look after you better,' muttered Eric. 'You can have some of the chips on the coach.'

'What did that peculiar boy mean about looking after you?' asked Charlie when the party moved off towards home.

'Nothing much; a would-be mugger who'd do better taking up art needlework.'

'How is it you always manage to find trouble, Lizzie?' His bald head wrinkled with anxiety. 'You worry me. I ought to keep you on a lead.'

'Don't even think of trying,' she said. 'Here, have a chip.'

* * *

After many fruitless telephone calls, Gus Early had been unable to find a hospital immediately willing to take in Mrs Worth. Nobody called him to ask for a home visit. His patients seemed determined to live out that particular day without his aid. He packed up Mrs Spratt's specimen ready for the post, threw out a sheaf of advertisements for new medicines and improbable electrical appliances, then put up his feet and fell asleep. Refreshed, he noticed that at Hannah's it would be teatime.

On his way to the lodge cottage, he called to check on Stella's condition. The door of her cottage was unlocked and the bed empty. Driving slowly, he looked for her on the High Street, but by that time she had drifted into the porch of the Community Centre where she sat on the floor, half-concealed by her hat and her empty bag, waiting until either the Duke's Head or the mini-market off-licence opened.

From the lodge, he phoned again to The Glebe. He was told that Mrs Worth was not there, but the police were, if he cared to speak to them. He didn't. She was a problem he would tackle again later. He could not force medical attention on the wretched woman, he was not her doctor, and the last thing she seemed to want was protection from herself.

At six o'clock, The Duke's Head and the mini-market opened their doors. Purged of their sorrow for the late princess, the women of Wynfred Abbas recalled the matter of their husband's supper and turned out to do their shopping. Neither Gus nor a cursory police search located Stella. She had retired with two bottles into the convenient cuts behind the High Street to quench her thirst. After a while, she passed out.

16

Bird heard the coach approach the turning into the village and went out on to the steps to welcome home the venturers. 'Police still here, I see,' said Tom, nodding towards the car parked in the drive. 'Any problems?'

'They're waiting to talk to Lizzie. How is everyone?' She hardly needed to ask. The weeping was over and, with all honour done to the dead, quiet contentment had settled on the mourners. Bunty, looking pink and astonished, extricated herself from the bosoms of the villagers, followed by genial farewells. Something — what? — had changed for her. 'Are you pleased that you went to London?' Bird asked.

'Oh yes,' said Bunty. 'No traffic, just flowers; a carpet of them to send the princess home. Lovely.'

Only Charlie Bean seemed less than happy. Turning to help Lizzie, he was forestalled by Eric and Trace, who handed her down with anxious care. 'Thank you for your help,' she said. 'You're quite sure you don't mind speaking up if they need you to give evidence?'

'No problem. I got no quarrel with the law.'

'What's the news of Rita?' she asked Bird.

'Still alive, though very ill. The police aren't allowing visitors yet.'

Eric grinned uncertainly. 'There you go, missus. Give us a buzz if you get grief from Wally. Respect to all!' The pair hopped back on the coach.

'That's a nice lad,' said Lizzie, making for the lift. 'Kind to old ladies. We had a good long talk in spite of Mrs Fred shoving her nose in. I must have a wash before supper.'

'Tom, you'll eat with us, won't you, when you've taken the Over Sixties down the hill?' As Hereward sat within earshot, Bird spoke quietly, aware that he would not have urged her into the arms of another man had he thought it a possibility. Ex-lovers had difficulty in believing in the death of desire. She contrived a smile of reassurance. Bunty sat down beside him and silently took his hand. They were joined by Miles, calm at last and full of his plans for the future.

★ ★ ★

Lizzie, refurbished and hungry, was intransigent in the face of police eagerness. 'Questions will have to wait. I want my supper and I want to talk over the day.' The sergeant was not pleased. He had thrown himself vigorously into a search of the grounds and outbuildings and found nothing. All the drugs in the pharmacy were accounted for. The bungalow lately occupied by the Worth hag had been scoured and, according to a nurse, made ready for redecoration. A patient, irritated by his questions, had advised him to shove off. And now an important witness refused to talk to him. The inspector ought to lean on her, but he was too soft. By the time that Lizzie had made a hearty meal, described the journey, given her opinion of the demeanour of the crowds and speculated about the effect of Earl Spencer's address on various members of the royal family, it was dark and raining heavily. 'He spoke up so sadly and affectionately about the way his sister was treated,' she said. 'It was just what the people were thinking and they let the world know it. Didn't give a hoot that it was royalty getting put down. There they were, tears running down their faces and clapping for all they were worth. Then you could hear them join in inside the abbey. I'm glad I was part of it.' The sergeant, interested in spite of himself, had just embarked on his third helping of apple pudding when Lizzie said unfairly, 'Now, do you want to hear what I've got to say, or are you going to sit there filling your face all night?'

The interview was bad-tempered. He recorded in his notebook her tale of Rita and the Spratt tomb and the plastic sacks in the shell grotto. 'Why didn't you tell someone about this before? Withholding information from the police is a serious matter.'

'Stuff and nonsense,' retorted Lizzie sharply. 'I don't have to tell you everything I do. If I'd known Wally was about to bash Rita's head in, I would have mentioned it, but I'm not psychic. Nor's she by the look of it.'

'That'll do, madam. Hours I've been searching this place and I was told that the grotto's kept locked at all times, being dangerous. How did you come to see inside it?'

Bird intervened. 'How did you, Lizzie? The key is in my office. Spratt borrowed it once; he'd been helping himself to flowers. I took it off him.'

Unintimidated by the police, yet Lizzie regretted having concealed her few scraps of knowledge from Bird, aware that Rita might have been protected from Wally had she spoken out. Miserably she said, 'There's another key. Spratt's got it. I ought to have said; I was going to, honestly, but you were busy and I wanted to wait until I knew what he was up to. I'm sorry!'

'I should just think you are, wasting valuable police time.' The sergeant had the bit between his teeth. Lizzie yanked it roughly out again.

'Mind your manners if you want to hear the rest. I wasn't apologizing to you. I'm an old lady, I don't have to talk to you at all if I don't want to. It's time I was in bed.' He glanced wearily at his superior, who merely smiled and continued to enjoy a last glass of port and one of Hereward's cigars.

'It's quite simple. One day Wally was locking up there and I got a glimpse over his shoulder. He didn't see me. The sacks were leaning against the wall just inside the door. They could have been filled with dung for all I knew, except that he didn't seem keen for anyone to get in there. He put the key in his pocket. When I passed the office, Mrs Dawlish's key was still on its hook.'

'All that tramping around: now I've got to start again. I suppose it's too much to hope there's a light in that grotto or that someone's got a good torch.'

'Don't be so daft. If you're thinking of drugs, there won't be anything there now, not after all the hoo-ha with Mrs Worth. Pity she got so pally with him,' said Lizzie. 'Rita thinks there's a hiding place in the family tomb. We were having a look at it, not realizing that Wally was hanging about in the bushes. We'd have been more careful if we'd known he was listening to us; at least, I would. With Rita there's no telling.'

The inspector took pity. 'Never mind it tonight, Sergeant. If the stuff's been moved there'll be traces. We can always get sniffer dogs in tomorrow.'

A resolute squaring of the shoulders rewarded him. 'Good idea, sir, and we can use them up at the churchyard too.'

'Hold on, lad. This isn't a case for Perry Mason, nor yet Miss Marple. Subtlety's wasted, as is undue effort. It's simply a matter of watching and waiting, that's all.'

Bird had noticed some constraint when Lizzie mentioned the palliness of Stella and Wally. Just how friendly had they been? Her view that these two were dangerous serpents in her Eden was reinforced. Tom Markham laid a large hand over hers. 'Now, my dear, leave the worrying to the police. Everyone's safely home and content.'

Hereward stood up abruptly and said a courteous goodnight. Connie Lovibond, correctly interpreting his feelings as a combination of helplessness and jealousy, shook her head as Bird made a move to follow him. 'He'll probably forget to take his pills again. It's been a long day. I might as well go up myself now and remind him,' she said.

★ ★ ★

Soon afterwards, Lizzie and Charlie Bean also went to their rooms. Charlie gave Lizzie an arm out of the lift, enjoying the comfort of her warm, plump body against his though he was irritable with himself on several counts. He had found the ceremonies unbearably moving. Dour common sense argued against getting caught up in the general hysteria, but the hushed mourners were not hysterical, they were uncommonly sane and temperate. He deplored still the implied rebuke to the Queen. Her loyalty to her family and to her country were bound to be paramount and not to be shaken by a girl who would not conform to the long-suffering pattern of her predecessors. Yet within that phalanx of disinterested love and sorrow, he could not remain entirely judgemental. Death had the last word.

He wished heartily that he had stayed at home. His sense of reason offended had increased when Lizzie invited an old gasbag to share her lunch. A poet and philosopher, so he claimed. While mopping up the chicken sandwiches he declared that they were present at a key moment, one of the occasional events that changes things forever. Never mind, he told her, that the change was small. Conscious memory would fail, but nerves and blood and bone were sensitized to the feelings of the unconsidered people. This seemed to impress Lizzie a great deal.

Charlie, wondering cynically how long it had taken him to work out his patter and find an audience, did not like her to be impressed by glib strangers. As if that weren't enough, she had encountered danger at the motorway services station and he had failed her. He wanted above all things the right to protect her. Not that she was at all an easy woman to protect, being more or less immune to good advice. He sighed. One large meteorite could, of course, wipe out this whole scene in an instant, and he half-hoped it would and put an end to his suffering. But the sky remained dark and empty and only the rain fell. Mapping the progress of cataclysms and human extinction had somehow lost its power as a charm against involvement. Some foreign emotion was distracting him. Thoroughly put out, he concluded that he loved Lizzie Greengrass. Worse, he would have to marry her if he were to live out his remaining years in contentment. How to ask? Suppose she refused? He dared not dwell too closely on those questions.

She did not take away her arm as they ambled towards their rooms. He said, 'You gave that young detective a hard time. It's not like you to be so aggressive.'

'He started it, trying to frighten me because I'm an old woman. How is he any better than the sewage that beats up pensioners for their few savings?'

'That's not fair, Lizzie, and you know it. We're all on the same side against Spratt, if he was the one who attacked Rita. Policemen have to ask questions.'

'There are ways of asking,' she said, a faint note of penitence in her voice; 'and I haven't shaken off the mood of the day yet. Why aren't they out there, looking for Wally Spratt? Life's too precarious to waste on footling about.'

'Aren't I always telling you that? We can't even count on tomorrow.' They were almost at her door and he had allowed himself to become exasperated instead of speaking of his feelings. He hesitated, then recalled something about Lizzie's statement to the police that had bothered him at the time. 'You didn't mention that business with Stella Worth. It might be a help for them to know about it.'

She stopped and withdrew her arm from his. 'And have them snigger and joke about her poor old sex-life? You don't seem to know the meaning of pity, Charlie Bean. If they're going to throw that sick, mad creature to the lions they'll do it without help from me; and if you say anything I'll never speak to you again.'

'But, Lizzie — '

'Don't but, Lizzie, me. I told you because I thought you were my friend. I wish I hadn't.'

'I *am* your friend,' Charlie said wildly. 'I love you. I want to look after you. How do you think I feel when you'll listen to any vain old fool who wants to impress you, but never to me?' The corridor was brightly lit. Blood flooded up into his face and over his balding head, spangling him with a light sweat. Lizzie, silenced, inspected her feet as though she had just grown them. At any minute she was going to start laughing, or say something that would crush him forever, and his words could not now be taken back.

Aeons passed. She spoke eventually, so quietly that he barely heard. 'Do you mean love, Charlie? Not just fondness or liking?'

'Dammit, I knew I was going to make a fool of myself. It's this blasted funeral again and all the ridiculous fuss. I didn't want to go and I wish I hadn't. Get to bed, Lizzie. Laugh at me as much as you like; you'll have forgotten about it by morning.'

From the hallway came the amiable rumbling of the inspector's voice and Bird's lighter farewell. The detectives were leaving. The front door opened, letting in the green scent of wet leaves, then closed. Bunty ran upstairs, singing 'Jesus Bids Us Shine', and disappeared into her room. A few moments later they heard Hereward rap on the wall with his walking-stick, then silence. 'Who's laughing?' said Lizzie. 'Don't try to wriggle out of it. You can say what you just said again tomorrow, properly.' She stretched to kiss him on the cheek. 'I don't know how I'd get on without you and I don't much mind whether your intentions are honourable or not. I only hope you have some. Goodnight, Charlie Bean. Sleep well.'

★ ★ ★

In her sitting-room, Bird kicked off her shoes and flopped down on the old sofa. It matched nothing else in the room. She had bought it secondhand for its comforting size and softness and had no intention of ever parting with it, though the springs creaked badly and the cover was hideous. Tom Markham also sat and took her feet in his lap. 'You're tired. Is there anything I can do before I go?'

'No, this is heaven. If you have any strong feelings about the royal family, please don't tell me. I can't face any more loose judgements.'

Too much had happened in a single week. Bird's initial amusement at her dubious beginnings as a Parstock bastard had given way to discomfort. It was all very well for Hereward. He had unburdened himself of guilt and transferred it to her, a favourite trick of men since Adam blamed Eve for giving him the forbidden fruit. Half-asleep, she considered the difficulty of becoming a convincing liar. The name and history of the lover invented by her mother for Hannah's benefit had slipped from memory and Bird felt half-inclined to tell her the truth, but not the whole truth. Her eyes closed. An array of social workers accused her of being unfit to look after decent people, being a deceiver and a notorious fallen woman. 'You must be punished,' Stella Worth said. 'Have some truth drug, dear.' Wally Spratt advanced on her with an enormous syringe when there was a knock on the door. 'That's for horses,' she said as she awoke.

Bunty eased her way into the room. 'Is it all right? I did say I would, but I began to wonder whether I ought to.'

'Can you explain a little bit? Perhaps between us we can decide.'

'The ladies on the coach asked me. Their instructor moved to Salisbury. Keep fit classes at the Community Centre. Once a week. They won't wear leotards, but don't mind shorts.'

'What a brilliant idea,' said Bird, looking at her fondly. 'You'll be a godsend to them.'

Bunty straightened. 'That's nice. I'll say yes then, shall I?'

Tom nodded gravely. 'It would be a pity not to, if you're up to it.'

'Up to simple exercise — no aerobics. Men can always decide, can't they, Bird? Bye bye for now then.'

He stood up and opened the door for her. Bunty, thought Bird, could not always have suffered from the extreme shyness that made her so solitary a figure. Sharing her photographs had served some need in her. Was it reasonable to hope that, with a new interest, the deliveries would stop? 'I ought to have done more for her instead of trusting to fate,' Bird said. 'Perhaps I really am a failure here.'

'You've done well and so has chance. If she hadn't gone on the coach trip, who would have thought of asking her? You think she'll be all right at her age?'

315

'Bunty's fitter than most of us and she has a load of unused energy. If this should shorten her life by a few weeks, and I don't believe it will, what does it matter as long as she's happy now?' She stifled a yawn. 'I think I'd better try to get some sleep before doing a last round.'

'Must you get up again? You deserve a private life, you know.'

'Stella Worth is missing. I don't think she'll come back here, she's probably looking for Spratt, but if the police can get any sense out of her over drugs, she has to be a danger to him. I shan't be able to rest properly until they've caught the wretched man.'

'There's a uniformed constable patrolling between the gates and the churchyard.'

'Not too hard for either of those two to dodge him. I'd rather not have more trouble here.'

Tom kissed her. 'Go to bed then. I'm not vain enough to think that you need me, but I'm staying the night in the conservatory, just in case.'

'Lovely!' Bird thought how pleasant it would be to wake and have a warm, reassuring presence beside her. Not to speak of needing to be loved.

★ ★ ★

Out in the wide world, as represented by Wynfred Abbas, the police guard on The Glebe gate was proving something of a nuisance to Wally Spratt, since he also blocked the way into the churchyard. In the ranks of criminals, Wally was playing well out of his league. Unfortunately for him, his stupidity far outmatched his cunning. All his earnings, legal and illegal, had been invested in the drugs venture, and his stock and most of his profits rested safely inside the table-tomb of his ancestors; which ones he neither knew nor cared. He wished ardently to retrieve his property without attracting attention. Had he been in any way an introspective man, he would now have been regretting the burst of fear and temper that had caused him to batter Rita Parry almost to death and waste good petrol in trying to burn the evidence. If he thought of her at all, it was only to curse her for buggering about around his family graves.

Wally was not built for stealth. Fortunately the rain had covered the scrapings, rustlings and heavy breathing as he climbed the railings at the side of the church and pushed his way through the bushes. Having drenched him it had now almost stopped. A sweet silence, broken only by the loud footfalls of the bored constable, enveloped the village.

Cautiously Wally tried moving the lid of the tomb a fraction. The squawk of stone on stone sounded like a strangling crow. At once the footsteps halted and torchlight swung across the ranked dead. He froze. After a while the watcher moved away. Wally swore under his breath. He pondered, and unable to come up with an alternative he climbed, while the clock struck midnight, on top of his treasure and stretched out to wait for dawn. For the second night running, Mrs Spratt slept alone. If she prayed, it was that this bliss might last forever.

★   ★   ★

Stella Worth, re-entering a blurred and unsteady world, struggled to her feet. Nothing about her was familiar. Her search for Wally Spratt and the comfort that he could bring had passed from her mind. Heading for home, she walked a long way. Alleys that she had not known existed kept opening out in front of her. In a place of one street and a hundred back entries she had managed to become thoroughly lost. Drenched and shivering, she groped her way across an abandoned timber-yard, collecting a splinter in a leg, and almost collided with a pick-up truck, property of Wally Spratt. It was without lights and the doors were unlocked. Stella climbed, weary and bleeding, into the front passenger seat and depositing her almost empty bottles with care, covered herself with a handy piece of plastic sheeting. She fell into exhausted unconsciousness.

At about this time, Rita Parry in her hospital bed, opened her eyes briefly. She shut them again before the policewoman noticed that she was awake. Rita's head and body pained her. Surreal images of flames and flight out of a Biblical Hell troubled her mind. She wrestled with her reluctant memory for a while, then gave up. Tomorrow was soon enough.

17

A quiet, grey Sunday morning, and as Connie poured her first cup of tea, Miles Alban knocked on her door. 'Will I be a fearful nuisance if I bring my tray in and chat for a few minutes?' Since his manner was calm and unexalted, there appeared to be no fear of soul-searching or epic poetry. She agreed. The room, as she glanced around, had a pleasant familiarity. It was scarcely believable that only a week had passed since she left Rye. More of drama and change had happened in that short time than she was accustomed to in months of sober routine. Connie, in what she had begun to regard as a previous incarnation as reclusive old maid, would much have preferred to find the strength of character to walk away from the untidy mess of Stella Worth and her connection with Wally Spratt. Yet change affected her also. No power for good or evil was going to tear her from The Glebe until all the outcomes had been resolved. It was asking too much of any woman. When Miles rattled in with his pot of herbal brew she was ready to listen.

'It's all settled,' he said. 'I arranged to meet some old friends in London. You remember Jeremy? I've always been particularly fond of dear Jeremy. He's involved in running an AIDS charity now and he wants me to do three sessions a week at their hospice for terminal cases. Basic stuff, feeding the weakest, helping them to bath and wash, just talking to them, that kind of thing. I'm nervous, Connie, but I feel that I must do it as a kind of recompense for all the wasted years thinking only of myself.'

Recalling Jeremy as a kindhearted man with an explosive sense of fun, Connie suspected that he had been half in love with Miles for a long time. And Miles needed a friend. Perhaps her deplorable meddling that had sent him soldierlike to fight his own small war would bring him more than a sense of purpose. She regarded him benignly. 'But of course you're nervous. Gentleness and compassion will see you through.'

'But I'm such a weakling, too easily scared, and terrified of infection.'

'So are we all, my dear; that's common sense. Princess Diana must often have been afraid, don't you think, yet she never hurt feelings by showing it. I have not been her greatest fan, I confess, but I admired her loving-kindness, which you share.'

That pleased him. He set out to entertain her with other subjects. Miles had an acute eye for detail and he had stored away his own impressions of the funeral, particularly the demeanours of important personages. These he described with no respect whatsoever. This one looked as though he were sucking a sour pickle and wondering what God thought He was about, bringing them all to such a pass; that one chronically constipated; the Queen herself stolidly enduring, as though she would have taken pleasure in giving all her tiresome offspring a clout round the head, whether they deserved it or not. 'One has to feel sorry for her, with her son and heir not exactly flavour of the month, but how much worse it would have been in any other country than England: screeching and keening and baying for blood, I suspect.' Eventually he said, 'The two boys were absolutely splendid. I hope that Earl Spencer will keep his word and not allow them to be turned into stuffed dummies. That world has passed.'

'I have to agree,' Connie said patiently, feeling disinclined for endless speculation on the fate of monarchs and princes. 'We should not give exaggerated adoration and respect to anyone, but we do. Moderation raises no false expectations. Prying into the lives of those youngsters for the entertainment of the moonstruck can only harm them, as it harmed their mother. Now, if you don't mind, I should like to dress. I shall just be in time for the eight o'clock service.'

She was not to escape so quickly. 'Will you mind if I join you? For absolute ages I used to pray to be straight and of course nothing changed, so I gave up on God. Jeremy hasn't. Church gives him a spiritual recharge when he feels that his work achieves too little to be worthwhile. It may do the same for me.'

'By all means come along,' said Connie. 'And Miles, if fortune offers you an opportunity for human love and fulfilment I trust that you won't reject it in favour of celibacy, which lays you open to sudden and unsuitable passions.'

He flushed. 'Ched, you mean? You know that I would never, never approach him in any way. I can't promise that I shan't think of him often. He will always be an ideal of beauty.'

Connie sighed, wondering how she had managed to become a counsellor in matters of love, when her one great passion had been for this fussy, self-absorbed man. She allowed herself to imagine having lured him into marriage. What hours of boredom she had escaped! And being as idiotic as most women over the once-loved, what hours of tedium she was now incurring. 'Precisely,' she said, a sharp snap in her tone. 'And he will always be an absolute misery to you until you make the best of what life has given you. Aspiring sainthood is a trial to others. I'm almost tempted to suggest that you pull yourself together.'

'How very sharp you are today. I'm sure you're right. You so often are, and I'm awfully fond of Jeremy, though he's rather plain.'

'None of us is perfect.' Connie slid her legs out of bed and stood up. 'Unless you want to witness the truly unlovely sight of me washing and dressing, scoot at once. Be ready in ten minutes if you're coming with me.' Miles actually laughed, and fled.

★   ★   ★

On Saturday evening, Hannah and Gus sat at either end of her sofa. She watched him lovingly, feeling nevertheless that there had been something deeply improper about her headlong rush into his arms. Hormones played hell with dignity. When Gus wondered aloud where the devil Stella Worth had got to and whether duty demanded that he should keep calling at her house all night, she knew that he didn't expect an answer. He would decide for himself. Irrationally distressed, angry and unnerved by Diana's fate, Hannah gnawed away at her own thoughts. Behind each of the princess's romances lay a hidden agenda of profit or power for the lurking, unspeakable pond-life of a capitalist society. Were it not for Joshua and Gus, she would happily march on London at the head of an army of like-minded women. To do what? She could change nothing. Who knew better that it was pitifully easy to make mistakes over love. Trusting too much brought betrayal and sometimes death, yet she trusted Gus, whether she should or not.

He yawned and stood up. 'Time we were both in bed. I'll have one more try at finding the tiresome Mrs Worth first, but I'll call for you at five to eight in the morning. We're going to church.' He had rejected the idea of a registry office wedding and was about to launch an assault on the vicar's reluctance to remarry a divorcee. It was not, perhaps, the best of moments to talk to Hannah of marriage.

'But I never go to church; I'm a Marxist Socialist; everyone knows that. It's embarrassing. They'll stare and gossip and I shan't know what to do. If you won't have a registry office, can't we wait until the banns are to be read.'

'No. That's like ignoring the neighbours all

year and then barging in on their Christmas party,' he said. 'You do keep Christmas, I hope, in spite of your political principles?'

'Of course I do. There's Joshua, and I quite like the decorations and the tree.' Her high forehead creased, giving her a slightly hangdog air. 'All my reasoning is wrong. I know in my heart that politics never helped anyone. I'm not even a party member.'

'Then stop havering, if you please. Tomorrow you can try the Established Church. It's restful, painless and a small sacrifice if you love me.'

'What about Josh?'

'He's a patient boy. Either bring him, or settle him with the children's programmes on television. He won't miss you for half an hour.'

'Suppose he — ?'

'He won't. Trust him a little.'

'I'm frightened. You're like a fairy-tale character,' she said, 'as good as you're beautiful. How can I possibly cope with that?'

Gus drew himself up to his full height, an unimposing five foot nine. 'You manage to make the words, good and beautiful, sound insulting. Does that mean that you don't want me after all? May I point out that the unseemly haste was entirely your idea?'

'Well, I didn't mean to do anything about it

since I rather got the impression that you disliked me. Most people do. I've always been impulsive and it sort of happened.'

'You're not the only one who's allowed to act on impulse. If you don't care for me, say so now.'

Wanting to marry him more than she had ever wanted anything before, she shifted her feet unhappily and glared at the carpet. What on earth had made her choose that pattern of manic sky-rockets? It was hideous. And why had she taken fright because of another woman's fate? We aren't alike in any way, the Princess and I, she thought; I am not an image of beauty and power; my death will never be convenient to the Establishment, curse them. Even now she was hedging her bets, in case this sudden blaze of joy should burn itself out and leave her desolate. She raised her head and looked at Gus, eye to eye. 'Another mistake would finish me. Those dreadful nights at the pub, the women sidelined with sweet martinis while the men talked football, the bored trapped looks if we interrupted. I couldn't bear to go through that again.'

'You certainly know how to puncture self-esteem,' he said. 'I thought I was quite a decent sort of chap. Not exciting, but reliable.' Flippancy did not quite hide the hurt in his voice. 'So which of us is going to tell the boy that you're too scared to marry me in case I talk about football?'

Put like that it sounded ridiculous. She smiled, though there were tears hovering behind her eyes. 'Nobody. I'm behaving like a fool again and I know it. That blasted funeral was too emotional and I kept thinking that the Fayed family would never have let Diana go, though it was an impossible alliance: she was too useful to them. Dying was her best way out. I ought not to have watched it, and I'm absolutely going to marry you if you'll have me.'

'Someone has to save you from being a social worker. Don't be late in the morning.'

'I wish you could stay.'

'So do I. Keep your doors locked. There's a policeman outside the gate, so they seem to be expecting more trouble.'

She kissed him. 'Goodnight, darling Gus. Do I have to wear a hat for church?'

'Please don't,' he said. 'Ladies in hats intimidate me.'

So at eight o'clock on Sunday morning, Hannah went to church. Joshua elected to go with her. 'There's ghosts in the churchyard. I told the policeman that I hear them when I'm in bed. He was very int'rested. I asked him if it's like Scooby Doo on television and the

328

ghosts are just men wearing masks. He said very probably.' She smoothed his obstinate hair and inspected his T-shirt for stains, vaguely wondering what in the world he was talking about.

*   *   *

Fate was treating Wally Spratt unkindly, ruining all his plans and wiping the complacent smirk from his face. Puzzling over the problems suddenly presented to him, he had spent the worst and longest night of his life, dozing on the tomb of his ancestors or trying to be comfortable among the roots of an ancient yew-tree. By dawn he was in spiteful mood. His bones ached with the cold and the damp and still he had not managed to retrieve his investment. Hollow rattlings from his empty stomach sounded like thunder in the quietness. He hobbled to a vantage point. Two policemen leaned on the church wall with their backs towards him. 'Inspector says we can pack up here in half an hour if it's still quiet,' said one.

'Where's he, then? Made himself snug, I bet, the crafty old sod.'

'Sorted himself a nice bed-and-breakfast outside this dozy hole. There's supposed to be a search going on today, so let's hope he'll give us a break and have a lie-in.'

'Then I vote we knock off now and see if that diner place is open. I'm wet, frozen and famished.'

They moved away at a smart pace. Wally's mind made some slow revolutions. A search? He had, he thought proudly, covered his tracks well and, as it was a weekend, he ought not to have been missed yet. Reassured, he decided that his only problem was to get himself, his stock and his money to a safe place under the noses of the police. The coast was clear for the moment, but for how long? The pick-up truck was still parked down by the old timber-yard and soon the whole village would be awake. How, then, to unite goods with transport? Planning had never been his strong point, but what he knew was that he did not care to be stopped by the police while in possession of illegal substances. He would have to risk walking down to fetch the truck.

He retrieved a crowbar from its hiding-place in the long grass. Once more he tried the lid of the tomb. It slid across the wet stone with little more than a couple of creaks. In a frenzy of haste he stuffed the package of money inside his jacket and buttoned it, then lifted out the plastic sacks and stowed them out of sight behind the yew. Blinds were still down in the church cottages. Wally passed by and slid into the first entry, trying to combine stealth with haste. Unusually there seemed to be people about, cluttering up the shortest route to the timber-yard. Beside the Duke's Head he heard movement and voices. The fuzz was still at it, sifting through the ashes, looking for clues, stupid buggers. He admired his own cleverness. They'd got nothing on him. An ancient atavism protected him from guilt. Rita Parry had been a witch and witch-burning was justified by the customs of his ancestors. He might have felt differently had he known that Rita was not dead. Pausing, he struck deeper into the maze of alleyways. And still he was not alone. Footsteps and voices rose from among the allotments and rubbish-dumps, forcing him into halts and retreats. The many detours wasted his energy. His feet hurt him and his corns began to twinge. By the time that he reached the timber-yard, his heart jumped and rattled like an old pump-engine and his fat face had the dull gloss of lard.

The summoning bell began to ring for early service. In ten minutes or so, he would have the High Street to himself. With a vision of the open road before his eyes and a quiet departure from the village when the fuss died down, he flung himself at the driver's door of the pick-up and wrenched it open. In the passenger seat, Stella Worth slept heavily, head fallen forward almost to her knees. Wally screeched with outrage. He limped around the truck, sustaining a nasty blow on the thigh from a sharp corner, dragged her out, still wrapped in his plastic sheeting, and threw her to the ground, helping her on her way with a punch that would have knocked her out had she not already been unconscious. She dropped head down on stones, groaned once, but did not wake. For good measure, he kicked her in the ribs with his steel-tipped working boots and threw the bottles at her before climbing into the cab.

It was then that he realized the extent of his own danger. Crazed as the woman was, she would pursue him and eventually she would talk. His money was in peril as well as his stock, and with their loss went his dream of Marbella among beautiful models and the very very rich. A wild idea of taking Stella out of the village with him and quietly finishing her off at some remote part of the Forest he dismissed reluctantly as too risky. At home, with the silent and incurious Mrs Spratt he could leave the money awhile. Just half an hour would be enough to pick up his drugs and slip away from Wynfred Abbas before the police caught up with him. Rolling the pick-up gently out of the yard and down the alleys to the High Street, he waited and looked. It was almost empty of people and traffic. A couple of women stood with their backs to him, gossiping outside the mini-market. The Duke's Head was still closed. Not a blue uniform to be seen. He accelerated across the road and backed into his own yard entrance and safety.

'What do you want?' asked Mrs Spratt, looking up from the *Sunday Mirror* and not as silent as he expected. 'Don't think you're going to leave any more stuff here, 'cos you ain't. The police are after you. They've already been here once, asking about petrol cans as though I didn't know you tried to kill old Mrs Parry.'

'What d'you mean, tried? She's dead, ain't she? They've got nothing on me, no witnesses.'

She smiled without pity. 'Trust you to mess up whatever you touch. The poor soul's bad and in hospital, but they say she'll get over it. How do you fancy twenty years inside?'

Mrs Spratt saw for herself what she had only read about in novels. As she described later to her friends, the colour drained from Wally's face, leaving it a dead white. 'If the rozzers come asking, I was here with you, get it? You stick to that and you'll be all right.

Open your mouth and I'll settle you, too. I'm leaving something here, but I'll be back for it and off again in no time.'

'Lie for you? You got a hope. Two nights you ain't come home and they were the best nights of my life. Stay away,' she added with benign lack of interest. 'Take that old crow in the fancy hats with you. Twice she came here, shouting through the letter-box, asking where you was. I didn't open the door.'

'She's nothing to do with me. She's mad. You do as I say or you'll be sorry.'

His threats were ineffectual. Mrs Spratt forgot dignity. 'Get stuffed, you mucky old pudden,' she said, and returned to reading the account of Princess Diana's funeral.

Wally began to lose heart. His day was far from over and he still had to run the gauntlet of the High Street to the churchyard and back before the service ended. At least he could save his money. 'Here, sit on this for a few minutes. If I don't get back at once, hide it somewhere safe.' She lifted her substantial rear and sat down again without pausing in her reading. Peering through the window, he saw a couple of cars go past, then the paper-boy labouring along on his bicycle. A group of men stood outside Fred's, talking and laughing. Half-an-hour passed. Wally waited and waited as panic rose chokingly in his throat. In the end they went inside. Now was his chance. Taking off once more, he ascended the High Street at speed, cursing the empty petrol cans clattering noisily under the tarpaulin. In spite of passersby, he dared not stop to secure them. Ten minutes and he would be away by the shore lane and heading for food and rest and a good long holiday. He had almost reached the church when an ambulance sped round the bend into the village, bell clanging, and almost ran into him. He gave a despairing moan. What now?

Morning service was ending and the verger opened the church door. At the evidence of new excitement somewhere in the village, the congregation erupted past the vicar's outstretched hand and stared after the ambulance. Desperate now, Wally pulled up and fell from his truck, leaving the engine running. Pushing past any unfortunate in his path, he snatched up his sacks and clasped them lovingly to his chest. Weak with fatigue and hunger, he leaned against the family tombstone and rested awhile to think. The noise of the ambulance subsided. Watched by the worshippers, he walked back to the road and threw his burden on to the seat from which he had evicted Stella Worth. Struggling a little, he turned around, and again rattled off. The small crowd hesitated briefly, then for no particular reason except dislike of Wally Spratt, they followed after him at a trot, picking up stones as they went.

★ ★ ★

One of the police constables, sitting at the window table in Fred's, was enjoying a quiet cigarette.

'We're off-duty in half an hour. We'd better give the inspector a bell.'

'No fear. He'll only find us something else to do. I'm not going to sweat while he lies in bed all day. Let's go while the going's good.'

The slur was unjustified. Not only had the inspector and his sergeant been up for hours, they had already found the unconscious Stella Worth. 'Cor, smell that booze,' said the sergeant to the inspector. 'Dead drunk, I reckon. Do we get her home or send for an ambulance.'

'She looks a bit bashed about to me. Better get the paramedics to have a look at her. If she croaks, we don't want any nasty little journalists shrieking about police brutality. Try to get the local doctor as well.'

The sergeant made some calls. 'Ambulance on its way, sir. Doctor's answering service says he's in church.'

'Go up and get him, lad, but if they're still

336

praying, ask nicely.'

'I hate churches,' the sergeant complained; 'they give me the creeps. *And* I hate Sundays.'

'Who cares what you hate? This is work; just get a move on. And keep an eye open for those two constables while you're at it.'

'No sign of the constables; I think they've sneaked off. But the doctor's on his way,' the sergeant said a few minutes later. 'He's with some haughty-looking bird and did she give me a look? His wife, I take it, poor bugger. And there's a kid.'

'That will be Mrs Dawlish's girl and her son. Getting divorced and engaged, she is.'

The sergeant became more aggrieved. 'How do you know these things anyway?'

'By looking and listening and not going off in all directions like a jumping jack as soon as you get near a crime.'

'What's a jumping jack when it's at home?' the sergeant asked maliciously.

The inspector smiled gently. 'Banned for some years, as you'll remember. Rip-raps, whizzbangs, those things you used to light and put through old ladies' letter-boxes, when you were a snotty-nosed brat. Ah, there's the ambulance and Dr Early too.'

Kneeling beside Stella, Gus examined her quickly. 'A nasty head injury, multiple abrasions and, from the bloodstains on her dress, I think you may find that someone's been kicking her,' he said, with content. 'She's not on my list, but I've been trying to persuade her to go into hospital for other problems. I certainly can't treat her here. Ask the hospital to ring me if they need any information about her.'

It was the sergeant, waving out the ambulance, who saw the white pick-up hurtle down the High Street and stop at the Spratt's front door. 'That's him, sir,' he shouted, 'Spratt and his blasted truck. And half this sodding village is behind, chucking stones at him.'

'Get up there and stop 'em, before they get under foot. The way those ladies are throwing, they'll be putting us in hospital and breaking half the windows in the parish.' The sergeant, making shooing movements as to a flock of sheep, did not hurry, though in pursuit of his quarry the inspector accelerated his dignified pace. In vain. Wally had seen the police cars. What he did not take into account was the animosity of the reconditioned Mrs Spratt. 'Get up,' he said. 'I want my stuff.' Obediently she elevated her backside and allowed him to retrieve the package then followed him to the doorway. Stones rained on him from the spectators. One hit him, but bounced harmlessly off his shoulder as he climbed into the driving-seat: the cricket-players were getting their eye in and finding their range. 'Don't forget to write,' called his wife derisively.

The inspector stood in front of the moving truck and raised a hand. He leapt for the pavement as Wally trod on the accelerator and shot past, missing him by inches. The watching villagers groaned, yelled and shook their fists. 'Come on in if you want, Inspector,' said Mrs Spratt, retrieving a large bundle of notes from the front of her apron. 'Have this. He's going to be dead disappointed when he finds he's got an old copy of the *People's Friend*. He never was much of a reader.'

'There's a good, clever girl. Do I smell baking?'

'We'd better get after him,' said the sergeant. Hot pursuit, siren blaring, blue lamp flashing between the forest trees, putting the wind up every crooked little pillock for miles. If he got out of the car smartish, he might even be the one to make the arrest and earn a well-deserved commendation.

'Cool down, lad. He won't get far. Put out a radio call and then come back here. The kettle's on and Mrs Spratt's been baking: force of habit to bake on a Sunday, she tells me, being on a diet herself. We have to help her out now she's lost her husband for a while.'

'There's nothing more to see,' the segeant yelled at the watching villagers. 'Drop those stones and clear off.' He was not going to be a hero, after all, only the lad, who wasn't allowed to do any real policing, just put up with a sly old bastard always making him look like a fool. The cooking was fine. Mrs Spratt certainly made a good cake; so did Mr Kipling. But where was the excitement and the challenge? To the depths of his police-man's being, the sergeant despised rural crime! No dogs, no stand-offs, no hijacks, no gangs, no dawn raids. If a wish could have wiped Wynfred Abbas from the map, the mini-mart, Fred's Diner, the Duke's Head, The Glebe, and all the tiny shops would have vanished into the ether. He sank his teeth into a piece of light lemon cake. Very nice. Mentally he began to compose a letter, pleading for a transfer.

18

To the disappointment of the stone-throwers, they were not able to witness the arrest of Wally Spratt, which happened almost by accident. Wally's not usually over-sensitive nerves were in a flux. Hampered in what was supposed to be a quiet withdrawal to bliss by the discordant music of the petrol cans, he stopped three miles from the village and began to toss them into a ditch. The approach of a motor-cycle did not penetrate his suffering consciousness. A large police rider, appearing at his shoulder and taking exception to his environmentally unfriendly activity, reduced him to a quivering, collapsed blancmange. ALL, said his overtaxed brain, IS KNOWN. He leaned his head against the yellow acreage of chest and began to sob. 'It's been a rotten sort of day,' he mourned. 'I gotta lie down; I gotta eat.'

The radio on the police bicycle began to squawk out a message. 'You just wait there a minute,' said the policeman, removing Wally from his bosom and resting him against the nearest tree. After a brief conversation, his eyebrows rose in astonishment. 'Well I be damned, proper little master criminal, aren't we? No wonder you need a lie down.' His captive showed no inclination for chat or flight, but to be on the safe side the rider found his handcuffs and secured Wally to the door-handle of the pick-up, then he settled down placidly to wait. A police van hee-hawing down the High Street, brought the villagers from their Sunday lunch to stare from their doorsteps and the inspector and his sergeant from a leisurely enjoyment of Mrs Spratt's cooking. 'They got the bugger then,' she said happily. 'I expect you'll be wanting to get along. Call in if you're this way again.' She thrust a bag containing a couple of steak pies and a tipsy cake into the inspector's hands and closed her front door behind them.

Wally, desperate with hunger and lack of sleep, went quietly. The only item on his person that puzzled the arresting officers was a sealed envelope containing a folded copy of the *People's Friend*. 'Fond of a nice love-story, are we, sir? Or is it the handicrafts?' He said nothing. This evidence of the perfidy of Mrs Spratt failed to move him; he simply wanted food as he had never wanted it before.

After so much excitement, Wynfred Abbas sighed and went back to sleep. The late flowering of Mrs Spratt provided a comfortably familiar source of conversation in the mini-market. 'They reckon Wally'll get ten years, if not life,' said the lady behind the till. 'And she's a new woman. On a diet under the doctor; low-fat yoghurt and raw vegetables. They give her wind cruel enough to crucify a donkey, but the doctor just says persevere.'

'*And* she wants to join the Keep Fit. Dulcie doesn't have the shorts to fit her, but she's getting them in.'

'Talking of doctor, seems he's courting Mrs Marsh,' a church-going customer put in. 'They were sitting together in church yesterday.'

'And her not divorced yet. Well I be damned. Our girls needn't get their hopes up, I suppose, though there's my Arlene, working her fingers to the bone for him, and pretty as a picture. Pure, too, if you see what I mean.'

'Oh ah?' The knot of women showed disbelief so plainly that the lady at the till reddened and added a penny here and there as she rang up their purchases, by way of punishment.

The residents of The Glebe, from the fit to

the infirm, were reluctant to accept that the sensations were over, discussing interminably what might come next. Only Lizzie Greengrass kept an uncustomary silence. For twenty-four hours she had managed to avoid being alone with Charlie, suspecting that he was equally determined to avoid her. As she inspected herself in the mirror on Monday morning, she took stock of herself: a strong, well-cushioned body and a face lined here and there, rather than wrinkled. Though greying now, her hair grew and curled vigorously. A mischievous light lurked in the dark eyes staring back at her. Nothing special there. She had not been loved by a man for a long time and her reactions needed to be sorted out. Consequently, Lizzie thought hard; about the liar and cheat she had married, the relief with which she had buried him, and her strong affection for Charlie. Without their alliance, life would lose its spice. His declaration of love had been made at an emotional time and by now he was probably regretting it. She would not prompt him. The risk that marriage might be the death of friendship was not worth the taking.

First she had to find and reassure him. He was hiding in the quiet room, an unfolded newspaper on his knee, gazing out of the window with the glum and hopeless air of a disappointed child. A rush of tenderness let her down badly. 'Now then, my dear,' she said, forgetting her resolve, 'where were we on Saturday night?'

'Oh lord, Lizzie, I'm sorry for bothering you. You must have thought I'd lost my senses.'

'Never mind. Do you love me, or don't you?'

'You're laughing at me. Forget I said anything.'

'That was supposed to be a winning smile,' said Lizzie with some irritation. 'Come on, Charlie, act on impulse for once and spit it out, there's a good man. I don't want you avoiding me for ever.'

'You can't possibly have any feelings for me. You're full of life and I'm a bore as you've told me often enough. I'm too old to change.'

She drew a deep breath. 'If ever I called you boring, which I deny, it was because you tried to stop me from making a fool of myself. You're the balance in our friendship, but how can we go on being friends with each of us frightened of upsetting the other?'

He closed his eyes, sighed and was silent for so long that she began to think he had dozed off. Abruptly he said, 'All right then, Lizzie, not only do I love you, but I'm *in* love with you like an idiot schoolboy. The thought of life without you is unbearable. I'm asking you to marry me. Now laugh to your heart's content and I'll never mention it again.'

Lizzie tried another smile, soft and mysterious this time to avoid confusion, and let him down gently. 'Thank you, Charlie. I seem to love you too, but are you sure that you're ready for marriage.'

'At my age I ought to be, for heaven's sake. And at yours, come to that. Just say no and I'll move out of here, if it's what you want.'

The return to irritability reassured her. This was the man she knew. 'Move out? I'd marry the devil before I'd let you. Don't look so shocked, that means yes, you fool.' Feeling that as an acceptance it lacked style, she added, 'You're supposed to kiss me at this stage, but don't if you'd rather not.'

He kissed her gingerly, blushing to the top of his bald head, then kissed her again with resolution, as an aspiring saint might set a foot on the road to martyrdom. 'Lizzie, you're a dreadful woman. You've never a good word to say for marriage. I expected you to refuse.'

'With your ideas of morality you wouldn't ask me to be anything but your wife, and I don't see myself as a chick, babe or live-in lover,' she said. 'You're a brave man, Charlie Bean.'

★ ★ ★

Absorbed in preparing her programme of health for the Over-Sixties, Bunty encountered a problem. Should she mention incontinence? On the coach journey to London she had noticed the agitation and the distressed expressions when the long queue for the Ladies moved too slowly. 'Hurry up in there,' they said, 'we're bursting.' Or, 'Haven't you finished yet? The coach'll be going in a minute.'

That week, in a magazine, Bunty had seen an article concerning the value of exercises to strengthen the pelvic floor. She read it again. At the League of Health and Beauty it had never been suggested that muscles in the front and back passages might require exercising, or even that such muscles existed. She tried to find her own and managed only to clench her buttocks (forbidden) or to pull in her stomach (also forbidden). The wretched things must be in there somewhere. A fascinating subject, yet two men had shown interest in the classes and if they had pelvic floors the muscles of their front passages must be even more mysterious than her own. Until she had learned to know her pupils better, she substituted a humdrum stretch-and-bend, twitching secretly as she tried to master the path to a healthy bladder.

She was absorbed and happy. The confidence that had somehow got lost in the aftermath of the war began to return to her and she was able to face memories that before had proved too painful: the strain, for instance, of nursing her parents through old age, and her sadness when they died within days of each other. By then Bunty had lost the habit of talking. Her friends had vanished and the music halls that she loved were virtually dead. The family home willed to her was over-big and expensive to keep up and she was now herself too old to be offered any but menial jobs.

She arrived at The Glebe by chance. On the day that she asked an estate agent to sell the house and began looking for a cheap room, Bird entered her life. In the close of Salisbury Cathedral, Bunty sat on a bench and shed tears over a cheese sandwich. People did not care that she was strong and athletic; all that they noticed was that she was old. 'You're very unhappy,' said the woman sitting beside her. 'Can I help?' The result was a small miracle. Driven into speech by desperation, Bunty poured her heart out, hoping that Bird might be able to offer her work. 'I'll do anything at all. I don't know how I'm going to live unless I can earn some money and I don't want to be put in a home.'

'There are homes and homes,' said Bird; 'I run one myself and I like to think that my residents are happy with me. You know, a large house in this area must be worth a small fortune. When it's sold you will be able to live anywhere you like.'

The passion for gracious living and desirable locations had not penetrated Bunty's seclusion. 'But it's quite run down.'

'All the better. Rich people love to renovate places and boast of their impeccable taste. But do consult your friends and get a solicitor to keep an eye on things.'

'I don't have any friends and I don't have anywhere to stay either.'

'You have me, now.' Bird smiled at her. 'If you can't find a place that you like, come to The Glebe for a while and stay with us.'

It was like meeting an angel, thought Bunty, and now I have my class. Her imagination began to range far from the community centre of Wynfred Abbas to team demonstrations throughout the county, London even — the Albert Hall. Lovely.

★   ★   ★

Miles no longer watched Ched in the garden. An eagerness to renounce his pleasant but dangerous idleness quarrelled with acute nervous tension as he prepared his anxious soul to re-enter a public place that rumbled with threats and alarms. He sorted through his things and packed a bag. Connie, his support, was taken up with the aftermath of the fire and with Rita Parry. He might well have thought of a cast-iron reason to go back on his word, except that each night his friend Jeremy telephoned and talked and made him laugh. Jeremy *accepted*, without complaint or campness. And he was a good man. He encouraged the weaker spirits, of whom Miles felt himself to be the weakest.

The manuscript of his novel lay on the desk. He read a page or two. Somehow he had lost the original inspiration, the pain and shame that had made him want to write the book: all that was reflected there was a dull lack of emotion and an attempt at self-justification. Jeremy opened his arms to embrace everyone, regardless of hurt to himself, creating a living drama of laughter and tears, pity and violence. Connie was right, without the stimulus of the world, the book could not be written. His mind at last made up, Miles opened a drawer, stuffed the mass of paper inside and locked it.

And what of his elegy? The outpouring of wounded love at the funeral, the tears and flowers, the anger of Earl Spencer, encouraged him to believe that one day his verses, revised and polished, would take their place beside Milton's *Lycidas*. Tenderly he folded the many sheets, put them in an envelope and stowed the charter of his immortality in a secure pocket of his suitcase. He thought that he might show his work to Jeremy.

★ ★ ★

While the lives of others buzzed into action, Hereward was isolated with his eternal question. Why? He read about the birth of planets and the beginning of life; but if no presiding power existed, gases and universes should not exist either. Space was as pointless as living and dying. So why anything? And why, at his time of life, had the damned subject come into his mind to torment him? No doubt others, philosopher types and egg-heads, applied their wits to imponderables, but they had never, as far as he knew, come up with a sensible answer to why. Nor could he. Science and religion had always bored him. It was inconceivable that if a god was at work he should waste time on setting puzzles for one entirely unimportant man.

Hereward brooded and drank too much

whisky. Where were all the damned women? Bird was forever chasing off after Rita Parry, or talking to policemen and solicitors and welfare workers, and never stayed with him for more than a minute or two. As for Connie, she seemed to have some bee in her bonnet about Winifred that made her uncomfortable company, with her dry, unemotional utterances. Even Bunty had stopped singing and posting photographs under his door. So weary was Hereward of the insistent, inaudible questioning that he would almost have welcomed one of Stella's mad visits. There was a weird creature, fixed on unattainable goals. At least, he thought, uncomfortably surprised, she had loved him in her fashion. Well, it was no use thinking along those lines. *He* was not to blame for her disintegration.

★   ★   ★

Relieved of the twin burdens of Wally and Stella, Bird sparked with energy. A joyousness in living brightened her eyes and gave a new vigour to her body. A week, she thought, so much has happened in a week; everything has changed. A coincidence, surely, that one tragic death had awakened the sleepers and released a flood of feelings?

There were things to be done. She drove to the hospital, hoping to see Rita Parry, who was mending, though slowly, but would not be well enough for visitors for another week. As an afterthought she enquired about Stella. 'Not a happy girl,' said the duty nurse. 'She won't talk to us, or eat properly, or do anything we ask. See her for a few minutes, if you like. The police have gone.'

'You'll soon be well,' Bird told Stella with professional cheerfulness in the face of an inimical stare. 'If you can keep off alcohol for a while your mind will clear wonderfully.'

Stella's contempt was plain. 'Boring, stupid cow,' she muttered wearily; 'I'd rather be dead.'

'But why?' There was a long pause. Bird thought that she was not to have an answer and turned away.

To her departing back, Stella said, 'You don't understand what love is. It isn't gentle and sweet, it's a torment. For thirty years I've loved Hereward and it's driven me to madness. I've done such things — anything to get him. But I'm not clever, behaving like that pathetic Diana child, imagining I could make him jealous with other men. Oh, I blew it completely.' She choked and began to cough, turning her face to the pillow. Her straggle of particoloured hair flattened like an alien weed to reveal the pink scalp beneath. A surge of pity for Stella's unloved old age reminded Bird of her own part in this ruin.

'I'll call a nurse.' Her voice was cold and defensive.

Stella struggled to speak. 'No you won't. It's useless anyway. There's no escape in drink any more. I just finish up alone, stone cold sober and longing for oblivion. And I can't die; I *cannot* die. Satisfied now?'

Bird walked back and touched her hand. 'About what? Truly, Stella, if I could unmake the past, I would. They'll look after you here and treat your depression. You'll feel entirely different.'

'Get off me. I don't want any of your bloody compassion. Save it for your freaks. For God's sake go away!' She wrenched the bed-clothes savagely over her head.

It was too late to be sorry. Stella could be given nothing; not comfort, nor help, nor even pity. Hereward, carelessly scattering his damned charm, had always wanted women to want him. Then, thought Bird, we become a nuisance and he denies our very existence, trying to pretend that we have never been, until he needs something from us. Outside the hospital, she wondered at her own resentment. The sting of the past had been drawn; she no longer loved Hereward or the memory of the man he had been. But Stella did. And, mad or not, every word she spoke, every action, drove him further from her. The rocket of joy that had lit Bird's sky sparked and fizzled out, bringing her back to earth, dull as a dead stick.

Ten days after her rout by Stella, Bird visited Madam Dulcie's to inspect the lady's modes and quality West End fashions. Wally's fireraising had been thorough. Rita's entire wardrobe consisted of a nightdress, a torn purple cardigan, a pair of directoire knickers in poor repair and an old raincoat, singed and bloodstained. Connie went with her. 'Wynfred Abbas is in grave danger of becoming exciting,' she said. 'Shopping will be suitably restful, and I should very much like a private word with Rita.' Between them they chose thermal underwear, a dress, a skirt, jumpers and a warm anorak. They then drove on to the hospital.

'She looks like something from outer space, poor old soul, but she's doing well,' the nurse said. 'Go in and see her.'

Rita slept a fierce sleep of mutterings and clenched fists. A large white dressing, perched on her shaven head, gave her the air of an elderly punk bride. After a while she woke. One purple, yellow and red eye opened. 'Where was you when I needed you?' she asked, mildly petulant. 'I warned you about that Spratt, didn't I? Pity you can't take a hint.'

'Your warnings are too cryptic by half for those of us who aren't favoured with visions and second-sight,' Connie said. 'Bird has bought you some new clothes. Everything was burned, including most of your hair.'

'It'll grow again or it won't. Show us what you've brought. I'm going to freeze without my woollies and mac.'

Bird produced their bags and parcels. 'Not when you're living in a nice bungalow with central heating. We haven't got stockings yet, in case you prefer tights or long socks.'

'I'm in then? No more dossing; I'll miss it in a way,' said Rita, turning over her new possessions, generally approving. 'Tights'll be best, and I'll tell you what I would like if you can stretch to it, a pair of blue jeans. I need pockets for me things.' Her colourful eyelids began to droop. 'Central heating, that'll be a novelty. I'm a bit tired. Come again when they let me up and we'll have a try-on.'

'Right. Next time we may be able to bring you home.' To Connie she said, 'I suppose I'd better make sure that Stella needs nothing while I'm here. I shan't go in. I only make her worse.'

'I've a question for Rita. You go on; I'll

follow in a moment.' Connie drew a chair close to the bed and asked her question.

Rita did not open her eyes. 'I knew you were going to ask me that. Fair enough.' A nurse pattered into the room and sat down at her desk and the answer that Connie wanted came in a whisper.

'Rat-bane?' she repeated.

'Hush, keep your voice down. Yes, rat-bane. I saw her pick up the tin and put it in her handbag.'

'Thank you. That helps me enormously. Get well quickly; Bird is anxious to have you home.' But now Rita really was asleep.

★ ★ ★

Bird had arrived too late at Stella's room, walking into a commotion of angry nurses and housemen. Weary of healthy living, weary of life, Stella had filched some clothes and a starched white coat and gone without notice in search of her preferred oblivion. 'She can't have got far without proper shoes. I only turned my back for a minute,' said the duty nurse. 'You'd have thought we were trying to kill her instead of saving her life. And the patient whose clothes she pinched is playing hell with us.'

A junior doctor shook his head. 'She's ill,

badly depressed and one of her wounds is still open, yet for her age, her strength seems to be phenomenal. It's a wonder she's survived this far. A thoroughly abused constitution, but she resented our care and if she isn't found we'll get the blame. We'd better have them search the grounds.' He spoke to Connie. 'Are you a relation?'

'Hardly. I doubt whether she has any. My only interest in her is that she was once involved with my own family in rather odd circumstances that I should like explained. I take it that she's sober and rational?'

'Sober, yes. Rational? Hard to tell. Either she has no memory of how she came by her injuries or she's not saying. If you see her, will you let us know, please?'

There was, however, no sign of Stella on the road to Wynfred Abbas. For Bird, any left-over optimism that the intervention of doctors and hospitals would relieve her of a sense of responsibility for her unwanted guest now vanished. Connie noticed a dimming of her vitality and said, 'Don't for heaven's sake let this worry you again. She's probably hiding in the hospital grounds or making for the nearest pub. They're bound to find her quite quickly.'

'I think not. A week ago I talked to her. Conscious, she can't bear herself or the world, and she would rather be dead than well. She has no idea that Wally Spratt's in prison either. She'll be searching for his brand of nirvana, and the first place she'll try is The Glebe.'

'What harm can she do now? If you're right, she'll simply leave and look elsewhere.'

Bird, remembering the bitter chill of Stella's desperation, was not comforted. Hereward, still the focus of her frustrated love, had a heart that shocked once too often, would stop forever. She jammed her foot on the accelerator, wishing to be home and in charge, until Connie said mildly, 'Ease up, my dear, if you please, or let me drive. These lanes are lethal.' After a moment she added, 'I count you a friend and I absolutely forbid you to waste love on Stella Worth. She is not and never has been your problem. If she can, she will damage you and all of us in pursuit of a chimera, a sick obsession. Should she turn up at The Glebe, *I* will deal with her.' Bird smiled, but did not answer.

★　★　★

Stella drifted aimlessly for a while through unfamiliar streets, half-stunned by draughts of air and the vastness of the sky. A shifting, dancing dizziness in her head gave her a lightness, as though she floated above the pavements like paper blown in the dust. All the roads led downhill from the hospital. She walked for a long time and in the calm September afternoon she came by chance to the coastal path above the sea. The bright horizon beckoned to her. She remembered, or perhaps imagined, that once, in summer seaside shows, she had been Stella Maris, star of the sea, dancing on skis, jumping through flaming hoops, leaping high to catch trapezes. A tireless swimmer, yet however far she swam, the brightness still lay ahead of her. On land she was doomed to live forever. One day, when she could no longer endure herself, she would give herself up to the water and strike out for the distant light, never returning. But not yet. In her sober, unclear mind was one purpose, to reach the shell grotto where she could find blissful forgetfulness, where the years went backwards and she had the power to command men.

The stolen clothes were too big for her and heavy. Stones tore at her slippers and cut her feet. But as she walked she forgot the tired aching of her body and remembered Hereward when he had loved her. The day began to die. Stella went on until the horizon had faded to a ghostly blue line on a black sea. For a while she dozed on a bench by the path. As the sky lightened to grey, she moved on, her slippers filling with fresh blood, recognizing nothing around her except for the waves receding, then advancing to break in white splendour along the shore.

Aimless as she was, yet instinct led her on. Where the path began to turn inland she saw below her rocks and a tiny beach, and ahead the slumbering High Street of Wynfred Abbas. The doors of Fred's Diner and the mini-market were still closed. The village men slept beside their wives or someone else's. Alone in the matrimonial bed, Mrs Spratt luxuriated in its space, slumbering sweetly. Nobody saw Stella, who was too weary to spare the houses a glance. Leaving a thin trail of scarlet from her lacerated feet, she trudged up the hill to the door of her cottage. She was home.

19

Stella tried the front door of her cottage and found that in her absence someone had locked it and drawn the curtains over the windows. She cursed under her breath. Frustrated tears filled her eyes, but she blinked them away. Sagging towards the doorstep, she drew from the depths of her exhaustion a last obstinate effort, and crawled under the bushes at the side of the house to the back door. It opened reluctantly and let her in. The narrow staircase reared up like a mountain into the gloom above. Briefly she rested, then began her climb, pulling herself from stair to stair with her sinewy arms. On the landing, she tripped over an open trunk that spilled evening dresses and coats, and opened another cut below her knee. The bed had been stripped and the dirty sheets and blankets piled in a corner. She was too weary to care. Resurrecting a mink coat from the trunk, Stella rolled on to the bare, stained mattress and slept for eighteen hours.

She awoke shivering and ill, wondering where she was. No light showed at the edge of the curtains and she noticed that the clock had stopped. It might have been any time, any place. Wincing from the soreness of the open blisters on her feet, she stood up and searched for the stimulating warmth of scotch, gin, rum, anything at all. The cupboards and every hiding-place had been emptied of food and drink. Driven by need, she drank water thirstily. After a while, she realized that for a reason she could not immediately fathom, she was dressed in strange clothes and wearing a cotton overall. A memory emerged from the clouds in her head. There had been a white pick-up truck and a man screaming at her, and after that, nothing that made sense until she woke to find a policewoman sitting beside the bed. How she came to be in a hospital baffled Stella. She took instant exception to being bothered with questions, disliking the woman's broad, solid body and square jaw.

'Can you tell me who hurt you?' she had asked in a tone that tried to be gentle but failed.

'Sod off, dear.' Stella felt her sore ribs experimentally, and winced. 'I'm not into lesbians.' The same question was asked again on several occasions, though not by the policewoman, who had taken umbrage. 'You tell me,' she had said. 'How many times do I have to say that I don't remember a damned thing about it.'

Then came a muddle of impressions — doctors, nurses, injections, voices, questions — and a descent into emptiness and near-despair. As if that weren't enough, Bird Dawlish had come to crow over her, looking beautiful and spilling over with unwanted loving-kindness. Damned hypocrisy, bringing back the past, *her* past, that she did not want to remember and could not forget. Stella noticed that she was shaking. She forced her reluctant muscles to move until the shuddering and twitching began to subside. She could not afford weakness. Unless she found Wally Spratt quickly, she would remain forever aware, reliving each day the miserable, the shameful mistakes of a lifetime.

While her description was being circulated seventeen miles away, Stella shrugged off the stolen clothes, kicked them under the bed, and put on the first dress that came to hand, a blue and yellow affair with wide stiffened underskirts. In its day, it had been her favourite, giving her a vivacious beauty, emphasizing her small waist, turning heads. For the briefest moment, she saw herself tapping along London streets in high heels, dark hair bouncing on her shoulders, collecting the stares of passing men and smiling. How long ago? What did it matter? The dress was lucky then. Her swollen feet could not be forced into shoes. Using her strong teeth, she ripped strips from one of the soiled sheets and bandaged them before trying her black trainers. The pain eased a little. Now for Wally. Stella shrank from knocking at his door and facing in her weariness the monumental hostility of Mrs Spratt. In daylight he never moved far from his supplies. The most likely place to find him then was the shell grotto, yet there was a reason, if she could only grasp it, why she ought not to go to The Glebe. A bright window opened on the confusion in her mind. She drank more water and the last of the fog cleared. The hospital: she had walked away from confinement and for all she knew they could force her to go back again, if they could find her.

The peephole from the grotto to the cliffs and the sea offered a bare hope. One good push would dislodge the grille, but the cave lay under a rock overhang and the path above it was crumbling. In her circus days she had managed such tricks, dropping from a high wire on to a tiny platform and catching a trapeze moving away from her. But without a steadying drink, she was uncertain of her strength and nerve. To fall was easy. Yet did it much matter to her if she fell? Below, the sea held out its promise like the arms of a lover, beautiful, cruel, all-embracing. No, it would not matter. Outside it was night without the promise of dawn. Stella sat motionless in the dark, wishing for some miracle to warm her blood. At first light she set out.

★   ★   ★

The village slept soundly. Denny slipped out of Dulcie's bedroom and into his own above the shop: her husband emerged from the embraces of Arlene and into the High Street. As Stella, unnoticed, was beginning the steep climb down to the floor of the chine and up again to the cliffs, Bird awoke thinking about her. She sat bolt upright, every nerve taut. For a minute or two the sense of a haunting was alarmingly strong, driving her to the window to look out into the moonless dark. The trees rocked and swayed in a strong breeze, bringing down a shower of dead leaves. Summer was over. The thought of a sick woman out there in the night made her unreasonably anxious. Within The Glebe all was well. The alliance of Lizzie and Charlie heralded a wedding. Her flock was thriving and convalescents were going home. Even her ninety-nine-year-old had become more animated with the prospect of his hundreth birthday party next week, complete with Press photographer and television cameras. And soon, when the police decided that they had finished with it, the shell grotto would vanish forever. Contractors had been hired to flatten and fill it, and Ched would seed the earth with grass, returning it to the green cliff. True, a general alert was on for Stella, who might be wandering anywhere. Yet, all in all, problems were vanishing fast. Bird faced the day hopefully.

Hannah telephoned during the morning to tell her that the divorce was expected to go through without a hitch. 'We thought of a Christmas wedding and a honeymoon later, as there's Joshua to consider. How do you feel about it?'

'Happy, and I agree that you can't leave Josh at Christmas.'

'We couldn't take him with us, I suppose?'

'On your honeymoon? Certainly not,' said Bird. 'That may be your one chance to be alone with Gus for years. Don't waste it.'

Hannah accepted this meekly. 'No, I won't. I do love him, you know. Properly. I expect you're busy, Mother, but would you, could you, come with me to find a dress? Gus insists on church and fuss. He's talked the vicar round, but white isn't appropriate and I haven't an idea what to wear.'

Of the many past losses, thought Bird, one, my daughter, is being restored to me and I must try to keep my excitement to myself. 'Of course,' she said. 'Let me know the day and we'll shop until we're worn out. Thank you for asking me.'

'There isn't anyone else to ask,' said Hannah, reverting momentarily to her tactless self. 'Oh dear, I only meant that I couldn't ask anyone, except my own mother. You've put up with a lot from me. It's my turn to thank you, and I do.' She hung up quickly.

The next call came from the hospital to ask whether Stella had been seen in Wynfred Abbas. 'Not so far,' said Bird. 'Do you want me to get someone, the doctor perhaps, to call at her cottage?'

'Your local policeman checked there an hour ago and found nothing helpful. She may have collapsed somewhere out of sight. Spotter planes are the best bet. Let us know if anything crops up, won't you?'

The gladness of the morning dimmed a little. Bird did not love Stella as Connie feared, but she felt that a sad and damaged old woman had not deserved to encounter the corruption of the baneful Wally. A vision of a Stella, picked up, dusted, washed, nourished, and gliding peacefully into her last decline, appeared, and vanished immediately into the land of impossible things. Untroubled by conscience, Stella would do whatever was expedient, with no regard to right or wrong. She would pursue her demon to the death, but whose? Bird determined that it would not be Hereward's.

★　★　★

Crossing the thickly wooded rift that lay between the village and The Glebe brought Stella once again to the point of collapse. There was no path. Between the elder and sapling oaks, shrubs and bushes grew unchecked. Brambles tore at her pretty dress and long swathes of bindweed snared her ankles. On hands and knees, clinging to tree roots, she made the ascent on the far side, and lay prostrate on the grass, glaring at the sky. Although the sun was up, damp penetrated her scant clothes; the open wound on the side of her head stung mercilessly. She had forgotten the nature of her errand, thinking instead of Hereward. He was not far away. He *must* love her now, seeing how much she had suffered to reach him. For a while she dozed. The team of a police spotter plane noticed her and thought that she might be dead. Although the heap of blue and yellow did not fit the official description, the observer radioed back the news of a possible sighting and the plane circled, watching her movements.

Waking, Stella, possessed now of a terrifying clarity of mind, recalled each detail of the hospital and that she had stolen clothes. She had become a fugitive thief, an outcast. Why waste time thinking of Hereward? However intensely he had desired her when she was young and beautiful and alive, he had not truly loved her, and now that they were both old, he never would. The grief that she had never managed to subdue was acute. But Spratt had the means to dull it and to keep her in a state of well-being for the rest of her days.

The next part of her journey was easier. Sea-birds, rising on the strong thermals, kept her company. Following the curves of the cliff-top, she came to the dolmen where Bird liked to sit, and the concealed gate into The Glebe garden. She was thirsty. Through the tangle of clematis vines she could see the seat where she had drunk her gin and watched and waited and slept. Even tonic water would be welcome. There was no sign of Wally, but people walked the path. One of them was Hereward, in a wheelchair pushed by a girl. Stella dared not go in, but wandered the last few yards until she stood above the grotto. A couple of steps below her lay the platform of rock beyond the cave, though it gave her little room to land if she judged badly. The face of the rock was smoothed by weather. Two slight projections might serve as fingerholds, but success or failure belonged to chance. A long way below her, the incoming tide frothed over sand and stones, driven by a dangerously strengthening wind that lifted the gliding terns and gulls high into the air. It must be now. Before fear could get to her, Stella half slid, half-dropped. Her heels were over the edge, but the trainers gave her a toe-hold while she threw herself forward into the cave and against the grille. The rusted metal broke free under her weight, dislodging earth and cement. She clambered through the ragged hole.

The darkness confused her. She groped along the wall, identifying the statue by its scabrous white patches, and there she leaned, assimilating the fact that Wally Spratt was not in the grotto. Somewhere by the door he stowed his boxes and plastic sacks. Covering every inch, Stella searched. One tiny packet was all she needed, just one, to cure the horror inside her head, and a few to hide away for whatever was to come. And after all her effort there was nothing. Then came the knowledge that she was trapped in a dank hole from which there was no escaping. Her resolution had ebbed. She could never climb the overhang and get back by the way that she had come. Hammering furiously at the door, she began to cry, open-mouthed like a disappointed baby. Great bellowing sobs rolled around the roof. She made so much noise, that she did not hear the agitated voices in the garden. Sinking down on to the floor, Stella wept on, cursing Wally, cursing Hereward, cursing Winifred Parstock and Bird Dawlish, and hating the force that kept her alive when she would much prefer to be dead.

★   ★   ★

'How can there be anyone in the grotto?' asked Bird. 'It's been locked up since the police were here, and they have Wally's duplicate key.'

'Just the same, there's a dreadful howling and hammering going on,' said Lizzie Greengrass. 'You'd have to be stone deaf to miss it.'

Hereward's young nurse, almost running

with the wheelchair, looked scared. 'Perhaps it's a ghost. I can't stay here if there's ghosts.'

'Idiot girl, of course it's not a ghost,' said Hereward crossly. 'Kindly don't bounce me around in that fashion, and if any of your tedious connections have seen ghosts, oblige me by keeping the details to yourself.'

'Would you like to go to your room now?'

'No, I would not. It's my exercise time. That grotto is infested with criminals and I want to know who's in there this time.'

Connie smiled at her. 'All right, Nurse. You can't do anything with him in this mood. It's probably nothing more threatening than a seabird. We shall find out.'

With an authoritative look, Lizzie collected Charlie Bean. 'We're coming with you.'

'Shall I fetch my revolver?' asked Hereward, shocking Bird. He had kept the existence of this weapon a close secret. She suspected that he intended to use it on himself if death heralded its approach with a long-drawn out agony. She resolved to find and remove it that day, when the intruder had been evicted.

As she fitted her key into the lock, she heard muffled maledictions followed by a faint scuttling sound. The door creaked inwards, letting in light. A dishevelled scarecrow in an umbrella of blue and yellow skirts peered from behind the statue. A voice moaned, 'Wally, is that you?'

'Good God,' Hereward said, peering over Bird's shoulder, 'I think it's Stella. Come out here at once, you tiresome woman.'

She backed further away, towards the hole in the cliff. 'I'm not going anywhere until you fetch Wally Spratt.'

'Stella, this is Bird. I need to talk to you, tell you about Wally. Do you mind if we come in? And do, please, take care; there's a sheer drop behind you.' Cautiously she moved a foot or two into the grotto.

'I can't imagine how you got here, but I dare say that you would like a drink,' said Connie, close behind, with Lizzie at her heels. 'Stay there, Hereward.'

'Why should I? I'm entitled to know what this is all about.' He put Bird aside and limped forward, holding out a hand. 'Come along. We can talk outside.'

Stella, who now had one foot in the grotto and the other in the cave, stopped. She forestalled his effort to lead her out by taking his wrist in a steely grip. Her voice was small and husky with weeping, but she made sure that he heard. 'You, entitled? Try not to be the complete prat, Hereward. She's right. I'm in a hell of sobriety, and at this moment I would gladly die or kill for a drink. Now, what's this about Wally?'

Bird told her, watching the grey face sag and shrivel with the retreat of hope. 'So you see,' Hereward said, 'you might as well get out of here. The police are searching for you. I'm sure Bird will give you gin, a bottle of it if you want, before you go back to hospital.'

Stella was too exhausted for full rage. 'Look at you,' she whispered; 'dried out like a stuffed monkey. You're too stupid to see that the only woman you were able to love properly was Winifred, who needed nothing and demanded nothing.'

'That reminds me,' said Connie, 'you poisoned my sister, did you not, with rat-bane that you found in the shed at Swan House?'

'Clever Connie, so I did. I don't suppose I meant to, or perhaps I did. I forget.'

'Why Winifred? She meant you no harm.'

'Why?' she echoed vaguely, shaking Hereward's arm until he winced with pain. 'I wanted to hurt *him*, one way or another. I don't think I expected it to kill; I didn't even know what was in it. But I suppose I had some mad hope that I could frighten him into turning to me.'

'Mad hope, indeed,' said Connie. 'White arsenic, that's what was in it. But do go on.'

'He talked Winifred into postponing the divorce indefinitely, and before that bloody

Nest turned up he had promised to marry me.'

'Bird, not Nest,' Hereward said. 'You murdered my wife? For nothing.'

A shred of past emotion seemed to revive in Stella's heart. 'It needn't be for nothing. I'll make it up to you; it's not too late. Come with me now, Hereward. We'll go abroad and I'll look after you for the rest of your life.'

The rescuers were stunned into silence. Eventually Connie found her voice. 'No remorse, then? What a dangerously stupid woman you are, Stella, dangerous enough to be locked up where you can do no more harm.'

She seemed scarcely to hear. 'Hereward?'

The disgust and loathing in his face should have answered for him. 'No, never. Let go of me, don't touch me. Please, somebody take her away before she kills me too.' He stumbled and sagged to his knees.

Still clinging to his arm, Stella, stood upright, contemptuous and suddenly beautiful in the dim light. The sea began to shake the cliff. A draught blew her torn dress into a coloured cloud around her. 'What is the point of it all?' she asked loudly. The words rang and echoed from the grotto walls. Deliberately, she stepped backwards from the ledge into empty space, dragging Hereward with her until the dead weight pulled him away. It was not quite her last appearance. The wind billowed out her full skirts and lifted her for an instant. She bobbed up, straight and blank of expression, staring without fear or kindness at those she was leaving behind. Then she seemed to float away like a grotesque pantomime fairy. Hereward lay inert and face down over the cliff edge as though he considered diving after her.

'I can't make out what's going on, or whether she's the woman we're after,' said the pilot of the spotter plane. 'She seems to be throwing her clothes away and there's a man trapped on a ledge. A helicopter can't get in past that overhang. Better radio the coast-guard.'

* * *

The onlookers in the grotto stood in shocked inertia until Lizzie Greengrass, to her shame, rushed back into the garden and was sick in a bush. 'It wasn't my intention to bring about a public execution,' Connie said, putting a hand on the dank wall for support and immediately removing it. She wiped away green slime on her handkerchief. 'Don't faint, Bird.'

'I'm not going to faint, and as far as

execution is concerned, I thought Stella singularly unmoved when she admitted to murder. I shall need help to get Hereward out of here.' She knelt down and made a quick examination. 'Get a couple of porters, will you, please, and a stretcher. He'll have to be carried. And you had better get Matron to call the police.'

'Again?' Connie said faintly.

At the subsequent interview, by unspoken agreement, both she and Bird confined their stories to the present time. Neither of them felt able to explain the events at Swan House in 1970, and as for an analysis of Stella's character and motives, Bird said, 'I doubt whether anyone really knew her at all. Certainly I couldn't say what she was like or what made her do the things she did.'

'An elemental?' suggested Connie, 'a ruined saint? Or simply a commonplace woman bereft of her soul? Pythagoras maintained that at death good souls turn into swans. If that is the case, I feel quite sure that it could never apply to Stella.'

'I don't know. At times I loathed her, but I also felt a little bit sorry for her.'

Connie disapproved. 'Try to stop being so very nice, if you please, Bird. You would be a little bit sorry for the Devil in Hell and it makes me feel inferior.'

'Ridiculous,' said Bird. 'You're far too analytical. I'm entirely ordinary and I certainly do not have Stella's emotional staying-power.'

'For which, we must all be grateful.'

Hereward could not be questioned. He arrived in hospital, clinically dead and, after his heart was restarted, he remained there for three weeks until the police had gone.

20

Stella's body was never found. The creation of her legend began at once in the Duke's Head, ensuring that, over the years, there would be an interesting tale to feed to visitors (always supposing there were any) in return for a free beer. There was something decidedly strange about a creature who could fly into a cave to kidnap her lover. A fisherman who had often seen her on the beach from his boat and noticed the phenomenal power of her swimming, decided that she was a sea-witch. 'Made out of wrack and spume, her was, and out for getting herself an 'uman, like my old nan used to tell. She were an ugly old bitch, notwithstanding.' His audience, discussing whether fags and petrol would be going up in the next budget, did not argue. They were not deeply interested. Stella would have to wait a while before she became a talking-point.

Recovering slowly from a massive heart-attack, Hereward had a different theory; that she was one of the undead. With a flight of the imagination that startled them both, he said to Connie, 'How did she manage to get into that cave, if she's entirely human? She'll be out there somewhere, plotting evil like a sorceress. My poor, dear little Winifred!'

'Nonsense,' said Connie, with scant regard for his health or state of mind. 'Stella may have had a defective personality, but her true misfortune was to go on loving you far too long. Sensitivity is not your strong point, especially with women. I don't doubt that she was swept out to sea and drowned.'

'Don't you care that she murdered Winifred?'

'Of course I do; I wanted the truth and now I have it. But she's past our punishing and her fate is scarcely enviable. Kindly get a grip of things, Hereward, and you'll pick up in no time. Bird is far too soft with you.'

'And you're a hard woman, Connie. I won't be bothering anyone for long. I'm a sick man.' The exchange had brightened him. 'Why?' he murmured to himself, 'why Stella? why anything?' But his unanswerable question had lost the power to alarm. He was pleased to be alive and back in his pleasant rooms at The Glebe. And, in retrospect, to be loved into old age, even by a half-human, had its flattering side. 'Ask Bird if I may have a little whisky, will you, please? I should like to sit in my chair for a while.'

Connie put in a sour last word. 'At this

rate, Hereward, you'll outlive us all and become another damned phenomenon.'

★ ★ ★

Even Bird preferred, at first, to believe that Stella had swum out to sea and reached her bright horizon, but she did not speak about it. Publicity of a mystical kind was bad for the residents. The new commotion over the presumed death caused her to wonder whether an unshakeable curse lay on The Glebe. Ashamed of her absurd sentimentality, she asked Tom Markham whether she should close down. His answer was definite. 'No, my dear. The curse boils down to one man, Wally Spratt, and that's the end of it. You need a holiday and you need a helper. I think you should marry me, if you love me enough.'

'Do you truly want me, Tom?'

'Yes, truly.'

Bird's smile blazed out. 'I can't think why you should, but I'm glad. I'm not sure about a holiday, but I'd like to marry you.'

'That's settled, then. When?'

'Will spring be all right? I don't want to tread on Hannah's toes, and there are awkward things I ought to tell you about my youth before you commit yourself.'

'Tell them if you want to, but it won't make

any difference. We'll make it spring, then, and don't say you can't take time off because we're going to have a honeymoon. You're tired.' He kissed her several times under the approving eyes of Lizzie Greengrass, who gave the news to Charlie.

'We could have a double wedding,' said Lizzie, enjoying his nervous air. 'I've arranged to get my hip replacement next week and I should be dancing by spring. Though perhaps separate would be nicer. What do you think?'

'Oh lord, don't make me choose. Something quiet. Just two witnesses.'

'Not on your life,' said Lizzie. 'We'll rock and we'll roll. And don't visit me in hospital until I get my teeth in. I don't want you to be put off before we get started.'

Charlie turned pink and looked terrified. 'Teeth, oh lord. Who cares about teeth?'

Lizzie dropped an affectionate kiss on his bald head. 'Don't get frightened. Ask your friend down to be best man. I hope Denny will give me away and I think I'll ask Bunty to be matron of honour if I can persuade her to leave off her boots.'

At Cut and Dyed, Denny said, 'What a heart-breaker you are, Lizzie Greengrass. Give you away? And I was thinking of marrying you myself.'

Lizzie leered at him in the mirror. 'Dulcie

wouldn't like that at all, nor would I. If you behave you can dance with me at the wedding, and in the meantime think me up a hairstyle that won't get squashed under a hat.'

★ ★ ★

The unusual circumstances of Stella's passing rated a small paragraph in the popular newspapers. 'It's awkward not having a body to bury,' Bird said to Connie. 'One or two people, actors, I imagine, though I've never heard of any of them, want to know when the funeral is.'

'We could arrange a memorial service between us, though it's likely to be a small gathering.'

'Don't you believe it. My old swans love a funeral as much as they love a wedding, particularly the ritual meal afterwards. Lord knows why. They can eat ham and drink port at any time, but they seem to be essentials at a wake,' said Bird. 'Hymns will be difficult. None that I know seem to fit Stella, except for things like 'Fight the Good Fight', or 'Rock of Ages', and we can hardly use those.'

'I think we'd better play safe with 'Lead us Heavenly Father, Lead us', and 'The King of Love my Shepherd is'. They are suitably general, and shouldn't cause any tittering in church.'

'Someone should say a few words, don't you think? Not the vicar. According to the verger, he made a pastoral visit to Stella's cottage and she opened the door in her French knickers. He never went back.'

'Who would?' said Connie. 'It's unkind to frighten an old man. Saying anything nice about her is beyond me; you too, I imagine.'

'It oughtn't to be personal, nothing about the marriages, and I don't know a thing about her stage career. Do you think I could ask Miles? I know he loathed Stella, but he *is* an actor.'

Connie nodded. 'Not a bad one either. I'll ask him, if you like, and make sure that he prepares a *short* address. He gets carried away by pen and paper.'

★　★　★

Hereward, still not convinced that Stella was dead, insisted on being pushed to church in his wheelchair. It would be like her to burst in on her own memorial service and give him another heart attack. He breathed heavily as the vicar read, 'I am the resurrection and the life, saith the Lord: he that believeth in Me, though he were dead, yet shall he live: and whoever liveth and believeth in Me shall never die.' Now, he thought, now it will happen. But the rites continued peacefully. Miles listed briefly Stella's theatrical triumphs, the last hymn was sung and the grace said. As the congregation began to leave the church, a broad smile of contentment lit Hereward's face. That was it. Stella had gone to her eternal rest and his burden had lifted. Poor girl, she had loved him, and though she had wantonly killed Winifred, he would always try to think charitably of her. He enjoyed the wake.

★ ★ ★

Bird noticed a change in Hereward's attitude towards her. He remained grateful for her care, though he no longer tried to claim her time or talk of personal matters. She wondered how upset he would be at the prospect of her marriage. Not very much, she thought. Since his collapse in the shell grotto, he seemed to have retreated into comfortable forgetfulness. If he spoke of the past, it was of Winifred and Stella, as though in death they had won him and were sharing him between them. Paris, Swan House, Bird (his once-loved half-aunt) and Hannah might never have been. Let the connection die, she thought. Tom doesn't care about the past so nor will I.

She mentioned as much to Connie Lovibond, who said, 'Confession may be good for the soul, Bird, but it creates awkwardness and destroys conversation. Hereward really isn't worth it. Has it ever occurred to you that, stripped of his charm, he's rather a dull man? He's never needed to work, never created anything. Marrying my sister and seducing you are the most adventurous things he's done in a lifetime.'

'There was Stella: she must have been an adventure.'

'More of a serious mistake. They were playing to different sets of rules. Hereward's contract with her will not have included her refusal to accept polite dismissal. Unlimited leisure is a curse. If I'm to stay on until your wedding, you must find me something to do. The grave is beginning to yawn.'

'The staff are competent, but I could use another driver. There's Lizzie's hip replacement. She won't let Charlie drive her, though he keeps a car here that rarely leaves the garage. He regards all motor vehicles as evil pollutants. And two of the convalescents have appointments with different consultants in Southampton.'

'What about Rita? Isn't she due out of

hospital tomorrow?'

'You would't mind collecting her?'

'Not at all. She can tell me what the grey ones from the sea have done with Stella.' Bird looked mystified. 'Don't ask me to explain. I'm reduced to making jokes in very poor taste.'

Connie duly delivered Lizzie to the surgeons and collected Rita Parry from the doctors. 'So this is it,' Rita said, inspecting her new home. 'I like the little kitchen. Blue's a good colour; it guards against evil spirits. I can dry my herbs there.' Her singed hair was slowly growing back into uneven wisps around the shaven patch of skull that Wally had fractured. She looked uncommonly clean and tidy in her new skirt and jumper, though she had to be persuaded to abandon the purple cardigan. 'I can mend it and there's only a few little bloodstains. The Good-As-Nu cleaners can get those out.'

'No,' said Bird, and meant it. Herbs, bloodstains! What other souvenirs of the past had she invited?

'Tell me again about that Stella Worth, then. You sure they haven't found a body?'

'You've heard it half a dozen times already.'

'Strange,' Rita brooded. 'After I saw her take that tin of poison, I've not stopped wondering about her. Who was she? No family background, no old friends, just a bunch of useless husbands; and I don't think she expected those marriages to last. It was Parstock she wanted and he was supposed to rescue her. She reminds me of that creature I met once who killed her own children and disappeared into the air in a fiery chariot. What was her name now? Medea, that's it.'

'Just stop it at once, Rita,' Bird said, as she hung clothes on hangers and stowed underwear in drawers. 'You know perfectly well that Medea lived thousands of years ago, if she ever lived at all.'

'And how would I know that?' Rita was decidedly nettled. 'I see what I see.'

'Not any more, you don't. Stella was simply a beautiful, selfish woman in love with a man she couldn't have. All this mystic nonsense almost got you murdered. You promised to settle down: no visions, no prophecies, no herbal cures, and definitely no frightening of my residents.'

'Beautiful, yes, she was that, but was she simply a woman?'

'Stop it, Rita.'

'It's going to be boring here if I can't do anything.'

'But safe. And there'll be a car available to run you around and coach trips too.'

Rita counted her blessings. 'There's that,

and Ched, and the Duke's Head, and I dare say they'll ask me to read the tea-leaves now and then. I'll lay out my things, then I'll go shopping. The Social have sent me some money. Madam Dulcie might have another of those cardigans.' At that point, Bird gave up. Civilizing Rita was going to be a long, slow process, especially since she wasn't at all sure that she wanted her to change.

★　★　★

The trial of Wally Spratt took place in November at Winchester. Rita, Bird and Lizzie Greengrass were required as witnesses, along with several villagers, including Mrs Spratt and the landlord of the Duke's Head with his wife. Charlie Bean also insisted on going to look after Lizzie, who had abandoned crutches and now menaced passers-by with a walking-stick. 'I shall come along,' said Connie. 'The city has some delightful places to lunch. And Bunty has somehow got hold of the idea that you are under threat. Will you mind if we take her too?'

The anti-Spratt contingent grew larger. 'We're going to look like a procession if we go in separate cars,' said Bird. 'I'll ask Tom to drive us in the small coach.'

'Quite a turn-out,' said their old acquaintance, the inspector, encountered on the court-house steps. 'All well, I trust? You remember my sergeant over there, looking miserable? He hates this case. For myself, I'm enjoying it. Our Mr Spratt is a first-class idiot in spite of his little store of cunning.' The inspector talked on amiably. Once fed and rested, Wally had repented of his confession and was pleading not guilty. 'He'll blame police brutality, of course, and make the prosecutor hate his guts, if you will forgive the expression. Now, if you will excuse me, there's a lady I want to have a word with. I owe her a good lunch if I can separate her from her husband.'

'Will you just look at that,' said Lizzie, craning her neck and tripping over her walking-stick. 'The pub landlady, looking like a smiling goddess. Doesn't she look like Minerva in those old statues, Charlie?'

He steadied her with a hand under her elbow. 'No, and watch your step.'

'I don't blame her liking attention. Her husband's a miserable git.'

'Keep your voice down and try to behave. People are listening.'

'Old ladies don't care,' said Lizzie.

The trial proved to be far shorter than anyone had expected. Prosecuting counsel stated the case against Wally and called the police witnesses; counsel for the defence struggled to refute their evidence and the court adjourned for lunch. By that time, Wally's gaze was locked with the inimical stare of Mrs Spratt, from which he seemed unable to break away. His stout frame had begun to wilt. 'He's losing the will to live, I hope,' said Mrs Spratt happily. 'I've brought cottage cheese sandwiches, but I think I might treat meself to a proper lunch. I've shed nearly two stone.'

'You come along with me and the inspector,' said the landlady of the Duke's Head, destroying Lizzie's romantic suspicions at a stroke. 'I know a place where we can get a smashing meal, and not too fattening if you keep off the chips.'

When the court reconvened, they learned that Wally had changed his plea to guilty and that the evidence of the witnesses from Wynfred Abbas would not be needed. 'Damn,' said Mrs Spratt. 'I was really looking forward to standing up and saying what a nasty apology of a human he is.' Her disappointment vanished when she heard him sentenced to twelve years' imprisonment. 'It'll do,' she said. 'I'd hoped for more, but it'll do.'

★ ★ ★

On the following day, the new slimmed-down Mrs Spratt called on Gus Early for her check-up. All in all she was a happy woman. 'Blood-pressure down, heart fine, circulation improved,' Gus said. 'Try to lose another half-stone, if you can. I shan't need to see you again for six months.'

'Good. So I'm well enough to get a job?'

'Certainly you are. What did you think of doing.'

'It's like this, Doctor, I don't have any skills, so to speak, but I can keep house and cook and manage bills and accounts. And I'm safe to look after children. You and Mrs Marsh will be getting married soon and I thought you might take me on when she and the boy move in to your house.'

'Well, I do have Arlene from the mini-market.'

'That slut's next to useless; setting her cap at you, though you haven't noticed, and those banister-rails are a disgrace; they never see a duster. She'll not do for Mrs Marsh.'

'I'll speak to Hannah about it and let you know. There won't be room for you to live in, I'm afraid.'

'Fine, Doctor. I'm getting out of my cottage — it smells of Wally and that woman who fell in the sea, and I'm going back to my maiden name, which is Tonkins, Adela

Tonkins. I thought of asking Mrs Dawlish if I can rent the lodge when it comes empty, unless she has someone in mind.'

Gus gave her an admiring look. 'Mrs Spratt, I'm proud of you.'

'To tell the truth,' she said, 'I'm a bit proud of myself.'

★ ★ ★

With the advent of Christmas and the wedding of Hannah to Gus Early, Connie had no need to fear going in idleness to her grave. Nor was she plagued by the sadness and depression that had settled on her each year since her sister's death. She had uncovered the truth and Winifred rested. Commandeering a group of junior nurses, she set about decking the halls with boughs of holly (tra-la-la-la-la). The result pleased her. 'It's a work of art,' Bird said, between telephone calls to the hotel where the wedding breakfast was to be held and the terrifyingly expensive milliner who was making her hat. 'Can the death of the princess really have brought these changes about, Connie? All the dramas and all the loving?'

'Coincidence, I should say, although a sudden death can act as a hurry-up: brief life is here our portion, so get on with it. There's no doubt that Hannah is more than ready. We haven't heard a word about our duty to the poor since her engagement.'

Bird laughed. 'Don't be unkind: her politics were those of a disappointed woman. This is certainly not going to be a Marxist wedding; capitalist to the last souvenir napkin-ring. My damned hat ought to be diamond-studded at the price I'm being charged, and you could buy a small house for the amount Hannah's paying for her dress.'

Connie had to concede that the cost was worth it. Wearing soft gold, Hannah warmed and burned like a second sun against the dreariness of the winter's day. Bird glowed with happiness and her hat was a triumph. Joshua was overawed. 'Mum's smashing, isn't she, Gran? Was I a good page boy?'

'Yes to both those, Josh. And Gus and his best man made very nice speeches. It was perfect and I'm proud of you all.'

'Can I be a page boy when you marry Tom? I do like weddings.'

'I wasn't going to have any attendants, but we'll see.'

'What about Connie? You could be a bridesmaid. Can't she be your bridesmaid, Gran?'

'It's kind of you to think of me, Joshua, but I am forced to decline.'

'Why are you forced to decline?'

'I don't share your passion for weddings, nor do I have the sweet and vapid appearance considered appropriate in a bridesmaid.'

'Vapid, rapid, vapid,' muttered Josh to himself. 'I like your appearance.'

'Don't bother Connie, there's a good boy.' Bird said. 'It's enough of a concession that she's staying on for my wedding, when she would much rather go home.'

Bird understood her eagerness to be gone. Connie had accomplished what she set out to do and declared herself refreshed. Yet it was plain that she did not altogether look forward to a quiet life of charity committees, coffee mornings and flower-arranging. Turning her house in Rye from a mausoleum to a home would scarcely fill the rest of her life. 'I wish I could persuade you to come back with me for a long break, but I know you won't,' she said to Bird. 'That leaves me in dire need of an occupation. Does it sound completely ridiculous to say that I might try my hand at writing a crime novel? I know a fair bit about the art underworld, which should help.'

'I don't find the idea in the least ridiculous.

All the best writers of detective novels seem to be women, and crime never goes out of fashion.'

'Then if I can invent an original kind of detective, I might well have a go at it when I have enjoyed your wedding. It's a relief that you're marrying Tom.'

'Why a relief?' Bird asked.

'At one point I was afraid that you would take Hereward back out of some misguided sense of duty, even marry him.'

'Do you think me that weak and stupid, Connie? I'm fond of Hereward still, but I'm not a complete simpleton.'

'Sorry! By nature you are overkind, and he's something of a tyrant. Too much love has always seemed to me a weakness, but disinterested love is your strength, thank heaven.'

'It's good of you to stay for the weddings. I'm pleased and so is Lizzie. She's hell-bent on livening up Charlie with a cruise and we've been talked into going with her.'

'A shared honeymoon? Isn't that a little odd?'

'Lizzie is no better at holidays than I am. If we are on a ship, we can't change our minds and come back. Her logic and Tom's! Hannah has volunteered to give Matron a hand here, with Mrs Tonkins, formerly

Spratt, on call if needed.'

'Ah well, two more sets of nuptials and then I can go home and find out whether I shall ever be a writer.'

The weddings took place in consecutive weeks, Bird's quietly, Lizzie's with a reception for most of the village, and Joshua again page boy at both. 'Might as well get some wear out of the suit,' said Gus, who gave Bird away. 'Hannah's a tiny bit pregnant, as you know, but I'm glad that it didn't disqualify her from being your matron of honour.'

'Gran's going on a cruise with Tom and Aunt Lizzie and Uncle Charlie. It's a joint honeymoon.'

'Quite improper.' Gus smiled at Bird. 'They'll be sharing cabins and having mixed bathing next.'

She said, 'It was Lizzie's idea. She thinks that two weeks alone with Charlie might be rather quiet.'

'Her new hip's certainly going to get a work-out, and no, Josh, I'm not going to explain why.'

★ ★ ★

On his wedding night, Charlie Bean dawdled, undressing slowly and carefully hanging up his suit. He put out the light and groped for his pyjamas. 'Hurry up,' Lizzie said from the bed. 'I'm falling asleep here.'

He had carefully not thought of this moment, fearing that he could only be a disappointment. Instead, he mentally reviewed his notebooks and tested the conclusions he had drawn from his researches. Out there civilization was crumbling, another watercourse was being polluted, radiation leaked into the sea, rain forests were steadily losing their trees, asteroids whizzed about in space, heading for earth. Now that he was a married man, such things had become less immediate. He did not want to consider annihilation or slow decay for Lizzie, who of all people was so thoroughly alive. 'What about your hip? Are you sure — '

'I'll manage. Come to bed, Charlie, there's a love. You'll soon get the hang of it.' Charlie went to bed.

★ ★ ★

Little craft gave way as the huge cruise liner turned from Southampton Water into the Solent. Lizzie and Charlie were at dinner. Leaning over the rail beside Tom, Bird shivered suddenly. 'You're cold,' he said, putting an arm around her shoulders. 'Let's go in.'

'In a moment. I'm not at all cold. There was something, a half-thought, but it went before I could get hold of it.'

Far below, the sea was scarcely visible. They did not notice the sodden piece of flotsam, washed-out, sun-faded from blue and yellow to a dirty grey, that floated to and fro with the movement of the tide. A wave sank it, then bellied it out like an arm rising above the surface, only to draw it back again. It had travelled a long way, in and out of harbours, past headlands, chines and river-mouths. Two men prodded at it from a small craft, lifting it briefly on a boat-hook in case it should turn out to be a body. But it was only an old discarded dress and they let it fall. The flow of the water picked it up. It journeyed on in the wake of the ship, going nowhere, going everywhere.